The strange and horrifying disappearances in upper New York State barely disturbed Manhattan. They rated just a few lines in the newspapers on this crowded island where rapes, muggings and murders were facts of life and death for people like beautiful young Joyce Dewitte . . . cynical Jim Hart . . . old Mrs. Haritson . . . a brutal gang leader named Snipe . . . and all the other city-dwellers about to discover that their most fearful dreams could not match the nightmare that was coming true . . .

. . . for the "children" were coming to the city . . . stronger, more savage, and far more ravenous than ever before . . .

THE CHILDREN OF THE ISLAND

Even *Strange Seed* and *Nursery Tale* did not prepare you for this!

D1598293

THE CHILDREN OF THE ISLAND

T. M. WRIGHT

A JOVE BOOK

THE CHILDREN OF THE ISLAND

A Jove Book / published by arrangement with
the author

PRINTING HISTORY
Jove edition / September 1983

ISBN: 0-515-07129-3

Jove books are published by The Berkley Publishing Group,
200 Madison Avenue, New York, N.Y. 10016. The words
''A JOVE BOOK'' and the ''J'' with sunburst are trademarks
belonging to Jove Publications, Inc.

PRINTED IN THE UNITED STATES OF AMERICA

This book is very much for Erika, my daughter.

ACKNOWLEDGMENTS

I think I would be quite remiss if I did not give high praise and thank you's to my editor at Playboy, Sharon Jarvis, who, over the last several years of our relationship, has exercised much patience and professionalism and to whom I am more than a little indebted for helping to bring me along as a writer.

And again, thank you, Bill Thompson.

AUTHOR'S NOTE

This is the third book of the trilogy begun with *Strange Seed* and *Nursery Tale*. I like to believe that each is more than a horror novel—at least I planned them that way. Whether or not the reader *sees* them that way is actually of little consequence, because the real purpose of occult fiction is entertainment; and philosophy, "message," must be secondary.

At any rate, some of what you will read here is based on fact, although all the people are entirely the construction of my imagination.

Lastly, who's to say that all of us are not Children of the Earth? Can we say we are anything else?

—T. M. Wright
Naples, New York
March 29, 1983

From *The Penn Yann Post Gazette*, December 6, 1978:

COUPLE INCINERATED IN HOUSE FIRE

Paul Griffin, 30, and his wife Rachel, 26, were killed last night in a fire at their 100-year-old farmhouse on the Tripp Road extension, ten miles north of Penn Yann. According to Deputy Volunteer Fire Chief Clyde Watkins, the fire apparently started when a gasoline-powered electric generator at the side of the house exploded. Watkins described the destruction caused by the fire as "total," and added that when he and his men arrived on the scene at approximately 3:15 A.M., the Griffin home was completely engulfed by flames.

According to Penn Yann resident John Marsh—who did occasional work for the Griffins—the couple had moved into the farmhouse about six months ago, hoping to make the farm profitable once again. "But there were lots of problems," Marsh explained. "I remember when they first moved in, for instance, that house was a shambles. Vandals got in there and just went wild."

Investigation has revealed that the house's previous

1

owners, a middle-aged couple named Schmidt, were found dead at the house in August, 1972, apparently as the result of a double suicide. Prior to that tragedy, Paul Griffin's father, Samuel Griffin, one-time owner of the house, died of a heart attack there in 1957. Mr. Griffin, formerly of New York City, leaves an uncle, Harold Martinson. His wife leaves her mother and father, two sisters, several aunts and uncles, nieces and nephews.

No local service is planned.

From the December 15th *Rochester Democrat and Chronicle*; fourteen years later:

BIZARRE TRAGEDY IN SOUTHERN TIER
BAFFLES INVESTIGATORS

The death toll now stands at 15 in what appears to be a baffling series of mutilation murders, suicides, and arsons in the newly developed community of Granada, ten miles north of Penn Yann. At least half of the deaths involve children, investigators say, many of whom may have succumbed to the great blizzard which passed through the area several days ago.

According to Chief of Police John Hastings, some of the children involved either were "runaways, or perhaps relatives of people living in Granada," because, he says, "our records indicate that only three or four children were full-time residents of Granada, and one of them has already been accounted for." That child, Hastings told this reporter, is ten-year-old Timmy Meade, whose parents, Dora and Larry Meade, aged 30 and 32 respectively, were among the victims in Granada.

Only two other residents of Granada appear to have escaped the incredible violence there—Miles McIntyre, 35, and his wife Janice, 29, who with Timmy Meade, are listed in good condition at Myers Community Hospital, suffering from exposure. John Marsh, a resident of Penn Yann, found both Mrs. McIntyre and the Meade boy on Reynolds Road, the night of the tragedy. Marsh himself was treated for exposure at Myers Community Hospital and released. He was not immediately available for comment.

Investigators theorize that the tragedy may have begun with the murders of Dick Wentis, 37, and his wife Judy, 32, who were found . . .

From The Rochester Democrat and Chronicle, November 8th; two years later:

NUMBER OF MISSING PERSONS ESCALATES IN ADIRONDACK AREA
by Jack Garner, D & C Newsfeatures Editor

The number of persons reported missing in the downstate New York area of the Adirondack Mountain Range has increased threefold in the last decade, according to Bob Quinn, head of the Missing Persons Department of the New York State Police. According to Mr. Quinn, this escalation apparently began late in the last decade and has involved some 125 persons in the decade since. "We have no hard and fast reason for these disappearances," Quinn said. "We do know that people have been hiking into the Adirondack region in slightly greater numbers in recent years, although this increase would apparently have little bearing on the much greater numbers of missing persons being reported."

The most recent disappearances—that of a young, newly married couple hiking through the Adirondacks on their honeymoon—is still being investigated. Quinn holds out little hope that the couple will be found: "Since this increase in disappearances began, we have found precious little in the way of evidence. My advice to anyone thinking of hiking in that area would be to exercise extreme caution. We do know that the number of black bears in the area has increased slightly, due to an unexplained increase in their natural prey. But whether this has any bearing, either, on the disappearances, is something we're still working on."

Part One

GENESIS

Chapter 1

Late Summer

Jim Hart wanted desperately to scratch his backside. The late-afternoon Adirondack sunlight, his heavy clothes, and the long hours of walking had drenched him in sweat. Despite the brisk temperatures, the sweat had caused a rash to start, and he thought he had never been in greater agony. But Marie was right behind him on the narrow path, and although she would probably think nothing of it if he *were* to scratch himself, she might think it was gauche, that it was something seasoned hikers didn't do, because they had long since accustomed themselves and their backsides to the walking, and so did not sweat, and she would, from that moment on, treat him as the outsider he realized he was.

But maybe, he thought, he was being unfair.

He said, turning his head to look at her, "Marie,"—and he grinned through his agony—"you want to go on ahead there?" He nodded in front of him. His grin grew apologetic. "Nature calls," he went on.

Marie smiled back. "Yeah," she said, "me too." And she stepped past him. "Fred?" she called to the big, moon-faced, red-haired man walking fifteen feet ahead of them. Fred stopped and looked around, questioningly. "Fred," Marie repeated.

"Yeah?"

"Jim and I have to make a pit stop."

"We're almost there, you know," Fred grumbled. "And that storm is right on top of us."

"It's just for a minute," Marie told him.

He lumbered back. He was Marie's brother, but the only resemblance to her was his red hair, and the several dozen freckles laid out prominently across the bridge of his nose. Marie looked up at him. "Just a short minute," she reiterated.

He sighed. "Yeah, well don't go too far—you can get lost in there"—he indicated the trees and thick underbrush crowding the path on both sides—"quicker than . . ."

"I know that," Marie interrupted.

Fred nodded briskly at Jim. "*He* doesn't know it."

Jim smiled again, foolishly, he knew. "I know it now," he said.

Two minutes later, after pushing himself painfully through the underbrush, after finding a small, sunlit clearing, after climbing out of his heavy backpack, and after scratching himself into ecstasy, Jim Hart realized that he was lost. He shook his head slowly, self-critically. He shouted, "Hey, you guys!" and waited only a moment, not long enough for a reply. "Hey, you guys—I'm lost!" He chuckled self-consciously. He heard someone—Marie, he supposed—call back, but her words were unintelligible. He grimaced and cupped his hands over his mouth. "Hey, I said I'm lost here." He waited.

"Where?" It was Fred's voice, and he sounded pissed.

"Here!" Jim called. "Over here!" He felt very foolish.

"Where?" he heard again.

"Here. North of where you are, I think."

"North?"

"I don't know. Follow my voice."

"Jim?" It was Marie, from behind him, at a distance. He shook his head again, and turned slowly.

Marie's voice again: "Jim, keep talking!"

"About what?"

"About how damned stupid you are!" Fred called.

"Yeah," Jim shouted. "I'm stupid, I'm *damned* stupid!"

Marie called, a bit closer, "Don't overdo it, Jim." And he imagined that she chuckled.

"Keep talking, goddammit!" It was Fred again, and he

seemed farther off than Marie. "Just keep talking, Jim. You can talk, can'tcha?"

"I can talk, Fred."

"You're not moving, are you?"

"No, Fred, I'm staying put." He paused; his throat was beginning to hurt from the shouting. He glanced about. "It's pretty . . . here, isn't it?" It was something to talk about; they *did* want him to keep talking. "I said it's pretty here, isn't it?"

"Just keep talking, Jim. I told you not to move."

"I'm not moving, Fred. I haven't moved an inch."

"Shit, too—I heard you move, Jim!"

"It was a deer, Fred," Marie called, and she sounded, Jim thought, as if she wasn't any closer at all.

"Hey guys," Jim called, "I've got an idea. Why don't I—" He paused to let a quick pain in his throat subside. "Why don't *I* look for *you*?" It was a good idea, he supposed. After all, he'd be searching for two people, while they were searching for only one.

"Asshole!" Fred shouted, and Jim heard several other words, but they were unintelligible. Fred, Jim realized, was moving away from him:

"Fred," he called, "you're going the wrong way!" He waited. Nothing. "Marie," he called, "Fred's going the wrong way!"

"Jim?" Marie called, apparently no closer.

"Marie, Fred's going the wrong way!"

"You're going the wrong way, Fred!"

"Marie," Jim called, "where's Fred?"

"Jesus, I don't know," she called back.

"Have you got a fix on me, yet, Marie?"

Silence.

"Marie?"

"No, I—"

Jim grimaced. Now Marie was moving away from him. "Marie, you're going the wrong way!"

"Jim?" a voice called from farther off.

"Back *this* way, Marie."

The rain started—large, random drops at first. Jim looked up, through the clearing; he caught one of the drops in the eye. It stung, like vinegar. He cursed, "Goddammit!", and rubbed the eye angrily. He glanced about. "Marie!" He waited a moment. Nothing. "Marie, I'm going to have to move." He waited. The rain strengthened; in moments it soaked his shirt through to the skin. He swore again. This, he thought, was getting very silly. "Marie, god-dammit, where *are* you!" He listened. He heard the steady, loud hiss of the rain—nothing else. Marie could be ten feet away, he knew, and still be unable to hear him.

"Marie!" he shouted.

He was angry, now—angry at them both. They should have known better than to drag him out here. This was alien territory; he had no right here—maybe they did, but not him. He was a city dweller. He had told them that. "New York may be a hellhole, I *know* it's a hellhole, but at least you know where to hide, and from what, and with whom!" For Christ's sake, that was true, that was . . . Modern American Anthropology, it belonged in *National Geographic*. "Marie, goddammit, where *are* you?!" And he had told them—slowly, steadily, as if teaching them something that required their deep attention—that people (people in general, but not all people) had long ago built cities in order to shield themselves from the wildness all around them. And gradually, over the centuries, they had produced children and grandchildren, and great grandchil-dren who were increasingly dependent upon the cities; until, at last, a whole new life form developed—the city dweller. "Marie, damn it!" Just like some birds were cliff dwellers, he told them, and some fish were bottom dwell-ers (but not all birds, and not all fish), so some people were city dwellers. But not all people. What was simpler? But they—Fred, and Marie, and their friends—hadn't un-derstood that, or believed it. They had told him he was intellectualizing his weakness; they had challenged him and laughed at him, and had, finally, dragged him here, where he had no business being, where the goddamned stinging rain was surely going to kill him unless he got out from under it.

The rain had stopped.

He glanced about, momentarily grateful, and saw that

he had wandered away from the clearing. He cursed. He had left the backpack there ("That backpack is more important than your damned *balls*!—you understand that, Jim?" . . . "Yes, Fred, I understand that."). He thought the clearing would be easy enough to find again. In his reverie he couldn't have gone more than a few feet or a few yards from it, at most. He did a full 360-degree turn, very slowly, his eyes wide, and searching, then realized that he had no idea at all where the clearing was. "Marie?" he shouted. He waited a moment. Nothing. "Fred? Marie? Can you hear me?!" He waited a full minute. He thought he heard an answering call, but it was barely audible, at a great distance, and when it was done he wasn't sure he'd heard anything.

He noticed that his backside was itching again, the rash there aggravated by his nervous sweat. He scratched the itch furiously. Embarrassment flooded through him—he didn't know why, at first. Maybe, he decided, Marie and Fred were playing a game with him. Maybe they were trying to show him how jaded he was, how basically . . . incompetent, how in need of their wise advice and counsel. And so, they had seen fit to put him here. In these woods. Alone (or so they would have him believe). So he could examine himself, and his life. While they watched from close by. Watched him scratch his backside. He shoved his hands into the pockets of his jeans. "Damn you both to hell!" he murmured, though not loud enough that if they *were* watching they would hear him.

He thought he heard a small, halting laugh from somewhere close by—actually more a giggle than a laugh. He snapped his gaze to the left, toward the source of the laugh. He said Marie's name, and Fred's, and knew, from his tone of voice, that he was getting a little anxious. He thought he couldn't blame himself for that. He said aloud: "Marie, Fred, I can't blame myself for that." He smiled dimly, and realized that the sound of his own voice comforted him.

"Marie!" he shouted. "Fred!" A stiff wind started and pushed the tops of the trees about. "I said I can't blame myself for that! I blame *you* assholes!" He found that he was walking, that something inside him was making him walk, slowly. He took his hands from his pockets. It wasn't smart to walk through the forest with your hands in your pockets.

He hoped he was moving east because the road was to the east. And the car, in a Holiday Inn parking lot, fifteen miles east—and that was a long way through the underbrush. It could take all night. But that was okay. It was forward momentum.

He heard giggling again, more like a laugh, now, and still close by. But he forgot it quickly as he walked; it was as alien to this place as he was; he decided that it was probably following him out.

Then he noticed two things simultaneously: that he was shivering—either because his shirt was wet, or the air had turned colder, or both—and that darkness was coming. He thought that was improbable—it had been late afternoon only minutes ago, before the quick rain started, and there had been bright, hazy patches of sunlight moving all around him through breaks in the trees. He looked straight up. He saw irregular, black pieces of sky, and he remembered what Fred had told him: "That storm is right on top of us."

He realized then that his anxiety had changed to fear. So he began to move faster (though not at a run; the thick underbrush wasn't about to let him run), very stiffly, very mechanically, not caring where he might be going, because he didn't know where he was going anyway. He stumbled several times, the underbrush opening small cuts on his knees and hands.

He found himself at the grassy shore of a small lake. He stumbled face forward into the shallow water, pushed himself up on all fours, looked out, across the water, and saw a pair of dim, yellow, rectangular lights—windows, he realized—through the darkness.

"He's a big boy, Marie. He'll be able to take care of himself."

Marie lowered her head and shook it briskly. "No," she said, and her voice quivered with emotion. She looked up at Fred seated across from her at the small, oak table.

"No, Jim is *not* a big boy. Not out here. Don't you understand that?! Out here, Jim is a very *small* boy!"

"He's got eyes, doesn't he? And a brain? And feet? And hands? Small boy, my ass! I've heard of kids—five-year-old kids—getting lost out here for days and turning up okay. You have, too."

"Yes, Fred, that's true. And I've heard of grown men—just like Jim—wandering off—*just like* Jim—and never coming back." She glared at her brother. It was at times like these that she thought she despised him.

He said casually, "You found your way good enough, didn't you? Well then, so can he."

"And what if he does find his way, Fred? How's he going to make it out here from shore? Is he going to fly? Maybe he can walk on water. Do you think he can do that?"

Fred studied her face a moment, and sighed heavily. "Jesus, okay. I'll take the damned boat back in the morning. I'll *find* him!"

She shook her head again. "In the *morning*, you can do whatever in the hell you want. But as soon as that storm lets up"—she nodded at the kitchen window—a heavy rain was pelting it—"I'm taking the lamp and I'm going to go looking for him."

Fred stood slowly. He leaned over, put his big hands flat on the table, and looked Marie squarely in the eye. "He's a candy-ass, Marie. You know it, I know it, *he* knows it. And I don't really give two shits if the damned fish have him for their damned dinner!" He straightened. He moved around the table, toward a door leading into one of the house's two bedrooms—he had already laid his sleeping bag out in it. He stopped in the doorway and looked back. "Do what the hell you want, Marie," he said, and he went into the bedroom.

Marie, seething, could think of nothing to say. She glanced toward the window again—the rain seemed heavier. She knew that the storm would last the night.

Jim Hart was singing—not very loud, barely above a whisper—a song his mother had taught him thirty years before. He had had occasion to sing the song only three times since his childhood, twice in Vietnam, and now here: "Hush little baby, don't say a word/Mama's gonna buy you a mockingbird" . . . and so on. He sang it with a wan smile on his face. He sang it because he was scared silly, because the song comforted him, because it carried him back; and when he sang it, he felt properly ashamed.

He was still shivering, though now more violently, and as he whispered his little song, a word came to him—*hypothermia*, the slow loss of body heat. Left untreated, it ended in death. He knew about hypothermia because the daughter of a friend had died of it one cold November night eight years earlier. She had gotten exhausted trying to find her way home in a freak, late-autumn snowstorm, and had fallen asleep twenty feet from a neighbor's house. She had been wearing a gray pleated skirt, red oxfords, and a sheer gray blouse. Jim had never met her, he had merely been witness to his friend's silent, staring grief.

And so he had learned about hypothermia, and knew that he had fallen victim to it, now. One of the first symptoms, he realized, was that he didn't care very much. It didn't hurt; he felt numb, and alone, and sleepy—not altogether uncomfortable. There were certainly far worse ways to die, far more painful ways. He thought he would have preferred to have been less wet, that it would be nice if the rain stopped and the stars came out. Everyone should have a look at the stars before death came—they were a nice reminder of eternity (he decided that for a city dweller that was a pretty profound way to think).

. . . "and if that mockingbird don't sing/Mama's gonna buy you a diamond ring" . . . He had always liked his singing voice; he wished he could really sing loud now, instead of merely whisper. He thought that whatever was watching him would be impressed.

Because he knew that he was being watched. It wasn't a guess, a shot in the dark—*there must be something else alive in these woods*. It was a certainty, he knew it—just as he had *known* other things throughout his life; that phones would or would not be answered, or that old friends would appear, or that pets would die.

He didn't know precisely what was watching him, only that it had intelligence, and that it watched with great curiosity, that—in its way—it was attempting to reach out to him.

"And if," he whispered, "that diamond ring . . ." He faltered, then went on, "turns brass/Mama's gonna buy you a looking glass/And if that looking . . . glass . . ."

He stopped singing. He knew that the thing had gone away, into the woods. He waited. Something else had taken its place. "Jim?" he heard. "Jim, answer me."

It was Marie. She was leaning over him. He wasn't sure if he was really seeing her.

"And if that looking glass . . . turns blue . . ." He thought he heard himself chuckle.

"Jim, I can't carry you by myself. You've got to help."

He felt her hands on his arms. He became aware that she was tugging at him: "Jim, *please*!"

"And if that . . . diamond brass turns . . . green . . ."

"What in hell are you talking about? Please try to stand up, Jim. Please!"

She grabbed his hand. She recoiled. He was as cold as a corpse.

"Wait here, Jim!" she told him. "Wait here! I'll go get Fred. Wait here!"

Chapter 2

The small gray frame house stood alone on the island; the people who had built the house fifty years before had discovered that the runoff from the streams feeding the lake put nearly half the island underwater at least once a year, which made the normally two-acre-size island much too small for more than one house.

It was a sturdy, single-story house, with an open porch, a shallow crawlspace basement (a full basement would have flooded regularly), a living room, two tiny bedrooms, a chemical toilet, and a kitchen with wood-burning stove and ancient ice chest. There was no upholstered furniture in the house (it mildewed too quickly in the moist air), only a few handmade wooden chairs and tables, and there were no beds, no electricity, and no telephone. And because it would have been impossible to reach the house in winter, there was no fireplace and no heating stove.

It was, as Marie (the former Mrs. Aubin, also the former Marie Williams, her maiden name—a name she loathed) had explained to Jim Hart a week earlier, in an attempt to convince him to come on the hike, "rustic living at its very coziest." To which Jim had responded, "Yeah? I know what 'cozy' means. It means spiders and black flies and frigid mountain air."

She took the cup of machine-made coffee he offered her. "Spiders? Sure." She sipped the coffee, grinned, then hurried on. "But the black flies are gone for the season. And we'll protect you from the spiders."

" 'We'?" he said. "Who's 'we'?" When she had first approached him with the idea of a hiking expedition—two days before—he had entertained the delicious fantasy that it would be just the two of them. Alone. The idea made him dizzy with anticipation. Now his shoulders slumped noticeably. "Do you mean that someone else wants to come along?"

"Uh-huh." She nodded grimly. "Fred does."

"Your brother?"

"My brother."

Jim's fantasies nearly exploded. He felt the same way about Fred Williams that, he had supposed more than once, most people felt about biting dogs and screeching nine-year-olds; he was afraid of Fred Williams, and Fred Williams made him nervous (or, as his mother had been fond of saying, "nervous and jerky," which was, he thought, a far more apt description).

"Fred doesn't . . . like me very much, Marie." He sipped his coffee and attempted a weak, apologetic smile at the same time. The coffee dribbled onto his white shirt.

"He hates you!" Marie corrected. She pulled a small handkerchief from her pants pocket and dabbed futilely at the coffee stain. "But that's okay," she went on matter-of-factly, "because you hate him." She put her handkerchief away and stared quizzically at the stain. "That's going to stay there forever, Jim. It's the fabric. Why do you buy shirts like that?"

He looked down at the stain. "I don't know," he mumbled. "A shirt's a shirt, I guess–"

She interrupted, "So, what do you say? This weekend? It'll be good for you." She glanced quickly at his belly, which was just beginning a long, slow hike of its own over his belt. "You need the exercise, Jim. And I promise" —she held two fingers up, scout's-honor style—"we won't let a spider within five feet of you."

He hesitated. She kissed him lightly on the cheek. "Please?" she said.

"Yes," he answered immediately. "Okay."

"Good." She turned toward her office. "You won't regret it, Jim," she called over her shoulder.

*   *   *

He wasn't at all sure about that now. Because he ached. Badly. As if every muscle in his body had been stepped on by someone in spiked heels. And although it was Marie's face over him, and her marvelous green eyes on him, and her soothing voice asking if he was all right, he found that his eyes would focus only on Fred, standing a few feet behind her, grinning as if to say what a fool he—Jim Hart—was, and what a stupid mistake it had been to bring him along in the first place.

Surprising himself, Jim heard these words slip from his mouth: "Go to hell, Fred!—you bastard!" And he realized, instantly, that the words had been unintelligible, that all Fred had probably heard was a long, slow, and undulating exhale. Jim felt very relieved.

"Try to stand up," Marie said.

"I can't," Jim whispered.

"Sure you can. You really should."

"Why?"

"What'd you say, Jim? I didn't hear you."

"Why?" Jim repeated. "Why should I stand up?"

"Because it'll get your blood circulating. Don't you want your blood to circulate?"

Jim supposed that he smiled; he wasn't sure. He saw Marie smile.

"He's got no blood," Fred grumbled, shifting his weight from one leg to the other. "He's got gin and tonic in his veins—isn't that right, Jimbo?!"

Jim hated being called "Jimbo"—it sounded too much like "Dumbo," or "Bimbo." "Don't call me that," he said aloud, and he felt himself moving, felt himself sitting up very slowly, saw his knees come up to his chin, saw his arms circle them. "Am I all right?" he said. "Did I get frostbite, or something?" He knew that he hadn't.

"No," Marie answered. "We put you in the boat and brought you back here. You fell asleep for a few hours, but you're okay."

He lifted his head slightly and focused on a bare, white wall several yards away. "Is this the house?" he asked, knowing full well that it was.

"It's the house," Marie said.

He felt himself grimace; shit, but if he could just shake the damned body aches, if he could just get in touch with himself again. He hadn't felt this way in a decade or so—ever since he'd last dropped acid—as if he was going to chuckle off to a fantasy-land at any moment. "It's still raining outside?" he asked, hoping that Marie would understand what he needed now—a hold on reality, because the rain was reality.

"It's still raining," Marie told him. "And you're okay, Jim. A touch of hypothermia, that's all."

Jim looked at her and grinned slightly, as if proud of himself. "I know what that is," he said. "I had a friend once . . ." He stopped grinning abruptly. "His daughter died because of it." He noticed, then, that his body aches were slowly dissipating, as if a hundred small vises were gradually being removed.

"You're outa shape, Jimbo," Fred told him.

Jim said nothing.

"Shut up, Fred," Marie said, though halfheartedly, because she knew he wouldn't listen.

He laughed low in his throat. "You're a candy-ass, Jimbo."

Jim closed his eyes. He imagined that he was back home, in his apartment on East 49th Street, and that the ceiling was leaking—as it always did when the woman upstairs took a shower, which was three or four times a day—and that the landlord was complaining that he'd have to raise the rent again ("It's the security problem; you know what I mean? We got to hire people, and when you hire people, you got to pay them money."), and that the odors of the deli across the street, rancid odors, mostly, were wafting up to him.

It was awful, sure. Half the time it was disgusting as hell.

But it was home.

Chapter 3

In Manhattan

At the same moment that Jim Hart was struggling his way out of a bout with hypothermia, sixty-eight-year-old Winifred Haritson was involved in a fight of her own: Her windows wouldn't open. It was nothing new. Whenever the temperature and the humidity rose—as on this late summer evening—the windows stuck. The superintendent, a man named Lou, had explained why: "The wood *expands*, Mrs. Haritson,"—he made pulling motions with his hands, as if stretching taffy—"especially these windows, because that wood"—he knocked twice on the window casing—"is so *old* it soaks moisture up like a sponge, Mrs. Haritson. So take my advice." He hesitated; she nodded. "Always keep the windows open a crack, anyway, then it won't be so hard to open them all the way when it gets hot like this. You understand?"

She shook her head, and told him, in a low, secretive tone, "If I do that, Lou, they'll get in."

"Who'll get in, Mrs. Haritson?"

"The thieves and the muggers!"

He sighed; he had heard all this before. "You're five floors up, Mrs. Haritson. Only Superman could get in here through those windows."

"They have their ways, Lou. I've *seen* them."

He sighed again. "I'm sure you have, Mrs. Haritson."

She thought of calling him now, then decided that at this hour—it was 3:30 in the morning—he might curse and

19

complain and she wouldn't be able to get back to sleep, thinking he was mad at her. She gave one of the windows a final, hard-as-she-could push. It wouldn't budge. Then she realized that even if she could manage to open the windows she wouldn't be able to sleep anyway, because she'd have to sit up and watch to make sure nobody got in.

She sat heavily in a nearby chair. Lord, but living was hard, sometimes!

Winifred Haritson was a nobody—an aging widow who kept herself all but barricaded in her Lower East Side apartment. She had no living relatives, no cats, no canaries, no real friends. She had once been very attractive, but that had all but faded away. She realized that she was pathetically lonely, and that she would probably stay that way till the end of her days, but it was a fact to which she had long since resigned herself.

She got out of the chair and made her way back to her small, memorabilia-cluttered bedroom. Despite the oppressive heat, she was asleep quickly.

She had no dreams.

Chapter 4

It was daybreak, and Jim Hart, standing just off the house's small porch, wanted to know who it was that was watching him from shore. He called over his shoulder, "Marie?"

She called back, from the other side of the house, "Yes?"

"There's somebody watching us."

"What?"

"I said there's . . ." And he stopped. Because whoever it had been was gone now. Just like that. As if the forest had swallowed him up. Or as if—which, Jim thought, was more likely—the morning sun, just rising, had momentarily blinded him, and the man on shore had merely walked away.

Jim heard Marie coming toward him through the tall grass that surrounded the house. He turned his head. "It's nothing, Marie. I thought I saw someone." He nodded toward shore.

"A hunter?" Marie asked.

He shrugged. "I don't know. It could have been a hunter, I guess." He paused briefly, then went on, "It could have been the Fuller Brush Man, for all I know."

Fred appeared from the western side of the island. He had a makeshift fishing pole in hand and a good length of nylon line attached to it. He grinned; "Hey, Jimbo, wanta do a little fishing? I thought we'd take the boat out. You afraid of boats, Jimbo?" He hesitated only briefly. "My little sister says you're afraid of spiders, so I figure you've *got* to be afraid of boats.''

Jim glanced at Marie and tried to conjure up a look of betrayal. Marie looked away quickly, as if embarrassed. ''Sure,'' Jim said. ''I'll come with you.''

Fred still was grinning. ''You know how to swim, Jimbo?''

''I know how to swim, Fred.''

''Okay then, let's go.'' And he turned and started back to the western side of the island. Jim followed, several paces behind. As he walked, he busied himself with figuring out the best way to sit in the boat. It was a small, three-seated wooden rowboat, and he thought it would be nice if he could find a way to face away from Fred. Then Fred wouldn't have to see that he had no idea how to bait a hook, or how to cast, or how to pull a fish in—should he catch one—because his body would block the view of all that. And then he realized, in the middle of these thoughts, that he was desperate and tense, and that this little hiking expedition had turned very sour.

Fred, keeping his eyes straight ahead, said, ''You're not having a good time, are you, Jim?'' There was only the very faintest trace of sarcasm in his voice. Jim decided that the question had been rhetorical; he stayed quiet. Fred kept his eyes straight ahead; the weeds here were waist-high, and the soil, spongy from the recent, heavy rains, squeaked under foot, making walking precarious. He went on, ''Think of it as a learning experience, Jim.'' Now the sarcasm seemed to have vanished altogether. Abruptly, Fred stopped walking; Jim reacted a second too late; the front of his foot connected with Fred's heel. Fred looked around at him. ''Where's your pole, Jim?''

Jim grimaced. He thought a moment, his eyes focused on Fred's hand, loosely gripping his own makeshift pole. He said, ''I assumed you had one for me, Fred. In the boat.''

Fred started walking again, a little faster. ''No, I don't, Jim. Did I tell you I did? You'll have to make one.'' He moved his hand slightly to indicate several thin birch trees a dozen yards to the right. ''That's a good bet,'' he went on, and quickened his pace even more. Jim stopped. Fred called back, "I'll wait for you in the boat, Jimbo." Jim watched him lope off. He thought he heard him giggle—a high, quick, grating sound, a child's giggle—then grimaced again. That giggle sounded ludicrous from a man like Fred Williams.

Jim moved slowly and carefully to his right, toward the cluster of birches.

Fred Williams would admit freely that he was a chauvinist and a bully. He would also go on to explain that because of this "self-honesty," he was "infinitely more at peace with himself" than other men.

He pushed his way through life like a bear, and anyone standing in his way usually got eaten. Slowly.

Like Jim Hart.

Fred mused that now he was probably just chewing on Jim Hart. In a day or so—when the hike ended—he would finish with him. It was what Jim needed. If Jim could be made to see himself as the candy-ass that everyone knew he was, then he'd be well on his way to becoming a much happier man.

So, Fred thought, there was therapy and goodness in chewing Jim up. Which was not to deny, of course, that it was also lots of fun. It was a man's right—and duty—to dominate other men if he could. The strong survived. The strong *had* to survive.

He stopped walking, leaned over, and set his pole in the little rowboat. He glanced around. Jim was nowhere in sight. He pushed the boat into the water, jumped in, and grabbed the oars. "Hey, Jimbo!" he called, and he rowed mightily toward the middle of the lake, where the water was deepest, and the chances for catching breakfast for all of them the best. "Hey Jimbo, it's okay!" He heard himself chuckle low in his throat.

He had seated himself in the middle of the boat; the bow was behind him. He saw Jim appear on shore, now about fifty yards away. He had a six-foot length of birch branch in hand, and a look of puzzlement on his face. It was a look that made Fred feel good. "Sorry, Jimbo," he called.

He noticed that the boat was moving very sluggishly, and that it was riding much lower in the water than it should have been. He saw Jim point at the boat. He heard Jim call, "Who's . . ." and a sudden breeze carried the rest of the sentence away.

"What'd you say, Jimbo?" Fred called. He saw Jim's mouth move, but because the breeze had sustained itself, and the distance to shore had increased to nearly a hundred yards, he heard nothing.

"Goddammit!" Fred swore, because the boat was moving so sluggishly—as if the water had suddenly become much more dense than water ought to be—and he had no good explanation for it.

"Fred!" he heard, very faintly, from shore. He looked. Marie was standing next to Jim; she had her hands cupped around her mouth. "Fred!" he heard again. And he saw her point frantically. At him, he thought. Then he corrected himself. No—not at him, at the front of the boat. She was pointing at something in the front of the boat.

He turned his head a little. He noticed first that the boat was angled slightly downward, toward the bow. He turned his head some more. He felt a chill go down his spine, and grinned as if in denial of it.

He saw the man in the bow seat for only an instant. He was tall, dark-skinned, dark-haired, blue-eyed; and he was naked.

"Welcome," the man said, "to my island."

And he leaped from the boat before Fred could get a word out. "What in the . . ." Fred murmured, then peered over the side of the boat. He lifted the oars from the water; a few bubbles undulated to the surface, where the man had jumped in. "What in the Christ–" Fred said. And the water grew still.

Chapter 5

In the Bronx

Georgie MacPhail was intrigued by the back room, just as any normally curious boy his age would have been intrigued. The room was kept locked most of the time, which had naturally piqued his interest (not that the lock prevented him from getting in; at twelve years old, he was an accomplished cat burglar—a skill his mother and three younger brothers depended on), and the fact that the building's janitor, Mr. Baum, had told him repeatedly to stay out of the room made it imperative that Georgie know everything there was to know about it.

He knew, for instance, that Mrs. Wain's parakeet was in the room, under a ten-year-old copy of the *Daily News*, though the bird was now just a pathetic pile of feathers and bones. Georgie had almost told Mrs. Wain about it, because it was sad, really, seeing her stick her head out her window twice a day (in the middle of the morning, and in the middle of the afternoon) and yell, "Peepers, here Peepers!" still expecting after three years that the bird was going to come back to her.

And he knew, also, that the back room was where the janitor kept his magazines. Georgie had never found the magazines, though he'd looked. He had seen the janitor slip quickly and quietly into the room and, five minutes later, slip quickly out, his movements a little stiff. Georgie had told his mother about the janitor's magazines, and his mother had said that the janitor was "entitled to his pleasures, Georgie, like everyone else." Georgie thought that was a nice way to think.

And he knew also about the ghost that lived in the room. He had never been sure what kind of ghost it was—whether it was a man or a woman—because he had never been able to talk to it, or get a good look at it. He knew only that it liked the two dark back corners a lot, and that it went from one corner to the other according to its mood. Usually, if it was raining outside, it would stay in the southwest corner and shiver quite a bit. Otherwise, it seemed to like the southeast corner. Occasionally, on very hot days, it stood very still right in the middle.

Georgie supposed at first that it was odd the ghost didn't scare him. Then he decided that it would be stupid to be afraid of a thing that spent most of its time shivering in the darkest corners of the back room. When he realized this, he realized also that he felt sorry for the ghost, and he wished he could do something for it. Something to bring it happiness.

Georgie MacPhail was a nice kid—good-looking and intelligent—who loved his mother, cared for his brothers, and prayed nightly to a God he called "Sir." The fact that he was a cat burglar, and would probably remain a cat burglar for the rest of his life, had nothing to do with Georgie himself. It was merely the road he had been forced by circumstance to walk on. He was no more to blame for it than he was to blame for the color of his hair—brown—or his shoe size, or his left-handedness.

Chapter 6

"Son of a *bitch*!" Fred Williams breathed. He took a long drink of the strong, lukewarm black coffee Marie had made for him. He shook his head briskly. "Son of a *bitch*!" he repeated.

Marie asked, " 'Welcome to my island'?" And she grinned slightly, despite her brother's obvious discomfort. "Is that all that man said?"

Jim Hart interrupted, "I thought this was *your* island, Marie."

She looked up at him. She was seated, with Fred, at the small kitchen table. Jim was near the door; it was closed. "It is our island, Jim." She pulled out the chair kitty-corner to her and nodded at it. "Come sit down, Jim. You're making me nervous."

He came over immediately and sat down.

"It sure as hell *is* our island!" Fred grumbled. He took another drink of the coffee. He wished fervently that they'd had the good sense to bring a bottle along. "And it's been our island from the damned Day One!" He jabbed the table with his forefinger. "The goddamned Day One, Jimbo!" He lifted his coffee cup and saw that it was empty. "Get me some more coffee, Marie."

Marie's eyebrows shot up in annoyance. "Sure enough, Fred." She stood and went to the stove with the cup.

Jim asked, "What was he talking about, then?"

Marie said, "A fly got in the coffee, Fred. Do you mind?"

"Why should I mind? Fish it out."

"It's raining again," she said. She was looking out a small window to the left and above the stove.

"Shit," Fred muttered, "that's all we need . . ." He listened as the rain began pelting the roof of the house.

"What do you think he was talking about?" Jim repeated.

Fred ignored the question. "We'll *never* get out of here! Jesus, I've got *orders* to fill—"

"He could be a squatter," Jim offered.

"A what?"

"A squatter."

And Marie said, her voice trembling, "He's out there. I can see him. He's out there!"

Fred and Jim looked over at her in unison. There was a short silence; then Fred pushed himself quickly, as if with great urgency, to his feet—the chair clattered backward to the floor. "What's he doing?" he said as he crossed to the stove. "Is he flashing you? If he's flashing you, I'll . . ."

"He's gone," Marie said. And Fred peered out the window. He saw the rain. It was falling straight down and it was heavy and gray against the backdrop of gray sky. He thought he saw a quick whisper of movement near a lone birch tree twenty feet from the house. "I'm going outside, Marie."

Marie said nothing. She watched him fetch his jacket from the back of his chair.

"I'll come with you," Jim said, though with little conviction.

Surprising him, Fred said, "Sure. Why don'tcha?! Two's better than one."

Marie smiled to herself as she listened to them shuffling about on the porch, obviously hoping the rain would stop abruptly. Fred and Jim—it was a strange and unlikely twosome.

She tried not to imagine what Fred would do if he found the trespasser, but there were too many other situations, past situations, to look back on, so she couldn't help but see Fred, in her mind's eye, working the guy over very thoroughly. And thoroughly enjoying every second of it.

She thought that Jim would raise a feeble protest; Fred would scowl at him, and grinningly invite him to join in the beating; "Be really good for you, Jimbo!" . . . "Teach you something about *survival*, Jimbo!" . . .

She took a sip of Fred's coffee (there had been no fly in it—that had merely been a feeble attempt at rattling him, a fact he had seemed to guess right away. Christ, if only he wasn't always so damned . . . aware of things!).

Unlike most of his kind, the creature had grown into adulthood. There were just a dozen or so others like him, all over the planet, including the female with him now. They were beings for whom the normal laws of change and evolution had been revoked, or at least altered: What would otherwise have taken eons, now took only decades.

Those who had cared for him, and had raised him, years ago—the ones he called "Grandpa," and "Grandma" —had given him a name, and he had kept it because the memories attached to it gave him pleasure. And pleasure in all its forms was one of the reasons he was alive (and he knew that when his life stopped giving him pleasure, he would gladly end it).

His name was Seth. It was a name he said often, in various voices and inflections, and in a number of the dialects he had heard through the years.

Seth.

When he said the name he often could see, in memory, the face of his Grandpa and the face of his Grandma; and it was delight he saw, and wonderment, and awe when at last they came to realize what he was, and where he had come from.

That was when he had taken them (and so, of course, they still lived—their blood was his blood, and their flesh his flesh; they had shared themselves with him—it was the perfect act of love).

Seth.

He was beautiful by any standards, because he was a creature that the earth had produced.

And the earth did not make mistakes.

*   *   *

Jim Hart said, "Why don't we forget it, Fred. I can't see a thing." The rain had strengthened until, now, it was deafening, and almost impenetrable.

But Fred hadn't heard him: He pointed to his left. "You look over there," he shouted, to be heard above the noise of the rain. He nodded to his right. "I'll go this way." And he grabbed Jim's arm and grinned maliciously; "If you find him, Jimbo, you just come and tell me. Okay?!"

Jim took hold of Fred's wrist and tried vainly to pull his hand away. Fred's grip strengthened. He repeated, "Okay?!"

"Okay," Jim said. Fred let go. Jim stepped off the porch. Within seconds, the rain soaked his clothes through to the skin and he whispered, with as much venom as he could muster, "Fuck you, Fred!" It gave him little comfort.

Chapter 7

Leonora Wingate (a name she despised because it sounded so damned cosmopolitan; she much preferred the nickname "Lenny") wasn't at all sure she was making the right move. After all, the job she'd had here—in the Utica Social Services Department, Child Welfare Division— was pretty secure, and the pay was good, the working conditions all right. Few women could really ask for much more.

She zipped up the brown vinyl two-suiter, and stared blankly at it a moment. *Life is chances*, she thought. She said it slowly, smilingly, as if to convince herself: "Life is chances."

The phone rang, jarring her out of her reverie. She snatched it up from the bedside table. "Yes?" she said. It was the man from the moving company. *Was everything all right?* he wanted to know. *Could his men come and pack things up, or was she having second thoughts again?* She briskly assured him that she wasn't having second thoughts, and that she expected her belongings to be in her new apartment, in Manhattan, the following afternoon. *That's our guarantee, Miss Wingate—next day delivery within 200 miles. And you got it, Miss Wingate.* "Thank you," she said, and hung up.

Now, she realized, she had cemented her fate.

She lifted the two-suiter, began mentally cataloguing its contents—dress, suit, underwear, deodorant . . . She lowered her head suddenly. *This is a mistake*, she thought. *This is a mistake!* And without looking back she quickly left the apartment that had been her home for the last five years.

She felt lousy.

Chapter 8

Jim Hart tried to find shelter under one of the island's three maple trees, but it was a very old tree, and its foliage was sparse, so the rain was nearly as heavy under it as out in the open.

He leaned disconsolately against the tree and felt himself begin to shiver. He took a long, slow, deep breath; the shivering abated. "Stupid!" he said aloud. "Stupid shitass, stupid, damn!" When he became frustrated or angry, as he was now, he often swore in a rambling, inarticulate, and uncreative way. "Crap, fuck!" he added, his enunciation very crisp.

He heard something rustling about above him. He looked. The rain stung his eyes and he turned his head quickly away; another string of curses erupted from him.

He realized, as he cursed, that he had seen something very odd in the branches overhead. He looked again, shielding his eyes as best he could.

The tree was empty.

Marie was feeling very uncomfortable. Not with the house, or the chair she was sitting in, but with the mood that had settled over her. It itched, it felt prickly and hot, like a wool blanket on a summer day. And there was a feeling of claustrophobia, too, as if she were wrapped in a blanket (no, she corrected, as if someone else had wrapped her in one) cocoon style, and there was no way of freeing herself. It was a mood she had felt only once before, as a small child, and there had been a vague, unremembered threat attached to it, something she had to hide from.

But here, she thought, there was only the rain, of course, and a late summer chill which had settled into the house (and maybe that was causing her mood—the rain and the cold. But she knew immediately that that was not it. She knew that if she looked deep within herself she would see that she was on the verge of panic. And she knew that she could think of no good reason for it. She knew that, with only the very slightest provocation, she would scream).

Fred could feel his fists clenching and his teeth gritting and all his muscles going taut. He, like Jim, was soaked to the skin, but, unlike Jim, he was feeling vengeful, and it was keeping him warm.

He was moving carefully and quietly through the tall grass. His plan was to first make a careful search of the perimeter of the island, and then to crisscross it. It was unlikely, he knew, that he'd catch the guy that way—he'd need a couple more good men to accomplish that—but at least the guy would be put on notice that he was not going to put up with any perverse fun and games here, on *his* island!

Jim had never been more exhausted than at this moment. He had stopped being angry and frustrated. The curses had ended. He merely wanted, ached, to be away from here. To be somewhere else, anywhere else, because all this . . . posturing—for Fred's sake, and Marie's sake, even for his own sake—was so terribly wearisome.

He was still leaning against the tree. He felt movement in it now, as if something inside—an actual part of the tree— had rolled over in its sleep. He dismissed it immediately.

It bothered Marie that she was talking to herself. She couldn't remember ever talking to herself before. She had seen others doing it, in New York City, although she supposed they talked to themselves for quite different reasons than she did, for reasons of insanity.

Her reason was fear.

She was glad that she'd finally admitted it. Now she could stop fighting it internally—she could relax a little. "Because, Fred, you see," she said to herself—her voice high-pitched, almost scolding—"you cannot go around doing that anymore." It was a speech she had practiced often. "It's not acceptable behavior. It'll get you into trouble. There are forces much stronger than men alone. Forces *we* created . . ." She trailed off. She wasn't listening to herself anymore; she was just mouthing the words out of a deep familiarity with them.

She was listening to the house instead. Listening to it wheeze in the rain and grumble beneath her feet. And perhaps, she mused, that was what frightened her—the house. "You can't go around doing that anymore, Fred. It's unacceptable behavior." She stopped. She realized that the awful mood which had been gripping her only minutes earlier had dissipated. The fear had replaced it. She much preferred the fear—it was at least recognizable, although it would have been good to know what, precisely, she was afraid of.

And then she wondered suddenly if she was afraid of the man she had seen. She forced herself to grin. There was nothing particularly frightening about naked men. If anything, they looked quite vulnerable, even silly (depending, of course, on the man).

"Of course," she murmured.

But *this* man—her grin vanished—had not looked at all silly. Not even in that downpour. He had looked very . . . honest.

And very human.

The creature sensed the emotion of others, even from a distance, with the same strength that other species sense a change in wind direction, or a rapid change in altitude.

The creature felt the emotion of others—he tasted it, reacted to it. If the emotion was pleasurable, he enjoyed it. If the emotion was painful, he examined it, took it apart, tried to understand it. And if he could not understand it, he absorbed it, and experienced the pain himself;

he cried out if the pain required it, wept if the pain required it. And then he understood it.

For his kind, it was a process similar to digestion, or respiration. It happened. And controlling it was nearly impossible.

The creature sensed the emotions moving around the house. For very brief moments, he could even see them as a kind of multicolored and very fine mist—here swirling and eddying about like miniature storms, there lifting lazily up, toward the roof of the house and finally evaporating. And all of it constantly expanding and contracting, as if it were itself a living and breathing thing. The creature took great pleasure in these momentary visions; his senses rejoiced in them.

Elena, the other creature with him, newer to the earth, could not yet see what he could see. It was a process that took time to evolve.

Jim Hart leaned, as if exhausted, with his back to the closed front door. He stared confusedly at Marie. "Marie?" he said. "What's the matter?"

She was still at the table, hands wrapped around an empty coffee cup. She had obviously been crying. She looked up at him. "We've got to leave, Jim."

He crossed the room quickly, sat next to her at the table. "I don't understand, Marie . . . What are you afraid of?" he said, because it was obvious—in the way her hands shook, in the way her voice quivered—that she was frightened.

"This place," she whispered, "isn't ours anymore."

Chapter 9

On Staten Island

Sam Campbell was saying something he felt was terribly profound, something his daughter, Marsha, should think about. He nodded at a bunch of kids playing Cowboys and Indians down the street. "They play Cowboys and Indians," he said, in his best observational tone, "the same way we did. Same sound effects, same rules. It's kind of interesting that there haven't been any changes." He paused. Maybe Marsha wanted to say something. She stayed quiet. "I remember," he went on, "I was playing it once. I was seven or eight. I was a cowboy, I think—not that it matters. It doesn't matter. And . . . I got shot. I was dead." He paused, memories trickling back. "But *I* wanted reality," he continued, a bit dreamily. "I mean *stark* reality. So I laid there, across this stump, my eyes and mouth closed—because I didn't know that people could die with their mouths and eyes open—for what seemed like an hour, at least, although it was probably just a couple of minutes." He paused again, reflected. "I was . . . carrying out the act of being dead, I think—as if death were something active, as if it were something for me to *do*!" He looked questioningly at Marsha. She looked questioningly back. "Do you understand what I'm saying, Marsha?"

She smiled a big, toothy smile. "I like Cowboys and Indians very much," she said.

He lowered his head briefly, and patted her small hand. "Yes," he said, "I'm sure you do."

*   *   *

Joyce Dewitte was almost sure of it now—Ginger was dying. She had watched the other cat—a Siamese named Amber—die only six months earlier, so she knew the signs well.

She stroked the cat, felt it purring softly under her fingertips, watched its half-closed eyes raise to meet hers. It would be another two weeks, maybe a month, then she'd have to bury it somewhere in the park. The hardest part till then, of course, would be in the watching, because she didn't have the courage to have the cat "put to sleep." She stroked it a little harder, felt the cutting edge of bone beginning its journey up, through the slowly dissolving fat and muscle. "It's not the leukemia virus itself, Joyce," the vet had told her. "It's the complications that ensue . . ."

"Jesus, cat," she blurted. It was all she could manage. She left the apartment quickly and went to work.

Chapter 10

At the House on the Island

"Of course this place is ours!" Fred proclaimed. "It certainly isn't his!" He nodded agitatedly to indicate the outside of the house, and the man he had been unable to find there.

"Jesus," Marie said. "I didn't mean it literally." She stopped, looked confused. "Maybe I did. I don't know. We've got to get away from here. Now! *That's* what I mean."

Fred had been leaning over, with his arms straight and his palms flat on the table. He straightened. "Damn it, Marie," he muttered. "Do you know what you're asking of me?"

"Yes," she answered immediately. "I do."

"At least it stopped raining," Jim offered, and he found that he was grinning vacantly. "We can light a fire, and dry our clothes over the stove, and then we can get out of here . . ."

Fred interrupted, "Well it's too much, Marie. Too damned much! Don't you realize what that guy's done? He's challenged me. He's said as much as 'Come out and prove yourself.'"

Marie said, "That's asinine. *You're* asinine!"

The fine mist around the house had grown thick and dingy gray in color. It vaulted high above the roof of the house and rolled toward the water; the miniature storms whipped into a silent frenzy in the tall grass; the grass did not move.

Seth watched without expression, his view of the mist a continuous thing because the emotions from within the house were so terrible now, and so strong.

Elena touched him lightly; she felt a tingle start in the tips of her fingers. The tingle became a dim paralysis that coursed up, through her arm, and into her brain.

Her other hand, lightly holding the wrist-sized branch of a tree, tightened involuntarily, in reaction to the emotion moving through Seth and into her. The branch snapped off. She groaned, as if in pain. "I want to kill you!" she screeched, because that, above all, was the emotion that was assaulting Seth, and so her, from inside the house.

"I heard something," Marie said. She held her hand up in a gesture designed to quiet her brother. "I heard something," she repeated.

"I think I heard someone scream," Jim said.

Fred looked around quickly at the door. "Is that locked?" he said, more to himself than to Marie or Jim. He saw that it wasn't locked. He ran to it, threw the bolt, backed away, glanced at his sister. "The gun, Marie. It's in my pack. Get it for me."

She hesitated only a moment, then said, "Yes, of course."

Jim said nervously, "Why do we need a gun? We don't need a gun. Someone's in trouble out there . . ."

"Shut up!" Fred hissed.

Marie pushed herself away from the table, stood, went into the bedroom. Moments later she returned, a blue, snub-nosed Colt .38 in her right hand, her arm bent at the elbow, the gun pointing at the ceiling.

"Bring it here," Fred ordered.

She crossed the room to him, hesitated. His back was to her. He still was looking at the door. He stuck his hand out stiffly behind him. "I said give it here, Marie, goddammit!"

He glanced around at her. She had straightened her arm; she was pointing the weapon squarely at his head.

"Shit!" he whimpered, and fell to the floor. She fired, her aim on the closed and locked door. "Shit!" Fred breathed. "Oh shit!" She fired again, and again, and again.

Jim found himself pushing the table over in his haste and panic, stumbling across the room to her, wrestling her to the floor.

Seeing this, Fred snatched the gun from her hand and scrambled to his feet.

She lay on her back, motionless, eyes wide. Fred, standing over her, held the gun pointed down at his side—she had emptied the gun into the door—and looked very confused. Jim had also rolled to his back; his eyes were closed lightly. "Jesus, God," he whispered, as if in prayer.

Darkness brought the motionless, silent cold of an Adirondack autumn with it. You'd stuff most of your body into a sleeping bag to protect yourself from that kind of cold. You'd curl up into a fetal position to protect yourself from it. And, almost without fail, a stiff, uneasy sleep would come quickly.

But Jim Hart was wide awake. He said to Fred Williams— in a chair on the other side of the living room, next to where Marie was lying in her own sleeping bag—"You think she'll be okay, Fred?"

"She's an epileptic," Fred answered.

Jim turned his head slightly to look at him. "I didn't know that."

"She had a seizure, Jim."

"Do you really believe . . ."

"I don't believe it. I know it. Now go to sleep."

"She never told anyone, Fred."

"Would you?"

"I'd tell my friends, Fred."

"How do you know she didn't?" It was a sharp, two-edged question, and it hurt.

Several moments later Jim answered, "From what I know of epilepsy . . ."

"Go to sleep, Jimbo."

"Go to hell, Fred!" But it was a tiny whisper, nearly too shallow for Jim himself to hear. He closed his eyes. He thought that somewhere, some time, in the last twenty-four hours, his life had taken a distinct and unpleasant turn. He didn't know exactly where it might be heading now, only that it would be impossible to go back.

Chapter 11

In Manhattan

Winifred Haritson was in a tunnel. Today, it led from the Social Security Office on West 39th Street, over to Broadway, to Third Avenue, Second Avenue, and finally to her apartment building. It snaked through the building's lobby, to the elevator, up to the fifth floor, down the corridor, and to her front door. It ended there.

Winifred Haritson despised the tunnel. It suffocated her, it made her deaf, and speechless. But it was a necessary tunnel. It protected her because no one could really bother her in it, though they tried. Sometimes they called filthy names at her, sometimes they touched her, prodded her, tugged at her purse, or her umbrella (her present umbrella was the second one of the year; the first had been yanked away from her in February by someone dressed in a tattered Santa Claus costume). She didn't care about the names (she let them slide past) and her purse rarely contained anything valuable, and what, after all, was more valuable than her life? If they really wanted the purse they would take it, so why resist too much?

She dug far into the pocket of her coat for her keys. She found them—they had fallen through a hole in the pocket and into the lining of the coat—squinted at them, chose the right one, pushed it into the lock.

"Hey, Mrs. Haritson!" she heard, from outside the tunnel. It was a young man's voice; she thought she recognized it in a vague, uncomfortable way. She turned the key in the lock, eyes straight ahead, on the elevator.

"Hey, Mrs. Haritson!" she heard again, much louder and coarser, so the walls of the tunnel shook and threatened to fall. She moved as quickly as her old legs could carry her, in small, shuffling steps, across the lobby. "I'm *talking* to you!" she heard. She hurried toward the elevator. She felt a hand on her shoulder, but just briefly.

"Get out of here! Now!" she heard. It was Lou, the superintendent, stepping in between her and the boy. The walls of the tunnel strengthened. She grinned very slightly. "And if I see your face around here again," she heard Lou say, "I'll make it uglier than it already is!" She heard running feet. The elevator doors opened. She stepped in, heard them close behind her. She would have to call Lou up later and thank him.

Chapter 12

Fred and Jim and Marie were asleep when Seth and Elena first appeared in the house. It was early morning, an hour before sunrise, and the rain had started again. Here and there, sleet mixed with it, like a random fall of whitish-gray ash; it melted nearly as quickly as it settled to earth.

The exhaustion caused by tension and by panic had brought sleep first to Marie, then to Jim, and at last, telling himself that it would only be for fifteen minutes, Fred nodded off. He still was in the chair, next to his sister, who was on the floor. His chin was down on his chest, and he was snoring in a loud, rasping, and unpleasant way. He had shoved the .38 into his right-hand pants pocket (it had remained warm from firing for quite a while and, nestled next to his thigh, felt like a small, quiet animal; it had comforted him).

He was not accustomed to sleeping in a straight-backed wooden chair, so when his brain told him it was time to roll over, he fell from the chair very quickly and heavily and hit the floor with a huge, resonating thud. His weight jammed the grip of the pistol hard into his wrist.

He woke suddenly and in deep pain, screaming harsh, spittle-laden curses.

And, at once, Seth, standing at the other side of the room, screamed and cursed too, followed almost instantly by Elena, beside him. It was an immediate, uncontrolled response—the blessing and damnation of their kind, and

45

only with immense mental effort were they able to quiet themselves.

Though too late.

Marie had been dreaming. She was in a cocoon, she was hot, and blind, and could feel, just beyond the cocoon's skin, that something was waiting for her to emerge, something that was very hungry. Her brother's scream had sliced into that dream like a knife.

And she woke screaming, too.

Jim had awakened before Marie, just as Fred had hit the floor, but before his screams had started. And in the few seconds since then, Jim had lain rigid and frightened, with his eyes wide open and his bladder threatening sharply to let go.

He had also heard Seth's scream, and Elena's.

He forced himself to turn his head slightly so he could see the entire room. Fred had stopped screaming—he was holding his wrist and uttering low, guttural curses. Marie had covered her face with her hands; she wept quietly.

And fifteen feet away, near the room's south wall . . . (Seth realized the man's eyes were on him. He merged instantly. Elena followed) . . . nothing. A wall, a window. The steady, hard rain beyond it. A pair of soft, almost invisible shadows shimmering in the near darkness.

Nothing.

"Fred?" Jim managed, his voice much too low and quiet. "Fred?" he said again, louder. "There's something in the house with us."

Fred continued cursing. He made no indication that he heard what Jim was saying.

Jim sat up very slowly.

Fred said, mostly to himself, "I broke my fuckin' wrist!"

Jim pushed himself halfway to a standing position. He felt movement around him, as if the air itself had become animated. He pushed himself quickly, confusedly back, away from the movement.

It ended.

"Fred?" he said, and looked over at him. "Something's . . ." And he saw the two shadows there, around Fred.

Fred screamed—a loud, high-pitched, ludicrously falsetto thing that caromed off the walls of the house and set Jim's ears to ringing.

Fred was clawing madly at his flannel shirt with his one good hand.

"Jesus Christ!" Jim breathed, because blood soaked the front of the shirt. Fred pulled hard at it; the buttons popped and sprayed out across the room; the shirt fell open. Fred grabbed the bottom of his freshly bloodied and ripped T-shirt, pulled it up to his chin, and looked down at his chest. In awe, he fell silent.

From across the room, Jim stared—disgusted, fascinated, disbelieving—at the narrow, jagged gash that ran diagonally across Fred's chest, from near his left armpit to just under his left nipple.

Chapter 13

In the Bronx

"Hey, Mr. Ghost!" Georgie McPhail called, and squinted into the darkness of the back room. "Hey, Mr. Ghost!" he said again. He had decided, on his previous visit to the room, that the ghost was a man. He had no hard and fast reason for this decision; it was just a guess, and now he was testing it.

Mr. Baum, the janitor, was at his sister's house for the day. "She's damn sick, Georgie," he'd said, not looking at all distressed, Georgie thought. "And I got to tend to her, ya know."

So, Georgie felt safe enough—no one but the janitor cared about the back room.

"Hey, Mr. Ghost—you wanta talk?!"

He thought he saw the ghost then, in the middle of the back wall, shivering and shaking. "Hey," he asked, "what you scared of? Nothin' to be scared of."

He thought that the ghost's name might very well be Hiram or Handy. He had no hard and fast reason for this, either, only that they both sounded like terrific names for ghosts: He tried them out. "Hiram?" he said. "Handy?" And he paused. Nothing. "Hiram Handy?" he went on, and he supposed that the ghost shivered more violently. He grinned. "Hiram Handy?" he repeated, as if hoping for confirmation that that was, indeed, the ghost's name. He thought the ghost was shivering more violently.

Georgie backed out of the room, reached behind himself, opened the door. He hesitated. "I got to go to work now, Hiram Handy," he said. "But I'll be back for sure. Then we can talk."

48

Chapter 14

In Manhattan

He called himself "Whimsical Fatman" (though he wasn't at all fat), "Whimsy" to his friends, and they numbered in the dozens. He was fifty-seven years old, penniless, white-haired, and he smiled almost constantly.

At the age of forty-five he left his wife and his two children—a boy and a girl, nice kids—and his job in Raleigh, North Carolina, as a Fuel Systems Design Engineer for a company serving the aerospace industry. He came to Manhattan and almost instantly fell into what he still called "the easy life."

For five years, as long as his personal savings lasted (he had left his wife and kids with the family account, which was substantial) he drifted from one sleazy hotel to another even sleazier, until at last he was forced to find, as he called them, "the meanest accommodations that Mother Fate has to offer"—the streets. Occasionally, if the weather was especially bad, he sought out an abandoned building or a particularly secluded part of the subway, but he liked to avoid these places. They were dangerous and lonely, and they went against the grain of what he felt he was doing (or had told himself twelve years earlier he was doing)—getting to know "the real people," the "naked ones"—the men that society had tossed away and who, therefore, lived "according to their wits and sinew."

He had gotten to know these men, and the occasional woman, as well as anyone. He had become one of them. And he had long since stopped using pretentious little phrases to describe himself and his ''ambitions.'' He admitted quite freely and happily that he had few ambitions beyond scrounging up his next meal and a place to sleep.

His name was William Devine.

Chapter 15

Fred Williams recognized in himself the symptoms of shock—weakness, lightheadedness, shortness of breath. He leaned forward in the chair and saw that the wound across his chest was bleeding again, though it was only a trickle (the air was cold, the wound was shallow, his clotting factor was good). He straightened in the chair, murmured "Jesus Christ," and his lightheadedness intensified until he thought he might fall out of the chair. He bent forward again. "Jesus Christ!" he repeated. And he realized that he was very frightened.

Marie was standing beside him. It had taken her a long while to struggle back from where her panic and desperation had carried her. And now that she was back, her fear had returned. "I don't understand," she said. "What could possibly have done that to you, Fred?"

"I don't know," he answered quietly, confusedly. "I was asleep, I fell out of the chair . . ." He trailed off, his confusion deepening.

"Maybe it was a nail," Marie said, and she began poking the floor with the toe of her shoe. She leaned over and moved the palm of her hand slowly across the floor. "A nail, Fred. It could have been a nail sticking up out of the floor." She stood abruptly. "No," she whispered. "I suppose not."

Jim Hart was standing close by, a little glassy-eyed. His memory was playing tricks on him; it was showing him things he didn't remember seeing when the wound had

51

opened on Fred's chest; it was showing him more than mere shadows; it was showing him, though very briefly—in milliseconds—the suggestion of arms, and legs, a pair of breasts, and buttocks—two bodies moving with such impossible quickness that they might as well have been invisible. But halting in their movements just long enough that, if only in memory, he could see them again.

It scared the hell out of him. And he wondered if he should say something to Fred and Marie. He didn't know what.

"It felt . . ." Fred began, and paused; he fingered the wound delicately. The bleeding had stopped. "It felt," he repeated, "like something bit me."

Seth and Elena's only concern was that the little ones be protected. The birthing was just days off now, and it was a process that had taken months to reach maturity, a process upon which the very survival of their species depended.

The big man in the house, the one called "Fred," could easily stop it if he were allowed. If he knew of it he *would* stop it. Without hesitation. He would try to destroy them, and the little ones too. Seth and Elena knew this. They had tasted him, ingested him (and so knew him better than he knew himself).

Killing would be an enormous and dizzying pleasure for him, as it was for them, but *he* would seek it out, beyond what was necessary. *He* would come back for more, again and again and again—

Seth did not smile of his own accord, from his own pleasure. He smiled only in imitation. When he felt pleasure, or anticipated it, it coursed through him like a drug and left his face as blank as stone and his muscles rigid.

Elena touched him. She felt the anticipation coursing through him, and responded in kind.

And, side by side, the backs of their hands touching very lightly, they stood in the early morning sunlight, a dozen yards from the house—a pair of stoical, naked, and wonderfully beautiful mannequins enjoying the massive pleasure that was soon to come.

* * *

Fred felt better about himself now that the lightheadedness was gone, now that he felt stronger and could think more clearly. The fear had dissipated. He despised those few moments when the fear had gripped him.

He stood. "We're going back to the car," he announced.

Marie smiled, relieved. "I'm glad you see it my way, Fred." She had expected an argument.

"In an hour or two," he told her, and glanced quickly about. "Where's the gun, Marie? Where's the goddamned gun?!"

Marie nodded at the table. "Over there," she whispered.

He crossed to the table, picked up the gun, checked it. It was empty. "It won't do me any good like this, Marie." He glanced at her. She said nothing; she looked very tense.

"I said this weapon won't–"

"I'll get the damned bullets," she cut in, and started for the bedroom.

Fred looked suddenly stupified. "You think I *want* to stick around here? You think I don't know how serious this . . . *thing* on my chest is?!"

She disappeared into the bedroom. Moments later she reappeared, a box of .38 slugs in hand. She held them out to her brother. "Go ahead," she told him icily, "blow his damned brains out!"

Then, surprising himself, Jim said, "There are two of them, Fred."

"Two of them?" Fred grinned slightly.

"Yes. I saw them. I *think* I saw them, anyway."

"Where, Jimbo?"

"Here."

"What do you mean, 'Here'?"

"I mean here, in this house."

Fred stopped grinning. "When?" he said.

Jim nodded at Fred's wound. "When that happened."

Fred looked down slowly at his bloodied shirt. He looked back up at Jim. He grinned again. "You're trying to tell me, Jimbo, that he . . . that *they* did this? Is that what you're telling me?"

"Yes, Fred, I think that's what I'm telling you."

Fred looked again at his shirt. He parted it, lifted his T-shirt, studied the wound.

And, at last, he saw two faces, just as Jim had seen two bodies—with the eye of his memory, in stark, brilliant flashes; two pairs of huge, exquisitely beautiful eyes open wide, two jaws parted and set, two pairs of lips pulled back from white, straight teeth—

Fred winced suddenly, as if in pain. He breathed one word, "Bastards!"

And a moment later he was out of the house, on the porch, and frantically loading the .38.

Chapter 16

He noted first that the air around him was moving fitfully, and that his view of the porch and the tall grass in front of it seemed clouded somehow, as if someone had put a pair of dark glasses on him.

He grunted in confusion—a sound that might or might not have been a curse—and heard it repeated instantly in the moving, dark air around him.

"Huh?" he said.

"Huh?" he heard. At his ear. And in his voice.

"Marie?" he whispered.

"Marie?" he heard, from close by.

"Marie!" he screamed. And the name came back to him an instant later: "Marie!"

His right forearm opened up—a wide, jagged gash across both the radial and ulnar arteries; it began spewing blood immediately.

He dropped the .38. He stared in awe at the blood flooding from his arm and onto the porch. He said "Huh?" again. And felt pressure at the side of his neck—light, at first, then much stronger—and he realized dully, because consciousness was rapidly leaving him, that another gash had been opened there, at his neck.

And in the last few seconds before blessed unconsciousness came, Elena stood quietly before him, her mouth and face scarlet with his blood, her body streaked with it, diagonally, left to right, across her breasts, belly, and thighs, as if she had rolled herself in him. And he whispered at her, very huskily—for reasons he would only vaguely have understood—"Well hello there, sweet thing," and passed from unconsciousness into death even before his eyes had closed.

They did not let him fall to the porch floor. They caught him, lifted him, carried him off . . .

Quicker than the angels—

Marie threw the front door open. It had been only seconds since her brother had screamed her name. "Fred . . ." she started. Her hands began to shake, and then her arms; her stomach turned over; acid crept high into her throat.

If she had been listening to herself she would probably not have heard the long, high-pitched, ragged screech that came from her because her hearing shut down in reaction to it—it was so incredibly loud, and close.

And she did not hear, either, the same scream repeated moments later, like an echo, from the island's farthest edges, fifty yards behind the house.

Evening

"We'll look again tomorrow," Jim said. He was sitting on the edge of the kitchen table; his body bent forward slightly, and his arms folded loosely at his stomach. He was trying hard to appear casual. Behind him, on the table, one kerosene lamp burned in the room. His body blocked its light, so Marie, who was sitting on the floor, ten feet away, near the front door, her back against the wall, legs outstretched, hands folded on her thighs, was in semi-darkness. She had said next to nothing all day, only this, several times; "I didn't love him. My own brother and I didn't love him," which had become a source of immense guilt for her.

"He might have just wandered off," Jim offered. "It's possible."

Marie stayed quiet.

"I cleaned . . . the front porch as well as I could, Marie."

She glanced at him. He saw the barest hint of amusement in her eyes. His brow furrowed; she looked away. "We'll find him, Marie." He paused. He realized that he was merely trying to fill the silence. And why not? "You never know," he went on, "maybe he'll come wandering back. That's possible."

She said nothing.

"Can I get your sleeping bag for you, Marie?"

"No," she answered tonelessly.

"Can I get anything for you?"

"No."

"Maybe some coffee–"

"No."

"We could use some coffee."

Silence.

"I mean, we've got to stay awake. One of us does, anyway."

Silence.

"We *will* find him, Marie. I can promise you that."

She glanced quickly at him again, her eyes narrowed slightly.

"So," he went on, "would you like that coffee, now?"

She looked away.

"Marie?"

"No." There was a hard edge to her voice.

"Food, then?" he asked. "We've got some tuna, I think."

Silence.

"Would you like some tuna, Marie?"

Silence.

"I'm going to fix some for myself."

"I don't want any tuna," she told him, and the hard edge to her voice cracked slightly.

"I don't think we've got any bread, Marie. I think we've got a couple of hard rolls. How does that sound?"

Silence.

"I've always liked hard rolls myself."

Silence.

"We used to bring them along on picnics. They were great on picnics."

Silence.

"We used to put hot dogs in them, and hamburgers—that was when I was still eating meat. I don't eat meat anymore; did you know that, Marie?"

Silence.

"I eat fish, sure. And chicken. But not meat—not animal meat, anyway. That sounds hypocritical, I know, but I've got my reasons." A brief pause. "You sure you don't want that sleeping bag, Marie? It's bound to get pretty cold tonight."

"No."

"Let me get it for you, Marie—why don't I get it for you?"

"No."

"I should probably get my own sleeping bag, anyway, if only to wrap up in it."

Silence.

"Marie?"

Silence.

"Can I tell you something, Marie?"

Silence.

"It's something I've wanted to tell you for a long time, something I'm sure you're aware of."

Silence.

"Marie, are you listening to me?"

Silence.

"Marie?"

"No."

"I wanted to tell you that I have . . . feelings for you." He lowered his head, as if embarrassed. "There, I've said it. It's done."

"It's done."

"Sorry, Marie?" He stepped away from the table. "I didn't hear you."

Silence.

He sighed, and went on, "I mean *deep* feelings. Feelings of love, I think."

"Jesus, don't!"

"I can't help it, Marie."

"Jesus Christ, don't do that!"

He stared at her, puzzled. What had happened to the light? "Marie?"

"Don't do that," she pleaded. "Oh please don't do that!"

He took a step toward her. Where had the light gone? Marie seemed to be in total darkness. "Marie?" he said.

"Oh my God don't do that!" she pleaded; it was a tight and harsh whisper.

"Oh my God!" Jim heard, in Marie's voice.

"Marie?!" he said, and stepped to his right. The light from the kerosene lamp flooded the area near the door, where Marie should have been.

"My God!" he whispered. And then he felt Fred's gun, still in the lower right pocket of his jacket, where he had put it after seeing to the mess on the porch. He stuck his hand into the pocket, felt it tighten around the weapon's grip: "Get away from her!" he commanded, his voice low, too low. "Get away from her!" he screeched.

And the two dark, frantically moving, naked bodies near the door, in front of Marie, stopped briefly. Two exquisite faces turned in unison. Two sets of pale blue eyes leveled on him. "Get away–" they started.

And in a fraction of a second, Jim pulled the gun out, trained it on the man's forehead, and fired.

Then he stared in dumb, quivering silence at what the light showed him in the next moment.

He stood very still for a long while. He felt tears begin.

And, at last, he whispered, "Marie, oh Marie, I'm so sorry, I'm so very sorry." He crossed the room to her.

Later, much later, he would tell himself that she had probably died instantly, and that there was something good to be said for that (it was quite merciful, no doubt, when— one moment to the next—the wall that separated life from death merely ceased to exist).

But, at that moment, with her head cradled on his right hand, and the bullet's exit wound there oozing blood at a quickly decreasing rate—because her heart had stopped pumping—he saw only all that might have been and he wept long into the night.

Chapter 17

Morning came and brought moist, late summer heat with
it. From high in the island's only white pine a goshawk
kak-kak-kaked in agitation at a great horned owl that had
perched momentarily on a branch nearby. At the island's
northern edge, an old and very large beaver ambled ashore,
shook himself frantically, sniffed the warm air, and ambled back into the water. In a dark corner beneath the
porch of the house, a black widow spider—one of a pair of
black widows brought unintentionally to the island in the
little rowboat several years earlier—began work on one of
its large, shapeless webs.

Inside the house, Jim Hart said to himself again—as he
had been saying to himself for an hour—"What am I going
to do?" He had no answer. He had even stopped listening
to himself ask the question.

He would have to do something with Marie's body, he
realized. He would have to bury it, probably, because he
couldn't carry it back fifteen miles to the car. Or he would
have to leave it here, the way it was now, under her
sleeping bag.

He thought, *This is not a nightmare.* Because nightmares were fleeting and unreal. Nightmares came and
went and left him sweating and afraid, but the reality of
morning always did away with them.

The morning could not do away with this. The morning
could only spin him deeper into it.

He put his hand on the top edge of the sleeping bag,

hesitated, pulled it back, exposing Marie's face. She had changed quite a lot during the night, he thought. She had grown very pale and gaunt; she no longer looked like she was asleep, she looked like she was ill, or malnourished, and vaguely in pain. He put the sleeping bag over her face again. He thought for a moment that he should say *I'm sorry* to her, once more, but decided that she probably wouldn't hear him.

Under the porch, a blue-bottle fly caught itself in the black widow's unfinished web. The spider seized it immediately, injected it with venom—paralyzing it—then went back to work. This would be a good day for the spider. In an hour, a beautiful, bright green luna moth, coaxed from its daytime sleep by the warm air, would blunder into the web, the spider would inject it, paralyze it, wrap it up in silk, and—the web finished, at last— would wait for more victims to appear.

The spider thanked no one for its usually full belly. It took what pleasure it could, accepted occasional hunger without question and, finally, when it was time, slid into death with no protest at all. That was its life cycle.

All over the island, similar life cycles were being repeated.

And, in several places on the island, the cycle was just beginning. The earth—stepmother to us all—was giving her children up.

And oh they were lovely—

Chapter 18

In Manhattan

"Seven hundred dollars?" Leonora Wingate said, astonished. "That's . . ."

"Highway robbery?" coaxed the rental agent.

She nodded briskly. "Yes," she said. "For one damned room—"

"Plus attached bath."

"For *one damned room*," she repeated, "it's highway robbery!"

The rental agent, a small, wiry, middle-aged man named Spencer, grinned a much-practiced, long-suffering grin. "You won't get an argument from me, Miss Wingate, no argument at all. But I'll tell ya, if you don't take it, someone else will. And that's a guarantee. Hell, we've got a waiting list longer than your arm . . ." He trailed off, his grin altered. "You're lucky you've got an in with the housing super, Miss Wingate." He gave her a quick once-over; it made her instantly uncomfortable. "Now, if you want to make a . . . similar arrangement with me, I'm sure we can—"

"What does that seven hundred include, Mr. Spencer?" Her tone was twenty degrees below chilly. "Does it include heat and electricity?"

He frowned. "It includes heat, Miss Wingate." He nodded at the room's only closet, near the front door. "Each apartment has its own electric meter. Yours is in there. You pay for what you use."

"And how soon is the room available?"

"Hell, right now, if you've got the month's rent and the security deposit—that's another month's rent. And there's a fifty-dollar lock fee, of course—that's if you skip with the keys and we have to replace the lock—and you got to sign a lease, too. Did I tell you about the lease?"

She eyed him suspiciously. "No one told me about a lease, Mr. Spencer, or a lock fee."

"Well, that was an oversight, wasn't it?" He grinned again: *I'm in charge here*, the grin said. "It's just a six-month lease, Miss Wingate. Pretty standard. No pets, no loud parties, that kind of thing. You'll see it." He paused briefly, then went on, "You got any furniture, Miss Wingate?" The room was unfurnished.

"Yes," she answered.

"How about a bed? We don't allow waterbeds in here. Had one break through a year ago."

"It's not a waterbed, Mr. Spencer."

"Good. You got a job, Miss Wingate? The super said something about you being new here."

"I've got a job, Mr. Spencer, with Admissions at Belle-vue Hospital."

His face broke into a broad smile. "Won't *that* be fun!"

"No, Mr. Spencer, I don't think so." Again her tone was crisp. "Where do I sign the lease?"

His smile slowly dissipated. "My office," he said. "A couple blocks over. You got a car?"

"No."

"Okay then, we'll walk." They left the apartment and started for the elevator. "It's good to have you with us, Miss Wingate."

She merely nodded.

In the Bronx

He was gone. Damn! "Mr. Ghost?" Georgie McPhail called. "Hey, where'd you go?" But he saw little in the dimly lighted room. The ghost had packed up and gone away—that was clear.

Not for the first time in his life, Georgie was sad. It wasn't as if a guy had so many friends that he could afford to lose one, and maybe the ghost didn't think of Georgie as *his* friend, but for sure it worked the other way around.

Georgie gave the room another long look. He said, "If you ever want to talk . . ." and backed slowly out.

The janitor, Mr. Baum, grabbed him by the shoulders. Georgie squirmed, but in vain. "Whatchoo doin' in there, boy?" the janitor growled.

"Nothin', Mr. Baum. Lookin', that's all."

"Yeah? At what? Whatchoo got to look at in there, Georgie?"

"Nothin'. I ain't got nothin' to look at in there, Mr. Baum."

"Damn right, Georgie. And I catch you in there again, you ain't gonna have nothin' to look *with*, either. You got my meanin', Georgie?"

"I do, Mr. Baum."

The man's grip tightened briefly. Georgie grimaced in pain. The man let go. Georgie hesitated, glanced around; Mr. Baum was grinning oddly at him. "You go on now, boy," he said, his tone suddenly one of great friendship. "I'll see you later, and maybe we can go shootin' rats. You think you'd like that?"

"Yeah, sure," Georgie answered. He was used to the janitor's mood-swings. "Any time you want, Mr. Baum." And he walked off, slowly at first. Then, when he'd rounded a corner and the janitor was out of sight, he ran back to his apartment.

Chapter 19

Winifred Haritson heard her voice rise, in anger; "I said I got the windows open and now I can't get them closed! Where's Lou?"

The young man's voice from the telephone receiver—a voice she didn't recognize—answered, "*Lou* is all tied up, Mama, but I'll be sure to have him get back to you."

Mrs. Haritson scowled: "Who is this?"

"This is the Easter Bunny, Mama, and I'll come up with my basket of goodies real soon, okay?"

Mrs. Haritson's mouth dropped open. She heard a laugh, short and malicious, from the receiver. "What have you done with Lou?" she demanded. "Where is he?"

"Like I said, Mama, Lou is all tied up, and I'm his new secretary. You understand?"

"I'm calling the police!"

"The po*lice*?!" He laughed again—the same, short, malicious laugh as before. "You don't want to do that, Mama. I wouldn't like that at all. My *co*workers wouldn't like it either. I mean, that would spoil the little party we got planned, you understand what I'm saying to you?"

Winifred Haritson said nothing.

"I said do you under*stand* what I'm *saying* to you?"

"I . . . understand," she answered.

"And you ain't gonna call no fucking police—ain't that right?"

"I . . . I . . ."

"Damned right you ain't!"

She heard the phone being slammed down, a silence cluttered by distant, random static, then a small, soft clicking sound. Then total silence.

Someone had cut the phone lines, she realized.

She set the receiver slowly on its cradle, and glanced at her front door. All the bolts were closed. She looked at the windows. She stared at them in terror. Earlier in the morning she had been able to open them halfway. She had sat in front of them for a while, had cooled off from the Indian Summer heat, had gotten up. And had been unable to close them again. Which was why she'd called Lou. So he could close them against "the thieves and the muggers."

They have their ways, Lou she'd told him time and time again. *I've seen them.*

And now, she thought, he knew how right she was.

Chapter 20

For Jim Hart, it had not been a "decision" so much as the sudden awareness of what he could and could not do.

He had to leave Marie right where she was. He'd been over it with himself a hundred times. He had to leave the island. He had to get back to the car. He had to notify someone in authority. For Christ's sake, he had to save his *own* life!

What he might do, he thought—what he should do, what he probably would do—was put her inside the sleeping bag and zip it up good and tight. And when he left he'd make sure the house was shut up good and tight, too. Then maybe the predators wouldn't be able to get at her. This idea made him smile because, he thought, it was a very good idea. It showed his continuing . . . affection for her. *Keep the predators out!* The raccoons, the foxes, the bobcats, even, for Christ's sake, the little goddamned *bugs* that might want to get at her. *Keep the predators out!* Because, after all, her body was a temple. *Keep the predators out!* At all costs *keep the predators out*!

Unless it just wasn't possible to keep them out. Unless, of course, they had hands, too, and a brain, like himself, and could not be stopped by whatever he might do to keep them away from her.

He didn't like to think about that—the same way a man doesn't like to think about a large and undeniably cancerous growth somewhere on his body.

He told himself he had seen only shadows, that in the

dim light the night before he had been fooled by shadows. He didn't believe it for a moment.

Which was why, now—an hour and a half after sunrise— he was still at the house. Because *they*—the two he had seen crouching over Marie—could be anywhere. They could be in the house with him, or just outside the door, or anywhere on the long, narrow path that led fifteen miles back to the Route 22A Holiday Inn, and Fred's car.

And so, his fear said, the best course of action at the moment was no action at all.

Better to stay here, with Marie.

And keep the other predators away.

It was a plan, he knew, that was born of creeping panic and insanity.

Chapter 21

On Staten Island

Joyce Dewitte thought there might be room for optimism.
Maybe she had misinterpreted her cat's illness. Maybe the
cat merely had a cold. Maybe it was going through
menopause. She was certainly the picture of health now,
bouncing around the living room like a kitten after the
empty cigarette pack Joyce had wadded up for her. And
even fetching it back.

Joyce reached down from her chair and scratched the
underside of the cat's chin. "Good girl, Ginger," she
said, and felt the animal begin to purr softly beneath her
fingertips. "Good girl." The cat tapped at the wadded-up
cigarette pack. "Oh," Joyce cooed, "you want to play
some more." She picked up the cigarette pack, wadded it
tighter, because the crinkling noise excited the cat, then
tossed it across the room. It landed in front of a bookcase;
the cat tore after it.

This was a moment that Joyce would treasure for a long
time because, for her, it was one of the few genuinely
happy moments of the past several years.

She had come to New York with one goal in mind—to
make it big!! It was an ambition, she knew, that a hundred
thousand other people shared—people with as much talent,
as much drive and ambition and spirit as she had. So, she
was involving herself in a shell game, wasn't she? The
chances that she'd win were ridiculously small, she knew
that.

Knew it, but didn't really believe it.

Because, of course—it was obvious—she was possessed of that little something extra, that something beyond talent, drive, ambition, and spirit. Lord knew what that little something extra was. Maybe it was luck. Dumb luck. Maybe it was an extra ounce or two of sex appeal. Maybe it was the little cleft in her chin, the small patch of green in her otherwise deep blue eyes. Or maybe she was simply blessed (the Reverend Thompson had told her she was, and if anyone was to be believed, he certainly was). And there had been the fortune-teller, of course, at the Watkins County Fair, fifteen years ago, when Joyce had just been entering her adolescence. "Oh my child," the fortune-teller had said, "I do most certainly see very great things ahead for you, oh most certainly," which had made up Joyce's young mind then and there. She would pursue the show business career that her parents, and her grandparents, aunts, uncles, and cousins had told her would be a sin not to pursue. And she would pursue it with a vengeance.

So, at the age of eighteen, she had come to New York.

Not until five years later did she begin to admit, reluctantly, that her dream was tarnishing.

She began by telling herself that she despised "show business types" (a phrase her mother had used). They were too pushy, too mincing, too single-minded, too damned *eccentric* for her essentially down-home personality. (It wasn't really necessary, was it, to smoke Tareytons two at a time—one in the ashtray, one in hand—in order to be a budding young cinematographer? And it wasn't really necessary, was it, to be "outrageously gay" in order to be a playwright? And what, for Christ's sake, was so damned chic about eating soyburgers instead of hamburgers? It was cheaper, for sure, but what was so chic about poverty?) She continued to believe in these stereotypes for about a year, until, one gloomy night, after a full day's worth of tryouts and not even a nibble, she had to admit that she was making excuses.

There was really nothing wrong with "show business types." They were really no more nor less eccentric than other New Yorkers (far less, actually, than some), and, as a group, they were fun to be with.

It was herself, Joyce Dewitte, who had become wearisome. Her pursuit with a vengeance of a show business career had turned her into a drudge. A very nice looking, very athletic, very healthy and talented drudge, to be sure, but a drudge nonetheless.

Talk about single-minded, she told herself, remembering the time one of her fellow dancers, a guy named Simon, had mentioned something about a recent headline—something, apparently, that everyone else in the world was acquainted with—and she had merely been able to smile dumbly at him and say, "Oh. Is that right?"

And so, over the months, and the years, after all the tryouts and the rejections and the disappointments, the dream tarnished.

So she gave it up.

"I hope you're okay, Ginger," she cooed, the cat now curled up on her lap. She thought, deep in her heart, that Ginger was okay, and that the two of them would continue to be fast friends for quite a while. But then, she'd been wrong about other things.

Chapter 22

At the House on the Island

Jim Hart knew it; he could feel it.

They were in the house with him. They were watching. Waiting. Sizing him up. Would he use the gun, or not? Would he run? If so, how fast? And where to?

Would he bring anybody back with him?

He wanted to know if they really thought he was so much of a fool that he had no idea of their intentions. Their intentions were murderously and obscenely clear.

He whispered, as low and as menacingly as possible, "Show yourselves, bastards!"

He pulled the .38 from his pocket and held it up so they could see it clearly. "I'll blow you both away. I will!"

It surprised him that he was not trembling or fearful, that his resolve was so plain. When they showed themselves he really would blow them away. Because it wasn't *he* who had stripped off the thin veneer of civilization. They had done that. So, civilization's laws did not apply to them anymore. This island was like a ship in distress on the high seas. He was its captain. They were the mutineers.

It was all very simple.

He would blow them away. He would blow a hole the size of his fist through both of them. And have loads of fun doing it.

He realized dimly that he had wet himself. He glanced quickly at his crotch, saw the stain there, and smiled crookedly. "I will!" he said aloud, "I surely will!" as if holding a one-sided conversation with himself.

Jim Hart had set one foot into madness.

No other course was open to him.

They ate what they could. It made little difference. They received pleasure not so much from eating—it nourished them and kept them alive—but from the chase and the kill, because it was then that their muscles sang and the air they breathed grew warm and vibrant with life, and, in this greatest act of love, they were able to come together with other creatures that shared the earth with them. And all of them grew a little as a result.

The big man inside them both, at that moment—and for the remainder of their lives—was not unlike many who had gone before. He was filled with hate (an emotion Seth understood but which Elena, newer to the earth, had yet to grasp) and he had killed for reasons even Seth did not completely understand (it had something to do with sex, he thought). But the energy within the big man, the energy which held him together and kept him alive, was enormous, dizzying, a thing of immense beauty and power.

He could have been one of their own.

Chapter 23

On Staten Island

Sam Campbell thought, *Cowboys and Indians—shit on Cowboys and Indians!* What had he been trying to say to her?

It had been twenty-four hours since he'd seen his daughter, Marsha. Twenty-four hours since his little, backward attempt to reach her through the wall she'd set up between herself and the real world.

"My God, Doctor—nine-year-olds don't try to commit suicide. That's not possible!" Sam had told the physician.

"Yes, Mr. Campbell, they do, and so do eight-year-olds, and seven-year-olds, and six-year-olds. Adults don't have exclusive rights to depression."

"Jesus, I knew she was depressed. I was too. I still am. But I thought children were supposed to be so . . . adaptable."

"It depends on the child, Mr. Campbell. And the situation. She was obviously very attached to her mother."

"She worshipped her."

"Then it should be obvious . . ."

"That she wants to be with her now—in death?"

"It's not an uncommon fantasy. We see it not only in children, but in older people, too, when a spouse has died. I imagine you yourself, Mr. Campbell, entertained similar fantasies after your wife's accident."

"Yes," he admitted at once, "but not to the point of . . ."

The doctor cut in, agitation in his voice, as if he was responding to some objection he'd heard all too often, "Let's get something straight, Mr. Campbell. You and your daughter are two, separate, distinct individuals. It's true that you're related by blood, and that you share certain physical characteristics; you even share certain personality traits, I've noticed. But you are still separate entities and you cannot assume that *your* strengths and weaknesses are necessarily *her* strengths and weaknesses merely because she's your daughter. Even identical twins, Mr. Campbell, are not one hundred percent identical. Do you understand what I'm saying to you?"

He lowered his head briefly, as if embarrassed. "Yes," he said, his voice low, "I do." He looked up. "How long will she have to stay here?"

"I have to be truthful, Mr. Campbell, and tell you that I'm not sure. She may come out of her depression next week, or next month, but it might take longer. Much longer. We have to get at the root causes, Mr. Campbell."

"Isn't there medication? I've heard about . . . antidepressant drugs—"

"The root cause would remain, Mr. Campbell. That should be obvious. And although the root cause appears to be the loss of her mother, there are signs that it might go much deeper . . ."

That conversation had taken place six months earlier, and although there had been some progress, the doctor said, it had been more "lateral than upward." Her smothering depression had been replaced by a kind of affable pliability.

"I like Cowboys and Indians very much," she'd said, conveniently overlooking everything else her father had told her ("I was . . . carrying out the act of being dead, I think, as if death were something active, as if it were something for me to *do*!"), and instead homing in on the bare outsides of the conversation—some kids playing Cowboys and Indians. Telling her father, in effect, *I don't want to think about what I tried to do, daddy. Please don't make me think about it.*

God, he loved her! And missed her! And he so looked forward to the upcoming Saturday, when he could again take her on an "outing."

Maybe he'd break through to her then. Maybe she'd break through to him.

Chapter 24

In the Bowery

Whimsical Fatman was on his back; he had been mugged and he hurt, bad. His attackers, finding only sixty-five cents in his pockets, which had required several hours of panhandling to collect, had taken out their frustrations on him—and they hadn't pulled any punches. He knew his nose was broken (not for the first time), and he thought it was possible that one or two of his ribs had been cracked—his breathing was necessarily slow, and very painful.

He thought wryly that the world was getting to be a really lousy place to live in. He tried to smile at that, but couldn't. Not from pain—though it would have stopped him anyway—but from a sudden and numbing realization: He, William Devine—Margaret and John Devine's darling little boy—was a *bum*!

He lay very still, tried to control his breathing, tried to remember where he was.

He remembered. He was in the old Elmwood Hotel, Room 402 (one of the few rooms in the long-abandoned building that still had a door and a door number attached). And he remembered that before the two creeps had appeared to take his sixty-five cents, Merlin O'Dwyer had been in the room with him (''That ain't my real name, but I like it. I don't really know *what* my real name is, Whimsy.'').

He moved his head so his gaze took in the entire room. Merlin was gone. Well, that was good, anyway; he'd gotten out, God bless him!

Whimsy tried to smile again. It was the pain that stopped him this time.

And, for a few, awful, fleeting moments he thought he would die here, in Room 402 of the old Elmwood Hotel. But then the pain subsided a bit and he was able to stand and move slowly to the door, his hand pressed hard to his rib cage.

He stopped there, in the doorway. His brow furrowed. His peripheral vision had shown him someone standing in the open closet to his left. He turned his head to look. Merlin O'Dwyer uttered one sentence before dying; "Shit, you got it all over your pants there!" Then he toppled face forward to the floor, driving the front inch and a half of the knife in his belly straight through his back.

Whimsy stared blankly at him. He thought that Merlin's killer must have been in a big hurry, otherwise he wouldn't have left that knife behind. It looked like a good one.

William Devine—also known as Whimsical Fatman (Whimsy to his friends, and they numbered in the dozens)—rolled his late friend to his back, at the same time avoiding looking at the man's face, pulled the knife out, wiped it on Merlin's shirt sleeve, gave it a long once-over (it was indeed a good knife; he might get ten or fifteen dollars for it), stuck it in his pocket, and moved down the hall to the stairway, hand still pressed hard to his rib cage, his gait agonizingly slow, and blood trickling from his nose.

Chapter 25

Jim Hart thought he could hear them, all around. He wasn't sure. There were more than two of them, he supposed. There were dozens, perhaps. Hundreds. Thousands, maybe. He wasn't sure.

He thought that the noises they made were very musical indeed. He thought he recognized certain melodies cast off here and there, as if in afterthought. He heard distantly, "Tie me kangaroo down sport/Tie me kangaroo down . . ." and he mentally finished it. And, "Old man river/He keeps on rollin' . . ." And, "Ninety-nine bottles of beer on the wall/Ninety-nine bottles of beer/If one of those bottles should happen to fall . . ." *Ninety-eight bottles of beer on the wall*.

But it was not all song that he heard. He also heard low, guttural, orgasmic grunts, and a shrill, high-pitched whistling sound that was almost like a wheeze, and, from close by, the sounds of someone who was apparently very much out of breath, and below that, a man obviously in deep pain.

He supposed that he had seen them, too—a hundred pairs of large, powder-blue eyes watching him through the early evening darkness as he made his way from the house to the boat, to shore, and then, after an hour's worth of looking, to the narrow path that would eventually lead him to the car.

They kept their distance. They sang their songs and

made their grunts. But they kept their distance. He wasn't sure why.

It was possible, he decided, that they didn't like him very much. And if it was true, his thoughts continued, he couldn't really blame them. He was a murderer, after all.

"Isn't that right?" he said, and heard it repeated from the darkness, again and again and again, until, like an echo, it faded away.

And then he thought, *They've always wanted to get at me*. Because he couldn't remember *not* feeling their eyes on him, couldn't remember *not* hearing their disembodied voices throwing curses at him. *They've always wanted to get at me!* Sure. That was the business of the city dweller, wasn't it? And these were the very worst of them.

He glanced about. He decided that they had taken the street signs down because they wanted him to become disoriented and out of touch.

They wanted him to blunder about stupidly. So they could pretend not to notice (it was what the city dweller did best), and laugh deep inside themselves. He resolved that he would not give them that satisfaction.

He knew where his damned apartment was, for Christ's sake!

He didn't need the street signs.

Only the streets.

Because he knew this city, his city, at least as well as *they* did, if not better. He could get where he was going with his eyes closed, if it became necessary.

It had all happened within the twinkling of an eye.
The birthing.
And now, en masse, the little ones were scurrying through the forest, snatching up what they could find and stuffing whatever it turned out to be—a moth, a spider, the occasional field mouse—hungrily into their mouths.
Seth and Elena shadowed them from a distance. The education of the little ones had to begin immediately. There would be cold days ahead, and colder nights.
And some of them would wither and die, it was true.
And some would lag behind.

But most would follow.

And as they scurried along they turned their heads now and then and stared at the man moving slowly on the dark path.

Seth stared, too. And Elena. Because the man puzzled and confused them (the same way that the sun would confuse them, even frighten them, if it came up one morning over the wrong horizon, or if the earth beneath their feet, the earth which was their mother, turned suddenly to granite).

They stayed clear of the man; the little ones because at this point in their new lives, it was instinctual to stay away from something so very strange and disoriented; Seth and Elena because although the man might be a threat to them, and to the little ones, they weren't certain what kind of threat, or how to deal with it.

Because when they reached out to him they found that he was not where they were, in these woods—he was in another place entirely.

A place filled with people and cluttered with buildings, and feverish with passion and violence.

Chapter 26

Winifred Haritson's front door, the only entrance to her apartment from the building's interior, was made of steel. The surrounding walls were made of cement. The door's four locks—two dead bolts, a chain, and a simple latch—would hold. She had no doubt of it. It was the windows that worried her. For the last half hour she had been trying with every ounce of her strength to get them closed. One had rattled in its casing and dropped a couple inches, leaving it about an inch short of the lock, and the other hadn't moved at all.

She pressed her face hard into one of the screens. There was a fire escape ten feet to the right, for apartment 436 (Mrs. Dyson's apartment, she remembered). The fire escape hadn't been used in twenty-five years. It had, she thought, probably long since rusted shut. But that gave her no comfort at all. Because *they* would figure out a way to use it. *They* were good at that kind of thing. *They* had done it before, a thousand times. *They* found nothing impossible.

She gave one of the windows another hard pull. It wouldn't budge. She heard herself curse. It surprised her. She couldn't remember cursing, not since shortly before leaving home nearly sixty years before (Oh, Christ, Daddy, please don't do that!'' In response he had merely grinned at her, a big, leering, malicious grin, and had continued beating her. She still bore scars from it).

She moved quickly to the south wall of the apartment, put her ear to it, listened. She heard nothing. She rapped

81

on the cement, softly at first, then much harder. She glanced at her knuckles; they were bleeding. "Mrs. Dyson!" she said, too softly. She hit the wall with the palm of her hand. "Mrs. Dyson!" she repeated, louder. Mrs. Dyson did not answer.

She cursed again, went to the phone, lifted the receiver, listened. It was dead. She set it down.

"Oh Lord, what am I going to do?" she blubbered. "What am I going to do?" She had no idea what she was going to do. She was as frightened and as tense at that moment as she had ever been.

So, when she heard the loud, demanding, double knock on the steel door, her fear elevated geometrically, adrenaline pushed through her veins, her blood pressure dropped. And she fainted.

The building where Winifred Haritson had chosen, out of necessity, to spend her declining years was three-quarters of a century old. It had been condemned several times by the New York City Bureau of Sanitation and the New York City Buildings Department, and had also been the scene of a dozen fires in as many years. Upon its construction it was christened *The Mohawk*, for undetermined reasons, but the name never stuck. Instead, the building's steady stream of transients (which had become a trickle shortly after Winifred's arrival) called it "The Stone," because its nondescript white cement walls and its plodding, unaesthetic massiveness made it look very much like a huge, rectangular white stone that someone had put windows in.

As a place for people to live, it was a failure from the start. Its complex and labyrinthine heating system had been poorly designed and installed. With substandard parts and workmanship (thanks to payoffs from the heating contractor to certain corrupt city officials), it was constantly in need of repair, and never seemed to work properly. The wiring (thanks to the same kinds of payoffs to the same city officials) was equally substandard and inefficient.

By decree of the city government, no one was supposed to be living in the building, but desperation makes people ingenious, and ways had been devised to reactivate the heating gas and the electricity, and even the telephones (though only as an intercom system within The Stone itself). For several years, the building had operated as a kind of sovereign entity inside Manhattan.

Lou Willis was its superintendent and troubleshooter. If The Stone had indeed been a sovereign nation, he would have been its benevolent ruler. He saw to it that the elevators were kept running, because all but two of The Stone's dozen or so residents were very old; that the "riff-raff" was kept out; that the inspectors were paid off regularly; and that, in general, The Stone did not come toppling down on the people inside it (an unlikely prospect because, whatever else could be said about it, The Stone was structurally sound).

Lou Willis, however, was no more. His body, still bound and gagged, languished at the bottom of the elevator shaft. He wore a look of great surprise on his face— probably because the five young men who had overpowered him had done it so quickly, or perhaps because they had decided with such suddenness to throw him down the elevator shaft, and then had carried it out with no hesitation whatsoever. *These boys aren't fooling around!* he thought, just before they threw him down the shaft. Lou was a realist.

And so, a bloody coup had been staged.

The Stone had a new ruler.

"Hey Mama, you wanna come outa dere or maybe you want us to come in?!" The boy, age seventeen, listened for a moment. He heard nothing from inside Winifred Haritson's apartment. He scowled. "I said you want us maybe to come in dere?" he growled, in a tone that had never failed to elicit a response from anyone. He listened again. Winifred Haritson's apartment stayed quiet. "Mother-fuck!" he hissed, and turned to the boy, age sixteen, beside him. "Get the can opener!" he commanded. The boy turned and started for the elevator at once. He pressed the Down button, but it failed to light. "Hey," he complained, grinning nervously, "this ain't workin'." He pressed the button again, much harder, and again, slapping it. "It ain't workin'," he repeated, and nodded quickly at the elevator door.

" 'Course it ain't workin', dumb shit, 'cuz we threw that asshole down it," said the seventeen-year-old, "and he screwed up the fuckin' cables."

The sixteen-year-old thought a moment. "Oh yeah," he whispered dimly, and remembered that they had used the stairs to get up here, to the fourth floor. "Yeah, I remember," and he turned and moved quickly, still nervous, to the stairway.

"The can opener" was a device employed by police and firefighters to free people trapped in their cars after an accident. It had a vague resemblance to a huge pair of grass shears and was used when the larger, gasoline-powered units were not available.

It was an ill-conceived device. It rarely worked properly; its long blades dulled too quickly; it required several men to operate it, one of whom had to force himself into painful contortions; and it was expensive. Consequently, the can openers weren't used very much, and sometimes were left, conveniently, at the scene of an accident. Which was where The Ravens—the particular street gang which had taken over Winifred Haritson's apartment building—had found one.

Jim Hart had a rather tenuous connection with The Stone. He had passed it several thousand times on his way to work, and had thought, once or twice, *That's damned ugly!* He had gone on to wonder what bastard of an architect could possibly have designed it.

Jim Hart would never see the building again.

Georgie McPhail's connection with The Stone was somewhat less tenuous. He had burglarized it twice, very early in his young career. He had come away each time with far less than he'd hoped for, and it didn't take him long to figure out that the few people still living in The Stone didn't have even enough material goods for themselves, let alone for the hungry family of a young cat burglar.

Joyce Dewitte had no idea The Stone even existed,

although her great-grandfather, Simon Lucretius Dewitte, was the bastard of an architect who had designed it.

Sam Campbell had no connection with it at all.

Whimsical Fatman had spent one drunken night in The Stone several years after coming to New York, before going, permanently he supposed, to the Bowery. An unnerving experience in the bulding that night convinced him that it was haunted, and so he had hurriedly left the following morning.

Fifteen years earlier; in a housing development near Penn Yann, New York:

Norm Gellis groped blindly for the latch on Joe's collar while Joe whimpered pathetically at him. "It's okay, dog," Norm said. "We'll get you inside and put you down in the cellar and you'll be warm as toast. What'd you think—I was gonna leave you out here to freeze your poor nuts off?" Norm wished frantically that he'd put his gloves on. The task of finding the small latch on Joe's metal collars—a task made difficult, anyway, by the storm, and by Joe's nervous twitching— was made almost impossible by the fact that his fingers had become numb already, and so were next to useless. "Fucking shit!" Norm hissed. Finally, he found the latch; he twisted it hard to the left; it wouldn't give. "Goddammit!"

Joe whimpered louder.

"Shut up!" Norm commanded, and whacked the dog on the snout with his open left hand. The dog stopped whimpering abruptly.

Norm twisted the latch again. It was frozen. "Chrissakes!" He took the tether in one hand and followed it to where it was attached to a post screwed into the ground twenty feet away. He put his hands on the post and winced at the burning coldness of the metal; he turned the post counterclockwise, aware—as it gave with agonizing slowness in the hardened soil—that the wind and cold were sapping his strength by the second. He thought about going back into the house for a breather, and to put his gloves on, when he realized that Joe's tether had slackened. "Joe?" he said. He pulled the tether; it was broken; in panic, Norm realized, Joe had broken it.

Chapter 27

John Marsh glanced in his rearview mirror. In the light from the dashboard he saw that he was smiling. It was no wonder why, he thought. He was a happy man—his search was nearly at an end, he was about to corner his prey, at last.

That, he supposed, was probably a fantasy. Seth Freeman was not about to be "cornered" by anyone, especially by an old man with an old score to settle. Seth Freeman was a magician, a superman, and bringing him down would require divine intervention. And John Marsh did not expect, or believe in, divine intervention.

But still he had no doubt that a confrontation would occur. And soon. He could feel it in his aged bones. He fancied that tracking the magician all these years had turned him into something of a magician himself. He liked the idea—Duel of the Magicians. Wouldn't that be something?!

He had thought it before and now he thought it again: It was probable, even likely, that senility was catching up with him; undoubtedly he was quite fortunate to have staved it off so long. It had claimed both his mother and father at relatively early ages (sixty-five and sixty-eight respectively) and his grandparents, too; so if it was flirting with him now, at age seventy-three, he really couldn't complain. Just so he could make a bargain with it. He would let it catch up with him—Hell, he'd welcome it!—if it would only let him finish what he'd set out to do fifteen years before.

"How's that sound?" he said to the German shepherd sitting up in the pickup truck's passenger seat. He reached over and scratched the dog's ear. "You think I got another six months, Joe?" Joe inclined his massive gray head into the man's hand. "Oh," Marsh said, "you like that, huh?"

The two had been together for over a decade, and they were inseparable. Marsh very much liked the idea that they'd "grow old together." He had even fantasized that they'd be buried side by side in the same coffin (a fantasy he'd shared with his sister, Margaret; her reaction, he thought, had been typical: "That's obscene, John!").

"I think I got six months, Joe. I think it's all we need."

Joe made slight, rasping noises deep in his throat, as if clearing mucous out; it was his way of showing pleasure.

Marsh scratched the dog's ear harder; the dog grinned.

"Maybe we don't need even that, Joe. 'Cuz I think we got him this time. I do think we got him."

Marsh wasn't sure if he really believed that. It was something he *had* believed several times, and very strongly in the past fifteen years, and he'd been wrong more than once.

Like the time he'd "tracked" Seth Freeman to a one-room apartment in Albany, only to find the apartment empty. "Ain't no one lived here for a long time," the janitor had told him. "Shit, who'd want to?!" Marsh had been running on his feelings then, his instinct—an instinct nurtured by several years of tracking the man and getting to know his ways and just missing him each time. "*He* wouldn't mind," Marsh told the janitor. The janitor merely shrugged—*This old man for sure had gone round the bend.*

And then, several years later, from a dirt road overlooking a farmer's newly harvested cornfield, he had actually caught a glimpse of Seth Freeman. He was at a distance, it was true, but there was no mistaking him: No other man could move so gracefully, and so quickly, the wildness in him as clear and unmistakable as his nakedness. Marsh's glimpse of him that time had lasted a couple seconds, no more. Then Seth Freeman had merged with the yellowish stubs of cornstalks surrounding him, and had vanished. If, Marsh realized, he had brought a pair of good binoculars along with him and knew precisely where to look, he might have seen the barest hint of a shadow moving swiftly through the field—if he'd been very lucky. But though he'd kept watching for another half hour, Seth Freeman had not reappeared.

Marsh had caught glimpses of him five times since then.

And once during those years he had spoken with him—in a little farmhouse ten miles from where he was now. He still called that farmhouse his home.

It had been late evening. Winter. A heavy layer of snow had built up from a two-day storm, and Marsh had just finished shoving the last of his firewood into the Franklin stove that heated the house (his pickup truck was useless in the deep snow and he hoped that by daybreak someone would come by).

Very quickly and very quietly, Seth Freeman appeared from a darkened corner of the room. He stood ten feet away from Marsh, who was kneeling in front of the stove. He wore a long gray wool jacket (Marsh thought it looked like a woman's jacket and he imagined that Seth had stolen it), and heavy, Timberland boots that were obviously several sizes too large. He appeared to be shivering. He said, his tone merely one of curiosity, "Why do you follow me?"

Marsh answered immediately, his voice quivering, "I . . . have to."

"You don't have to." Seth's tone now was instructional, as if he were talking to a very young child. "You are in the last of your years. Enjoy them while you have them."

Marsh stood and took a step toward Seth. Seth's face went blank, he took one step backward, not in fear, but, ironically, in warning. "I know what is in your head, and in your heart, John Marsh. You want to destroy me." There was no anger or animosity in his voice—his tone was still one of instruction—but now it was mixed with rebuke. "And you cannot destroy me, unless I wish it.

And I do not wish it.'' He raised his arm slightly to indicate the Franklin stove. ''I need that heat.''

''So do I,'' Marsh said.

And Seth grinned very slightly, with only one side of his mouth. It seemed unnatural—and it was chilling. He said, ''I believe there is enough for both of us.'' Then he backed up several steps, into the darkness at the edges of the room, and was gone.

''What do you think, Joe?'' Marsh said now, and he reached over and scratched the dog's ear affectionately. ''You think we got him?''

Joe moaned deep in his throat, in pleasure. Marsh took it as an affirmative, and it sent a shiver of happiness and expectation through him.

Chapter 28

In the Bowery

At the opposite end of the room Whimsical Fatman sat in, there was a huge dark chest of drawers six feet tall and three feet wide. It was missing all but its bottom drawer, and inside that drawer a small, rangy Calico cat had made a nest for itself and its six recently born kittens. Whimsy, in an old gray wing chair, could hear the kittens purring softly. He had the knife that he'd taken out of Merlin O'Dwyer in his right hand, blade pointing downward, and his feet were propped up on the chair's matching ottoman, which was minus most of its stuffing. He was remembering his wife and his children, and finding himself in awe of the fact that somewhere in his quickly atrophying gray matter his son's name still lurked. But he could not, for the life of him, fish it out. He could remember his daughter's name—it was Melissa, a name his wife had chosen, over his objections that it was too "fussy," but which he had slowly come to accept. But his son's name eluded him, and it made him angry.

He ran his thumb along the blade of the knife, opening a tiny slit in the skin. He studied the finger for a moment, but no blood appeared. *Ivan*, he thought suddenly. *My son's name is Ivan!* He chuckled low in his throat; it became a quick, gurgling cough.

"Ivan!" he grumbled, when his coughing fit finally ended. "Shit! Ivan!" His voice, a low tenor, had once been comforting, almost sweet, but over the years, and after countless gallons of lousy booze had snaked down his throat, it had become harsh and ragged; and now, the Calico cat, hearing it, leaped from the chest of drawers, one of its kittens still clinging to a nipple. The cat ran for the open front door, then through it. The kitten fell off halfway to the door and lay on the scarred old wood, mewing pathetically.

"Ivan!" Whimsy growled. His gaze settled on the kitten. "It's not 'Ivan,' cat!" The kitten's head bobbed about in a blind search for the source of the voice.

Whimsy chuckled again, and again it became a quick, gurgling cough, the kind that seems the distinct province of old, unhealthy men and of bums. And when it ended, a name floated up to him, as if it had been anchored under black water and the coughing fit had set it loose: The name was "William, Jr." and it made him angrier still. A loud, brittle curse erupted from his throat, which made the kitten mew more quickly, in panic. And then he let the knife fall over the arm of the chair, to the floor, buried his face in his hands and wept.

"I am an educated man!" he said into his hands, through the weeping. "I am an educated man!" And somewhere deep inside him, in some small, cluttered back room of his brain, he thought that that fact, the fact that he was educated, was very, very funny, because it really didn't make any difference now.

The kitten continued mewing. Whimsy continued weeping. At last the mother cat reappeared, approached the kitten very cautiously, sniffed it a couple times, picked it up by the scruff of the neck, in the time-honored manner of mother cats, and carried it back to the nest.

A half hour later, Whimsy pushed himself, with effort, out of the wing chair, went over to the dresser, peered down blankly at the mother cat and its kittens and said, "I wish I could tell you it's been nice." He left the room quickly, favoring his left leg—because of a touch of arthritis in his knee—and made his way out of the building.

He wondered about making it all the way to 181st Street, through Harlem, to the George Washington Bridge.

He wondered how long it would take him to walk to North Carolina.

He wondered if anyone there would recognize him after so many years.

And he wondered, most of all, why he gave a damn.

Chapter 29

Jim Hart could smell pungent, Sicilian-style pizza baking and he knew that he was near home because Nino's was just a few doors down from where he lived. He saw the tip of the Empire State Building far in the distance, the gaudy, brightly lit Con Ed Building off to the right:

And so, through Jim's eyes and brain, did Seth.

And Elena too, through Seth.

Jim murmured, "You can take the city dweller out of the city"—he chuckled quickly—"but you can't take the city out of the city dweller." Dimly, it made good sense.

Because, dimly, he knew he was not in Manhattan at all. Dimly he knew he was on a narrow path in the Adirondacks, that he was several miles from Fred's car, that all around him, hidden by the darkness, there were things watching him, sizing him up, and waiting.

He knew all this.

But just dimly. As if it were some long-suppressed memory from childhood trying to creep back. He knew, much more concretely—with confidence—that he was actually in Manhattan. And that he was near home.

Seth's big, powder-blue eyes followed the long, slowly merging vertical lines and the contours of the great buildings around him. The lines undulated, as if he were seeing merely some reflection on swiftly moving water. He recognized the buildings. He recognized the city. It was a black splotch on his memory. It smelled bad, and the air moved leadenly about in his lungs, as if it might solidify.

It was a place of death.

Not the kind of death that serves and nourishes the Earth. But the kind that is sudden and needless; the kind that leaves behind it a heavy, and sweltering grief—an emotion which Seth had felt in others more than once, and had found confusing.

There were a thousand similar places on the earth, like the place which this man—Jim Hart—called home.

The island.

Manhattan Island.

The place which, before the buildings had been put up to cut the sky apart, and before the subways sliced through the earth, and before the dark blanket of streets and parking lots smothered the soil, had been the place of their birth. The place where they had first sprung up. The place which had nourished them, and given them pleasure. And watched them die. And then spring up again. And die.

The place which, at last, men had found and driven them from and claimed for their own. The place which men had changed into something foul, something that hurt underfoot, and assaulted the ears, and had a strange, harsh unliving pulse all its own.

"It burned down. It didn't burn up, it burned down."

And suddenly Seth was listening to the voice of his memory; listening to his "Grandpa" talking to him. Fifteen years ago.

"Huh?" Seth had responded.

And "Grandpa" repeated himself.

"Oh," said the boy Seth. "Anybody get killed, ya think?"

"You're a morbid sort, aren'tcha?" "Grandpa" asked.

That had been only minutes before Seth had found out what, and who, he was. It had leaped out of him like a scream, and then had come back on him like a hungry animal.

He hadn't understood it then.

It had taken him five years to understand it.

But he understood it fully now. And he understood that there were others like him. Fully grown.

The survivors.

The children of the island.

The first to whom the Earth had given life, a half a thousand years ago.

Ten thousand of them, or more, in that first season.

And all but a handful dead with the first winter.

And in that second season, another ten thousand, twenty thousand. Stronger. And swifter.

In that second winter, all but a handful dead.

And in that third season, thirty thousand. All but a handful dead with that winter's passing.

But some had survived.

Some had survived to this moment. And they were waiting—as confused and as terrified as he had been fifteen years ago—to be told what they were, and what their purpose was.

Waiting, Seth was certain, to take back the island that had given them life.

Jim Hart saw faces in the windows to his right and left, faces that were as blank as water. They came and went quickly; they watched for a moment, the span of a heartbeat, then they dropped, as if the dark body beneath were dropping to the ground again. And again. Dropping to the floor of some lousy, cluttered, and expensive apartment— little more than a cell, really, a place to peer out of and watch the taxis go by, and the hookers, and the dealers and users.

A place to watch Johnny Carson reruns.

A place to make love. To fuck.

A place to eat.

And a place to wait.

A place on the island. A couple hundred square feet on the island.

Home.

Jim Hart began to laugh. Low at first, down deep in his belly, as if his stomach were turning over and complaining about a bad meal. And then louder, so his throat got involved, and his mouth. And quickly it became manic, shrill, and the faces in the windows heard it. The faces in the windows repeated it.

And a quarter of a mile away, a hiker bedding down in his lean-to for the night heard it. A chill moved down his back. His testicles tightened up in fear. A sudden sweat started in him, despite the cold air.

He listened for ten minutes, until the laughter slowly faded, and the other sounds of an Adirondack night returned.

Chapter 30

The seventeen-year-old trying to force his way into Winifred Haritson's apartment did not mind pain too much. There were times, in fact, when he almost enjoyed it, when he bore it as a kind of badge of honor.

His mouth, for instance, was an area of agonizing desolation. For the past several years he had been able to eat only the softest and mushiest of foods (though he occasionally braved a Wendy's Double with fries). He was, at the time of his takeover of The Stone, suffering from several virulent gum diseases at once, though he was not aware of it because the constant pain, caused by his chipped and decayed teeth, dominated. As a result of these various conditions, it was not a pleasure to be close to him and to have to talk to him, as did the sixteen-year-old who'd fetched the "can opener."

Together, they had wedged the huge blades of the awkward device into the doorknob side of Winifred Haritson's door and were now trying to get some kind of bite on the door itself. They weren't having much luck, so the seventeen-year-old was cutting loose with a constant string of spittle laden curses, and, at the same time, subjecting his friend to a virtual fog of disease-caused bad breath. Despite himself, the sixteen-year-old was becoming nauseous.

You got bad breath—it smells like somethin' died inside ya! he wanted desperately to tell the seventeen-year-old, just as a matter of self-defense. But he knew that the seventeen-year-old would beat the hell out of him for it.

The seventeen-year-old stopped cursing for a moment. He closed his mouth. The sixteen-year-old breathed a small sigh of relief.

"This ain't gonna work!" said the seventeen-year-old.

"Yeah," agreed the sixteen-year-old.

" 'Cuz you're a pansy!" observed the seventeen-year-old.

The sixteen-year-old stayed quiet. He lowered his head a little. He tried holding his breath against the fog of halitosis spreading over him.

"You know you're a pansy, ain't that right?!"

The sixteen-year-old murmured, "Yeah, I know."

"Your old man's a pansy, too, and your brother's a pansy, and your sister's a whore. Ain't that right?!"

"Yeah, that's right."

"That old fuck inside there—she could probably wipe yer ass all over the street. Am I right? Am I right?"

"Yeah, Snipe, you're right."

"Snipe" was the seventeen-year-old's nickname, but he was hard put to remember how he'd acquired it. As close as he could recall, his father—dead several years then—had been the first to use it. He wasn't sure what it meant, but he liked the way it sounded, the pointedness of it, and he thought that it fit him.

Snipe stepped back from Winifred Haritson's door, leaving the sixteen-year-old to hold up the heavy "can opener."

"We're gonna wait her out," Snipe said.

The sixteen-year-old struggled with the can opener, freed it from the door, and let it drop heavily to the floor. "Wait her out?" he asked.

"Sure; she's gotta eat, don't she?"

"Yeah," nodded the sixteen-year-old.

"So we wait her out."

"Then what we gonna do with her, Snipe?"

" 'Do with her'? We ain't gonna *do* nothin' with her. Whatcha think, you think I'm some kind of pervert-asshole?"

"No, Snipe, I don't think that, you know I don't think that."

"We're gonna make her sign her checks over. Like all the rest are gonna do."

"Oh," murmured the sixteen-year-old dimly. "Yeah."

"And maybe we'll have some fun with her, too."

The sixteen-year-old grinned expectantly. "Are we gonna throw her down the elevator shaft, like we done with the super?"

Snipe grinned back. He stayed quiet.

" 's that what we're gonna do, Snipe? We're gonna throw her down the elevator shaft after a while?" The idea excited him; he remembered the way Lou had fallen—quickly, and solidly, like a large sack of meat, which, he thought, was exactly what Lou had been.

"Sure," Snipe answered finally. "Why not? We'll throw 'em all down the elevator shaft after a while. How's that sound?"

The sixteen-year-old did not answer immediately. He was imagining trussing up each of the dozen or so people that lived in The Stone, carting each of them to the brink of the elevator shaft, giving each of them their "last words," and then, whoosh!—tossing them in. "It sounds good, Snipe!" he whispered, as if he were tasting something exquisite.

Snipe grinned again. The sixteen-year-old stared at the desolation that was Snipe's mouth. He thought suddenly that Snipe sure was a damned beautiful son of a bitch!

Nine people stood side by side in The Stone's lobby. Most of them were well into their sixties and seventies and they looked very tired and resigned to whatever The Ravens had planned for them. Mrs. Dyson, a thin, balding woman of seventy-two, was there. She'd been coaxed from her apartment with graphic threats of starvation and violence. Beside her stood a tall, silver-haired, and normally very distinguished-looking man named Wanamaker, who had once been a pediatrician. Now he looked decidedly foolish, dressed only in a pair of white boxer shorts and a ruffled white dress shirt (it had been Snipe's idea. For all his shortcomings, he was an excellent judge of the way people thought of themselves. He had seen that

Wanamaker thought of himself as "aging and poverty stricken but, above it all, distinguished," and so had decided to take that away from him. He knew that if you took away a person's dignity, you took away his willingness to fight).

A man named Carter Barefoot stood just to the left of Wanamaker. Carter had always assumed because of his last name, that he was part Indian, though his red hair suggested otherwise. He was barely five-and-a-half-feet tall, wiry, in his early forties. And he was scared. He'd seen what had been done to Lou, and it wasn't hard to imagine that he would be next, merely because he was male and therefore a threat. He was living in The Stone because he was penniless, and surviving on whatever menial, part-time or temporary work he could scrape up.

Standing very stoically next to Carter Barefoot, hands folded in front and his eyes straight ahead, was a stocky, sixty-five-year-old man dressed in a tattered, although clean, gray pin-striped suit with only a T-shirt on beneath. He called himself "Mr. Klaus." He was not scared. He expected that The Ravens would kill him sooner or later, but he was not scared. For very good reasons, death meant little to him. He supposed that he would accept it with thanks.

The rest of the nine people standing side by side in The Stone's lobby included a bag lady who called herself "Ms. Ida Cooper," a former longshoreman named Bill Meese, who was clutching a $125.00 pension check in his quivering, skeletal right hand, a seventy-five-year-old former radio personality, Wilson Gruscher, who had bid goodbye to radio three decades before, a sixty-five-year-old gray-skinned black woman who called herself "Aunt Sandy," and, to the far left of the group, clutching her pension check to her ravaged bosom, sixty-eight-year-old Connie Tams. She was saying over and over to herself, mentally, her hard gaze on one of The Ravens who'd been put in charge of guarding the little group, *May your mother's eyes scald in hell!*

Snipe appeared suddenly from the emergency exit stairway, the sixteen-year-old just behind him. He moved

very slowly, with consummate grace, to a position about
ten feet in front of the center of the group. He stood very
still, hands clasped behind him, as if he were a drill
sergeant inspecting his platoon. He looked first at Mrs.
Dyson, who looked away, then at Wanamaker, Carter
Barefoot, ''Mr. Klaus,'' Ida Cooper, Wilson Gruscher,
''Aunt Sandy,'' and Connie Tams. He held his gaze on
each of them for half a minute, his mouth set in a tight,
nearly horizontal grin. Finally, he said, ''I wanta know
one thing from you and it don't matter who tells me: I
wanta know if this is all there is or if there's more of
you.''

''Yes,'' said Carter Barefoot at once; several pairs of
old eyes settled quickly and condemningly on him. ''There's
Mrs. Haritson, too.''

Snipe's grin broadened until what was left of his teeth
were clearly visible. ''Yeah, I know about Mrs. Haritson.''

''Oh,'' said Carter, obviously disappointed that he had
not been much help.

''And the super ain't here no more,'' Snipe went on. He
paused, glanced again quickly from one face to another,
saw some questioning looks, a look of shock on Carter's
face. ''He's down in the basement—he's food for the
rats.''

Snipe heard a gasp from Aunt Sandy. He caught her
gaze, held it a long moment, then looked away. ''Any of
you think you wanta be food for the rats, too?''

Carter Barefoot answered humbly, ''No, sir.''

Ida Cooper shook her head briskly.

The rest of the group stayed quiet.

Snipe's grin faded. He told them angrily, ''I said,
'Any of you think you wanta be food for the rats, too?!' ''

There were a few no's, a few heads shook. Mr. Klaus
stayed quiet, as did Wanamaker. Snipe stepped quickly
over to Wanamaker; he looked him squarely in the eye.
Wanamaker stared back: His view of Snipe was just a
vague, oval patch of pink skin and dark hair because he
was wretchedly farsighted. Snipe hissed at him, ''Yer
name's Wanamaker, ain't it?''

Wanamaker nodded once.

"You wanta be food for the rats, Wanamaker?"

Wanamaker said nothing.

Snipe repeated, in exactly the same tone he'd just used, "You wanta be food for the rats, Wanamaker?"

Wanamaker hesitated a moment then shook his head ever so slightly.

"Huh?" said Snipe.

Wanamaker shook his head more briskly.

"You wanta be food for the rats, Wanamaker?" Snipe said again, in exactly the same tone he'd used the first and the second time.

Wanamaker shook his head even more briskly. "No," he whispered.

"Huh?" said Snipe.

"No!" said Wanamaker, aloud. "No." He shook his head fiercely.

"You wanta be food for the rats, Wanamaker?"

"No, I don't want to be food for the rats, I don't want to be food for the rats."

"Huh?"

"I don't want to be food for the rats." He was on the verge of pleading with Snipe now. "I do not want to be food for the rats."

"You wanta be food for the rats, Wanamaker?"

"No, I don't—" Snipe planted his fist hard in Wanamaker's belly. The air went out of the old man. His hand clutched at his stomach. He crumpled to his knees and began coughing fitfully.

"They're gonna eat you alive, Wanamaker!" Snipe growled. He took hold of a scruff of the man's white hair, pulled his head up. The man continued coughing, though now with greater effort because his head was being held at a harsh and unnatural angle. "No," he managed. "I . . ." He could manage no more.

Snipe was pleased. He let go of Wanamaker's hair. Wanamaker fell face forward to the floor, groaned, turned his face to the side, and vomited.

Chapter 31

On the Staten Island Ferry, Halfway to South Ferry

Sam Campbell had been riding the Staten Island Ferry for nearly a decade. It was a routine that was firm and set in his life: He got on, read the *Times*, and got off. The routine had grown comforting in its sameness.

Now, though, with his wife gone and his daughter Marsha shut away in Bellevue, it had grown chill, because it sprang from a way of life that was forever behind him. Still, he clung to the routine, as if somehow, *because* of its sameness perhaps, it could bring back that past.

Halfway to Manhattan, he lowered the *Times* suddenly and let a long, shuddering sigh escape him. "Jesus!" he breathed. At once he felt self-conscious because he could see several people, opposite him, turning their heads as if embarrassed, and a woman, just to his left, looking questioningly at him. He turned his head a little and smiled at her as if to say there was no problem. She continued to look questioningly at him. Normally, he would have been annoyed by her concern, because he was normally a very private person. But she intrigued him—not merely because she was attractive; he'd been a widower for too short a time for her attractiveness to mean much—but because there was an unmistakable air of genuineness about her. He said to her, "I didn't mean to disturb you."

"You didn't," she answered simply. He liked the sound of her voice; it was soft and pleasant and seemed to carry, even in just those two words, the same kind of genuineness he had seen in her face. "Are you okay?" she went on.

He smiled broadly, as if in apology; she liked his smile.
"Yes," he said. "Just some . . . memories crowding back."
He felt suddenly that he was saying too much. "I haven't
seen you on this boat before."

She shook her head. "I used to take the ten o'clock. I'll
be riding this one for a while. I hope."

He asked, "You work in Manhattan?"

"Uh-huh," she answered. "I'm a dance instructor . . .
an *assistant* dance instructor. Today's my first day. How
about you?"

She was making him feel comfortable. "I'm a editor,"
he said, without much enthusiasm.

She nodded at the *Times*, which was folded in his lap.
"A newspaper editor?" She seemed vaguely impressed.

"No. Books. Fiction—novels, mostly."

"You've been at it a long time, haven't you?"

He grinned. "Does it show?"

"Only in the way you talk about it, as if you'd rather
not talk about it." She smiled. It was an open, pretty
smile, very nice to look at.

He smiled back, easily. "Ten years ago," he began, "I
actually sought out people to talk with about it. I really
thought I was hot stuff—you know, hobnobbing with the
greats and the near-greats, discovering wonderful new writ-
ers buried in the slush pile–"

"The slush pile?"

"Uh-huh, over-the-transom manuscripts—the stuff that
comes in uninvited."

"Oh," she said, and he thought he saw something
playfully accusing in her big, green eyes. "The *slush
pile!*"

He grinned. It occurred to him that he hadn't done so
much spontaneous grinning and smiling since well before
his wife's death. "Uh-huh. But that was ten years ago,
and it didn't take me long to find out that the greats and
the near-greats of this world are, after all, really–"

"Just people?" she interrupted.

"Just people," he confirmed.

She stuck her hand out. "My name's Joyce Dewitte.
What's yours?"

He took her hand, shook it, held on to it for a few moments because he liked the firm, warm touch of her skin. "Sam Campbell," he told her.

"It's good to meet you, Sam Campbell." She hesitated, looked away momentarily, then looked back. She smiled again, warmly. "Would you like to have supper with me, Sam Campbell?"

He smiled back, hugely pleased. "Yes," he answered. "Yes, I would like to have supper with you."

The boat docked at South Ferry fifteen minutes later.

Chapter 32

In the Bronx

Georgie MacPhail worked the night shift. He had worked
the night shift for several years. He left his apartment in
the Morrisania neighborhood by 1:00 A.M., and got in by
6:00. They were hours, he'd found, when people were
least apt to be awake and/or sober.

He allowed himself a total of an hour commuting time—a
half hour each way—and took the subway exclusively. It
was quick, dependable, and cheap, all very important
considerations.

Tonight he was working the South Park Apartments, a
big, rambling complex on the lower east side of Manhattan
which had lax-to-nonexistent security, and a good percent-
age of dayworkers and drunks. It was the drunks who
usually forgot to latch their doors and lock the foldaway
iron grating that was a fixture on practically every window
in Manhattan.

Georgie was an accomplished acrobat; it was a talent
he'd developed because of his work. Had circumstances
been remarkably different, he might easily have been a
future Olympian with fawning, proud parents, and a promising future endorsing exercise mats and sneakers.

He weighed in at eighty-eight pounds, but his heavily
muscled legs could easily have supported several times
that much. His arms were long, and incredibly strong; he
had, in fact, once challenged his Uncle Jim—a beefy man
of thirty-five—to a bout of arm wrestling. After nearly ten
minutes of struggle, Georgie finally lost, but he made his

uncle feel very weak indeed, and angry that a twelve-year-old had proved to be such tough competition. "You're sure a lean, mean son of a bitch, aren't you, Georgie!" he'd said. And Georgie said to him, "I ain't mean, Uncle Jim. I ain't mean to no one."

Tonight, at the back of the South Park Apartments, he sensed that he was going to have trouble. His senses were usually correct. He didn't know what kind of trouble he was going to have (trouble getting in, trouble keeping himself hidden, trouble with the cops) and the feeling wasn't strong enough that he'd consider going somewhere else, but it was an uncomfortable feeling, like wearing unwashed underwear, and he thought that he should finish this night's work quickly and put it behind him.

As a cat burglar, Georgie had several self-imposed restrictions. Most importantly, he would never burglarize someone who was obviously poorer than himself. That was simply fair play. He also never carried a gun. Guns were meant to kill people, and Georgie wanted harm to come to no one. His third rule was that he would never take anything too large to safely carry out of the building, and then safely carry or conceal on his way home, in front of the transit police. Cameras were good targets, as were portable radios, headphones, jewelry, watches, and the literally hundreds of other items he could shove into a pocket, hang around his neck, hold to his ear, or put around his wrist. Georgie wasn't greedy. His needs were simple—to feed himself, his mother, and his two brothers; to pay the rent; and to have a little bit left over to go to a movie every now and then, or to the Bronx Zoo, which he was fond of telling visitors to the city was "the best zoo there ever was." His philosophy and outlook were unique in the world of cat burglary. His methods, however, were more traditional.

Beneath his "work clothes"—tonight, a loose-fitting, ragged though clean, dark red flannel shirt, and black, early-sixties vintage, double-knit slacks—he was smartly dressed in a crisp, apparently brand new Izod polo shirt, and clean, also apparently brand new, designer blue jeans. His thinking was the soul of logic: If the transit police, or any other police, for that matter, saw a kid who was obviously poor carrying an eight-hundred-dollar Nikon, they'd look twice, and maybe ask some questions. But if that same kid looked like some kind of Mama's boy from Riverdale—the Bronx's most fashionable neighborhood—then the Nikon would be right at home. Consequently, the pretty-boy outfit. His shoes—impeccably brushed Wallabees—were good for climbing and for staying quiet, and also completed the outfit. Georgie went through lots of "working clothes" (which he wore, in the first place, to keep his pretty-boy outfit clean) because it was sometimes not possible to carry them back home, and so he had to toss them into the nearest trash can.

He got into apartments the same way most cat burglars did—up a rear fire escape, and then through a window that was neither barred nor latched. Simple. Of course, he'd spent more than a few nights just *looking* for the right apartment, and never finding it. And he'd more than once had to beat a hasty retreat when a just-awakened apartment dweller came into the room and hit the light. And then there were the fire escapes that would barely hold the weight of a cat, let alone an eighty-eight-pound cat burglar. And there were the apartments that were easy to get into, sure, and where the owner was sleeping off a drunk, sure, and where there was lots of fine stuff laying around— cameras and watches and so on—but it was clear that everything was marked, and marked merchandise was worthless.

But once, sometimes twice a week, Georgie got lucky, everything clicked, and he got home at 6:00 in the morning with enough merchandise to put away something for the rent and buy food.

Tonight, though, Georgie's luck would turn sour.

Chapter 33

Jim Hart sat a full half hour in the driver's seat of Fred Williams' baby-blue late model Ford Thunderbird—the windows closed and the doors locked—and finally realized that he had no keys for the damned thing. Fred had the keys. And Lord knew where Fred was.

Jim leaned forward so his chin touched the top of the Thunderbird's steering wheel. He looked through the windshield at the Con Ed Building just ahead, all lit up like some huge garden madonna. Then he looked to the left at the Empire State Building, and the twin towers of the World Trade Center far in the distance. He whispered, "I love you, Manhattan." And he smiled wistfully.

He sensed that there were faces pressed against the Thunderbird's side windows.

"What are you doing?" he heard.

The faces of the islanders, of course.

And then he heard, "Something wrong, fella?"

He kept his eyes on the Con Ed Building. He wondered what time it was. He knew that at 10:00 they turned off the lights that lit the building. Then the island would be plunged into darkness. Pitch darkness. Darkness, he thought, as black as the inside of his brain.

"Unlock the door, fella. Unlock the damned door!"

"Jesus," someone else said, "he must be roasting in there."

It was a warm morning, especially for so late in the

year. Already it was eighty degrees, humid, and cloudless. It would get a lot warmer.

Jim hated the darkness. He saw *things* in it. Dark, formless things. Things that looked for all the world like huge, shifting mounds of black cotton.

He turned to one of the faces pressed into the driver's window. He smiled amiably. "What time is it?" he asked.

"What'd you say, fella?"

"I think he wants to know what *time* it is."

Jim went on, "They shut the lights off at ten. What time is it now? It's about nine-thirty or nine-forty-five, isn't it?"

He heard, "What in hell is that guy talking about?"

"He wants to know what *time* it is."

"It's ten-thirty, fella."

Jim shook his head slowly, the amiable smile still on his face. "No," he said. "No, that's not possible. They turn the lights off at ten."

"Jesus, he's nutty as a fruitcake."

The temperature climbed to eighty-one in that moment. Inside the Thunderbird it was much hotter than that, and Jim began to sweat.

"Your fucking watch is wrong," he heard. "It's ten-forty-five"

"I still say that guy's nutty as a fruitcake."

"My watch isn't wrong. It's a Seiko!"

"I think we should get that guy out of there."

A drop of sweat rolled over Jim's eyebrow, into his eye. He blinked, rubbed the eye, cursed. He turned his head to the right, looked out the passenger window. A woman appeared there—she was young, very pretty.

"Marie?" he said.

The woman said nothing. She looked questioningly at him.

"Marie?" Jim repeated.

"We gotta get him outa there." A man's voice.

"My name is Carol," the woman said through the closed window. "Is there something bothering you?" Her voice was soft and soothing, too soft and too soothing for Jim to hear all of her words through the window.

"Marie?" he said again.

"Carol," she said, louder.

"He's wacko, the guy's wacko!"

"I resent that word," someone said. "I really do resent that word. It's crass, it's insensitive—"

"It's ten-thirty-five, not ten-forty-five. My Seiko's always right."

"Is there something bothering you?" Carol asked again. "Please, is there something bothering you?"

"Marie?"

"No, Carol." A pause, then, "Why does he keep calling me 'Marie'?"

"I told you, he's wacko!"

The temperature climbed another degree, then began edging inexorably higher. Sweat covered Jim's face like an oily mask. "Marie," he said, "I'm so sorry."

"Carol," the woman told him again. "My name is Carol."

"Would you believe," Jim went on, his tone straining for the conversational, "that I had never, *ever* fired a gun before, never in my life. It was chance, Marie. Chance! If I'd been aiming, of course, if I'd been *aiming* I would have missed, I would have missed by a country mile—"

"I think he's talking about killing someone, that's what I think."

"He's talking about *shooting* someone."

"D'joo shoot someone, fella?"

"You think he's got a gun in there with him right now?"

Inside the closed car, the temperature pushed to 95.

"I would have missed for sure," Jim said to himself. Then he turned his head quickly to the left and confronted one of the faces there. "But I didn't miss," he told the face. Then he shouted at it, "I didn't miss!"

The face retreated; a look of shock and dismay fell over it. "Jesus, he *did* shoot someone!"

"We gotta get a cop over here."

"I think I saw a State Trooper in the restaurant. You want me to go get him?"

"Yeah. Quick. We'll keep this guy in here till you get back."

"Jesus, I don't think he's *going* anywhere. Hey fella, you *going* anywhere?"

The temperature reached 96 inside the Thunderbird; Jim was feeling lightheaded. He saw Manhattan begin to melt in the heat, and his mouth fell open in awe. Several of the faces outside the car turned to follow his gaze and saw only a deep blue Adirondack sky sliced by evergreens, a couple of billboards, a tall, neon sign that read HOLIDAY INN.

"What do you see?" Carol asked Jim.

Jim didn't hear her. He had just watched the lights on the Con Ed building blink out. "No," he murmured, panic rising in him. He saw the lights blink on again, then off. "No," he said again, sharply. And in response the lights blinked on.

"What's *wrong*?" Carol asked; she was feeling very frustrated.

He turned, looked at her sadly, and mouthed the words, "It's melting!"

"What?"

"It's melting!" He said the words aloud now; she heard them.

"What's melting?"

He turned his head back. "Manhattan," he whispered, but no one heard him.

"Anybody here got a gun?" someone said.

Silence.

"I said, anybody here got a gun?"

"Why do we need a gun?" It was Carol.

" 'Cuz *he* might have one. And he's *wacko!*"

Again, silence.

"So, like I said, does anybody have a gun?"

"*I* don't have one," someone said.

"The State Trooper will be here in a second, so let's not–"

"Hey . . ."

"Why don't you open the door?" Carol said to Jim.

"Hey, I just saw a goddamned streaker."

"Why don't you open the door," Carol said again, more soothingly now. But Jim didn't hear her. "Manhattan is melting," he told her and he began to weep softly, as if in resignation, or defeat.

"Jesus," someone said, "he thinks he's in *Manhattan*!"

"I saw two of them, I saw *two* streakers!"

"I think that trooper's coming."

"Maybe we should all back away from the car, don'tcha think? Hey fella, you gonna shoot anyone?"

Jim continued to weep; he had his arms folded on the top of the steering wheel.

"I think we should call the fucking white coats!" someone said.

"And I say we should all just back away, very slowly . . ."

"Damn you!" Jim breathed.

"D'joo say something, fella?"

"Damn you!" he said aloud.

"Why's he swearing like that?"

"He's nutsed up, that's why."

"I think we should just back away . . ."

"Damn you!" Jim shouted. "Goddamn you!"

The crowd that had gathered around the Thunderbird backed away quickly.

The children knew well what hunger was. They had sprung from the earth knowing what it was; the ache, the need—and satisfying it was passion itself, as much a part of each of them as breathing was.
They ate to stay alive.
They ate so their species could stay alive.
And they ate whatever the earth provided them.

The tableau which had developed in the Route 22A Holiday Inn parking lot—fifteen miles from the house on the island—was growing increasingly tense. At first, for the dozen or so people who had clustered around the Thunderbird a half hour earlier, it had been merely a break to the morning's routine: *Hey, look at this—there's some guy sitting stiff as a board in his car here, and he won't say nothin'.* It was something to speculate about—"He must be on dope." . . . "Maybe he's having some kind of fit." . . . "He could be diabetic."—just a few minutes of casual entertainment.

And then someone had remarked how "scruffy the guy

looks,'' and someone else had suggested that Jim was probably just ''a bum sleeping off a quart of Pinot Chardonnay,'' which no one found particularly funny. At last, the humanitarian in the group had pointed out that it was probably going to get pretty hot in the Thunderbird.

Which was when Jim had realized he didn't have the car keys.

No one in the Holiday Inn parking lot saw Seth, or Elena, or the children. They had merged into the perimeter of the surrounding piney woods and they were seeing what Jim was seeing, and feeling what he was feeling. And the mist swirling out from inside the car, from inside Jim Hart himself, and the rich, dark colors and striations of madness in it.

With Jim, Seth and Elena and the children were watching Manhattan melt into its horizon.

They were watching an Adirondack horizon rise up in its place.

And because they were trying very hard to understand what they were seeing, they had set aside their vast hunger. For the moment.

''Didn't you say the trooper was coming? I don't see no trooper.''

''I thought it was the trooper—it was the bus driver.''

''The *bus* driver?''

''Question is—what are we gonna do with this guy? Look at him.'' Everyone looked; they saw that Jim's face had turned beet red. ''He's gonna die unless we get him out. It must be a hundred degrees in there.''

Carol spoke. ''Open the door,'' she shouted at Jim. But Jim didn't answer. He was sitting up in the seat, and he was mumbling something—no one could hear what. ''Open the door!'' Carol repeated.

''It's called heat prostration,'' the man next to her said. ''I had a dog die of it once. My wife left him in the car . . .''

''I got a gun!'' someone announced suddenly, and shrilly.

All faces turned toward the voice. They saw a short, thin, middle-aged man, dressed in a baggy gray suit. He was holding his right arm out, wrist bent, and there was a small black pistol in his hand. Its barrel was pointing downward. The man looked like he had little idea what he was going to do with the gun. He looked, in fact, as if he was sorry he'd brought the whole thing up.

"I don't think we need it," someone said.

The thin man stared a moment at the gun. Then his grip tightened around it. "You can never tell for sure," he stammered, "when you're gonna need a gun. Not for sure." He grinned, pleased with the analysis. He lowered his arm, so the gun still pointed at the ground, but now his finger was on the trigger, and his grip was very tight. He made his way through the cluster of people to the passenger's side of the car. He smiled grimly at Jim. "Hi guy," he said. Jim didn't turn to look. He continued mumbling incoherently. "Cat got your tongue," said the thin man. Jim still didn't turn to notice him. The thin man's smile faded. He brought the gun up to the window, placed it flat on the glass. "You can see this, can't you guy?!" Jim still did not turn to notice.

"This is foolish!" Carol said.

"This is *not* foolish!" hissed the thin man, and Carol fell silent.

"Marie?" Jim whispered.

The thin man knocked the gun against the window. Once. "Open up, guy." He gave Jim a long and thorough once-over and saw what he supposed was a bulge in the pocket of Jim's jacket. "Hey guy, what you got in there?" Jim had nothing in the pocket. It bulged because the fabric had decided to bulge.

The thin man turned to the others in the group. "I think he's got a gun in his jacket pocket."

"Marie," Jim said. "Oh, Marie!" he shouted, and threw his arms down, against the steering wheel, and buried his face in his hands.

It took the thin man by surprise. He jumped back, spread his legs wide, straightened his arms. He had the gun pointed directly at Jim's head. "Get outa there!" he screeched. "Get outa there!" He was very nervous.

Jim took no notice of him.

The thin man fired. Once.

Carol screamed. One of the men screamed. Behind the group, the State Trooper bellowed, "Drop that weapon!" and the thin man turned toward the voice very quickly.

Had the trooper not taken him by surprise, the thin man would have done as ordered—he would have dropped the gun. But because he had been taken by surprise, he kept his arms straight, and the gun level. And just as he finished turning, and had begun to explain, grinningly, what exactly he was doing—"I thought it was advisable–" —the trooper fired. A .38 caliber slug tore into the thin man's chest. It zigzagged around in his lungs for a moment, slammed sideways through his heart, and exited through his back. It came to rest in the Thunderbird's front left tire, which began to deflate immediately.

The thin man slumped to his knees. He fell face foward to the pavement.

Carol screamed again.

The State Trooper cursed beneath his breath; "Goddammit, Jesus Christ, Goddammit!"

A man screamed.

And, at the perimeter of the piney woods, Seth screamed. And Elena. And so did the children gathered around them.

The trooper looked up from the thin man's body. "What in the hell?" he breathed.

Seth forced himself into silence. But Elena could not. Nor could the children. And so their screams, like a chorus of shrill echoes, continued.

"What in the hell *is* that?" said the trooper.

"My God!" someone else said.

"An echo," Carol said. "An echo," she repeated, although she knew well enough that it was not an echo. She was a remarkably sensitive, intelligent, and gentle woman—the mother of three, an up-and-coming commercial artist, highly thought of in her little community.

She was the first to die that morning at the hands of the children.

Chapter 34

It was without a doubt one of the very best ways to die. Not because it was quick—for most it wasn't; for most it was slow, almost fantastically slow. And not because it was painless—it wasn't; it was alive with pain. But because it was so easily denied. Death just could not happen that way. And so it had to be something else. It had to be a fantasy, some kind of dream, a hallucination or an illusion, some sort of awful fit, perhaps.

But it could not be death. It certainly could not be death!

In the midst of it, when the pain was screaming through her body and her forearms had been opened up wide, down to the bone—as if being made ready for surgery— and her belly had been ripped away, revealing the crowd of organs within, Carol thought of her children, and the swimming classes that her youngest was scheduled to begin the following day, and how glad she was of that. And then blessed unconsciousness overtook her and she made the transition from life into death with plans for tomorrow in her head.

A man named Albert, looking on from close by, found that he was smiling, as if some kind of performance were being staged for him. He saw shadows moving swiftly around him and he remembered that he had seen similar shadows—on windy days, when low, small clouds scurried overhead, and the sky was blue and bright behind them.

He saw Carol fall amidst these shadows; he saw her being opened up and reduced to her vitals, and then to her bones, and from one moment to the next he felt that he could see faces turn, and stare up at him from what was being done. Faces that were small and dark and layered with Carol's blood. Faces which, he knew, without that mask of blood would have been exquisitely beautiful, as perfect as anything the earth can produce.

The faces of children.

And the trooper, lying face down on the pavement, his eyes opened wide in awe and shock, and the pain searing through his legs (where the children had begun their meal) thought deep in the recesses of his brain that he'd be up until midnight or later filling out reports on this one, and that he didn't want to be up past midnight filling out reports. Because he had other plans.

And someone passing by in an old Buick, on Route 22A, a hundred feet east, slowed to a crawl and said to his passenger, "Hey, looka that! I wonder what the hell's going on there!"

His passenger looked. He saw the same shadows that Albert had seen, and through them, as if he were looking through a veil, he saw the suggestion of bodies heaped about, arms and legs turned and maneuvered into improbable positions. And all around, something like a dark rain was falling—rising up, shifting sideways, falling. "It's some kind of dust storm," he said, knowing even as he said it that it wasn't a dust storm at all. He turned his head quickly; "Don't stop," he said to the driver, very urgently. And then he looked again at the scene in the parking lot. "It's just a dust storm of some kind," he repeated. And then, as if to himself, "Don't stop," he whispered. And the driver sped on toward New York.

Fifteen years earlier; Near Penn Yann, New York:

The creature had fallen seventy feet to the bare earth from the upper branches of an aged honey locust. The creature had climbed the honey locust for no other reason than it could climb it; and it had fallen because it knew nothing about old trees and decayed branches. It knew only about itself—what pain was, and what cold was—and how to protect itself from the cold—and it knew about heat, and hunger, and about desire. It knew what the earth said it must know.

The creature did not know it was dying. Since its birth only weeks before, it had killed, and it had seen death, and it had experienced life. But it could not give names or meanings to anything—its brain was not set up for clutter.

The fall from the honey locust—which would not have been fatal had the creature jumped instead of fallen wildly out of control—had broken the creature's back. One lower rib, as well, had pierced its heart. And so it was dying. Very painfully and slowly.

Its eyes followed the subtly changing patterns of light and shadow all around. That changing pattern was what it had first seen, weeks before, when the earth was done giving it life.

The creature could not smile. If it were human, it might. But it wasn't. So, blankly, it watched the changing patterns of light and shadow; it experienced the pain. And, in time, life stopped within it.

Forever.

The new creature pushed itself up to a half-sitting position. It stood. It felt the soft creepers of the hard wind that was pushing the tops of the trees about; it heard the busy, quick noises of squirrels and rabbits and raccoons, and a thousand others, making ready for the winter. It saw the changing patterns of light and shadow all around.

And it felt its muscles moving gracefully over its bones; the air swelling its lungs.

The others present at the birth touched and prodded the creature. Wonderingly. Because the creature was alive, and warm. As they were. And because they could see. And hear. And taste. And smell. And also touch.

Because they had sprung from the earth. And they were alive.

Chapter 35

At The Stone

Snipe had good ears. "Ears like a dog," he was fond of telling people . . . and it was almost true. A small accident of biology had blessed him not only with ears that were slightly outsized, but also ear canals and eardrums that were several decibels and several octaves more sensitive than those of most other people.

It was a little past 8:00 P.M., and Snipe was in the middle of giving the nine people he had brought together in The Stone's lobby another pep talk about "staying in line and staying alive." He stopped talking in midsentence and turned his head quickly to the right, his gaze on an open concrete stairway about forty feet away, a stairway which led to the second floor.

He had heard a stomach growl.

One of his "lieutenants" (a designation that, by inference, made Snipe feel very important indeed), a boy nicknamed "Cheese," because he seemed to carry the faint, but unmistakable odor of cheese around with him, said, "D'ja hear something, Snipe?" Snipe did not answer. Cheese elected wisely to stay quiet.

After half a minute, Snipe nodded once toward the stairway. "There!" he commanded. And immediately three of his lieutenants ran to the stairway and started up. They stopped as one when Snipe shouted at them, "Alive! I want that sucker alive!" Again as one they nodded and ran up the stairway.

*   *   *

121

Georgie MacPhail could taste the blood seeping into his mouth from his lacerated gum. He liked the taste. He remembered something from "The Wild Wild World of Animals" about a tribe in Africa drinking cow's blood regularly and he thought that that was all right. If it tasted anything like people's blood, then it was probably habit-forming.

He was trying very hard not to think about the events of the past few hours. About the poor, dumb kid who'd chased him down the fire escape. About the ugly *whump!* the kid's body had made after falling three floors to the damned blacktop behind the South Park Apartments. About the lousy, time-wasting tug of war that had gone on in his—Georgie's—mind when he'd seen the kid lying there, moaning and bleeding in his damned jockey shorts. "Goddamn you, kid!" Georgie had whispered at him.

He told himself that it was a matter of priorities. This poor dumb kid's life, or the lives of Georgie's mother, and his little brothers, who depended on him for support. Because if he stayed and helped the kid, then he'd get caught. And if he got caught he'd be out of work for a year, maybe longer. And in that time, anything could happen.

He had come upon the solution quickly, surprising himself: He stooped over, picked up a large piece of chipped blacktop, and heaved it at the nearest window. The chip of blacktop broke apart against the iron grating, but a chunk just large enough got through and the window behind the grating shattered beautifully. A light went on almost immediately. Seconds later, a female head appeared; "What in the fuck . . ."

"Call an ambulance!" Georgie yelled, and pointed frantically at the dumb kid's body at his feet. "Please . . ." The head disappeared, the light went out. Another light, in the apartment just above, went on; a man's head appeared.

"Call an ambulance!" Georgie yelled again.

And then he ran.

He told himself now that the man *had* called for an ambulance (anonymously, of course—which was the way things like that were done in New York). He told himself that the poor, dumb kid would be all right, that he'd just had the wind knocked out of him.

He didn't believe a word of it. Because anybody who falls three floors like that, head over heels, onto blacktop gets more than just the wind knocked out of him.

And so Georgie ran.

Down 89th Street, to 79th, then to 2nd Avenue, and, finally, a half hour later, to the back of The Stone, where he stopped, breathless.

He had recognized the building, vaguely—the way he might recognize an uncle he hadn't seen in quite a few years. And because he recognized it, because he had a good idea what kind of building it was, it became, instantly, a place for him to hide. For a couple of days, anyway. Just in case the poor, dumb kid lucked out and pulled through and was able to describe him. The cops had his picture on file, after all, and there was no sense taking chances. And maybe he had that look about him—the look that said loudly, "Hey, I just done something wrong!" But he wasn't sure. He didn't think he had that look. He thought he just looked scared, and maybe that was bad enough.

Getting into The Stone had been a piece of cake. Up a badly rusted fire escape, and in through a window. No iron grating. No bars. Just an open window, and a screen behind it, which had pushed open with shameful ease.

And then inside.

In the darkness, he had fallen over Winifred Haritson.

THEORIES NUMEROUS ON CAUSES OF ADIRONDACK
DISASTER

(Sept. 19) (UPI): In the wake of the recent unexplained, grisly accident which took fourteen lives at a Holiday Inn parking lot in the Adirondacks, 45 miles northwest of New York City, state and federal investigators are putting forth several theories as to the cause of the tragedy.

A Chief Accident Investigator from the FAA was quoted as saying he has seen similar accidents involving the rotor blades of helicopters—most recently in

Manhattan several years ago, when a helicopter tipped over on top of one of the World Trade Center Towers: "The carnage then was incredible, unbelievable, and this accident seems similar in many ways, although we do not yet have any reports of missing helicopters, or rotor blades."

The same investigator explained that certain jet fuels might, under some conditions, have the effect of denuding bodies of flesh, as was seen in the Adirondack tragedy. He goes on to say, however, that the chances of such a spill from a passing aircraft are "extremely, almost impossibly remote," and that, at any rate, it would be difficult to accept in the light of the fact that the parking lot itself was not damaged, nor were several cars in the immediate vicinity—most notably, the car in which the only survivor was found.

An attack by a horde of "army ants" was also offered as a possible cause for the tragedy, and quickly dismissed. Army ants are not native to New York State; they are native to various southern states; and have not been encountered above Maryland. It also seems implausible, experts say, to believe that army ants could be the cause of such incredible destruction . . .

Chapter 36

Whimsical Fatman knew that he was dying, and the thing that amazed him most was that he *cared* that he was dying. Goddammit, he'd had another twenty years in him, at least. If he'd mended his ways. There were places he'd never been to, people he'd never seen—his children all grown up, for instance. And it was possible, altogether possible, that his father was still alive, and it would have been a blessing to have seen him again.

But the cops had done a good job. They were smooth, and well trained.

("Just a little twist, right at the end of your kick, Tony—just before you make contact, and I guarantee it'll snap clean as a whistle.")

They'd broken his kneecap almost without effort.

("See, wasn't that easy? Like I said, it's all in that little twist—that's what does it. Just like you're throwing a punch, Tony. But with your foot.")

And seeing to it that he wouldn't be able to call for help had been easy, too.

("Know how easy it is to break a man's jaw, Tony? Real easy. Thing is, you don't try and *break* it so much as *dislocate* it, and that's just a matter of the correct angle. Kind of up, and over, and you make contact right close to his chin so you get the leverage—know what I mean?")

Whimsy groaned very softly; he could do no more than

125

that—his jaw hung open, uselessly, a little to the right of where it should have been.

("So we'll let him rot here, Tony. It's better than letting him rot in New York, right?")

Whimsy supposed that the cops hadn't actually wanted to kill him. He supposed that they didn't care enough about him for that. They had merely wanted to give him some pain, lots of it, and if he happened to kick off, who was to care? And if someone found him, and he told a wild story about a couple of Manhattan cops beating the hell out of him, and then dumping him in a field just outside Fort Lee, New Jersey, who was to care, either?

The cops had had their fun. And now they could go back to chasing bad guys.

Whimsy closed his eyes. Not only against the pain in his jaw and in his kneecap—a pain which alternated from one moment to the next between the two points—but also from an incredible exhaustion which, all by itself, he thought, could take his life from him.

Consciousness stayed with him, though barely, as if he were tied to it by a very thin thread. And, distantly, he could hear what sounded for all the world like a dog growling.

The dogs which he had grown accustomed to dealing with in the past decade or so had been very much like the people he'd grown accustomed to dealing with—lean, and scruffy, and desperate. Dogs that would never curl up next to somebody's armchair, or fetch a Frisbee, or get used to twice-daily feedings of Alpo. He had learned to stay away from these dogs, and to let them have their own turf.

He thought that the dog growling at him now was much like a street dog because it had a street dog's smell, and a street dog's aura of desperation about it. And he knew that with a lot of street dogs, it was instinct to go first for an enemy's genitals. Whimsy wanted very much to slip into death with his genitals intact. He thought that he deserved at least that much.

And then he heard, "Hey, whatcha got there, boy?" And the beam of a flashlight stabbed into his eyes.

Chapter 37

The old couple never thought much about being in love. They'd been in love for nearly sixty years, and so it had become a state of being for them, a way of life. Life itself.

Occasionally they still held hands.

Occasionally they embraced, without apparent reason. And kissed each other.

They still slept in a double bed, and while they slept they reached for one another. And touched.

A pale blue, gentle mist—visible only to Seth, who was watching them—surrounded them both. It was nearly the same blue that was in the eyes of the children. And in his eyes, and Elena's.

The place the old couple walked in daily was called Laufer's Woods—a twenty-acre stand of spruce and pine, plus several varieties of maple and oak trees that was crisscrossed by footpaths, and dotted in several spots by small wooden bridges that spanned narrow gulleys lush with vegetation.

The old couple had been walking regularly in Laufer's Woods for half their married life, ever since coming to Purling from an ancestral home in New Hampshire. They walked the woods nearly every day of the year, except for several days during winter, when the snow was too deep.

They had speculated once that when they were gone their ghosts would continue to walk the woods. It had made them laugh, and it had made them feel good. They did not really believe in ghosts, but they knew very well about wishing.

Seth and Elena and the children took them with the speed and urgency of the moment. And afterward, Seth could feel and hear inside himself the lives of the old couple:

Oh, Marcus, yes, I'll marry you! Lord, yes!

His name had been Marcus.

I can't promise you much, Emma. Only myself, and my love . . .

. . . Some camomile tea, Marcus? . . .

. . . I think the Stickley loveseat would be perfect, Emma . . .

. . . I love you, Marcus . . .

I love you, Emma . . .

All the beautiful, hesitant, quickly spoken whispers of two lives coming together over six decades came together inside Seth and gave him pleasure.

"They talked about ghosts, Elena," he said, and something that was close to a smile appeared on his lips. Elena did not understand.

And some of the children, who had formed a circle near Seth and Elena, repeated Seth's words: "They talked about ghosts, Elena," the children said, though they had no idea at all what the words meant.

They soon left Laufer's Woods and headed south, toward Manhattan.

Chapter 38

John Marsh was tired and angry. Seth—the magician, the superman—was toying with him. He knew it. He could feel it. As if Seth were reaching out, probing, telling him, shouting at him—*Yes, I am near!* And then nothing.

Marsh swore beneath his breath. Joe, his German shepherd, sitting close by, whined deep in his throat as if asking what was wrong. Marsh reached out from the big, overstuffed chair and scratched the dog's chin. "You're lucky they let you in here, Joe," he said, and the dog inclined his head into Marsh's hand.

Marsh let his body relax in the chair; "I could sleep a month of Sundays, Joe," he said. "That man out there is playing a game with me, he's having his fun, and it's wearing me out." Joe whined again. "It's been a hell of a long haul, Joe, but my guess is that it's coming to an end." He closed his eyes. Joe came over and curled up next to the chair. Marsh reached down, stroked the dog's head. "We'll keep goin' south, Joe. *He's* moving south. I know that." And Marsh wondered momentarily if he really knew anything about Seth. He called him "The Magician," and "Superman," but they were only words, and they actually meant very little.

"I'm getting old, Joe. We're both getting old, aren't we?"

Joe licked the man's hand. Minutes later, Marsh was

asleep. It was a fitful sleep, full of short, nasty dreams, and just before sunrise, he woke, went to the window, and looked out.

He left the guest house two hours later, and drove south, toward Manhattan.

Chapter 39

"She tried to kill herself," Sam Campbell said, and he settled back in his chair, away from the chess table. Joyce Dewitte moved her knight's pawn ahead one square. She was trying hard to think of some response to what he'd just said, because she desperately did not want to let what he'd said lie there so flat, and cold, and ugly.

"And so," she asked, "she's in Bellevue?" and felt at once that it was a pretty lame remark.

Sam leaned forward and took one of Joyce's pawns with one of his bishops. "Yes," he answered tonelessly, "she's in Bellevue."

"You miss her, don't you, Sam?"

"I miss her a lot, Joyce. A hell of a lot!"

"I mean . . . your wife, Sam."

He looked blankly across the table at her, momentarily confused, and idly moved one of his chess pieces. "The hurt is fading, Joyce. The memories aren't, but the hurt is."

"Yes," Joyce whispered, "I understand that." She put back the piece he'd just moved. "It was my move, Sam." She looked the board over.

He said, "Would you like to come with me next week, Joyce?"

"Come with you?" She moved her queen. "Come where, Sam?"

"To see Marsha. At Bellevue."

Joyce looked quickly at him, then away, as if he had

131

taken her by surprise. "Do you really think that would be . . . a good thing to do, Sam?"

He thought a moment, sighed, shook his head. "No," he answered, "I guess not."

She reached across the table, touched his hand lightly. "I think you should talk to her about me, first, Sam."

He nodded. "Yes, I think so, too."

"And then, when she's gotten used to the idea that there's . . . that there might be . . . someone else . . ."

He took her hand, squeezed it, nodded again, "Yes, that's a good idea, Joyce. Yes." He was clearly upset.

"Or am I way off base, Sam?"

"No, Joyce"—he lowered his head, as if to avoid looking at her—"you're not off base. God, not at all!"

"You sound as if that bothers you."

"It does bother me. It bothers me a lot. It makes me feel lousy. It makes me feel . . . I don't know—adulterous, for Christ's sake!"

Joyce said nothing.

"And feeling adulterous, Joyce, feeling *adulterous* about . . . us makes me feel like a damned fool!" He sounded as if he was pleading with her.

"I can understand that," Joyce said.

"I know you can *understand* it, Joyce, but that doesn't make it . . . good. That doesn't make it *normal*."

And she said crisply, "Oh Christ, Sam—fuck 'normal'!" She grimaced. "No, I'm sorry . . ."

He smiled, closed his eyes lightly. "Yes," he whispered. "Thank you, Joyce. Thank you."

From *The Purling Post*: September 24th:

COUPLE REPORTED MISSING

Long-time Purling residents Marcus and Emma Wheeler have been reported as missing by their grandson Jason, according to Purling Town Constable William Sears. The couple, both 79 years old, have lived in a house at 432 Butternut Tree Lane since the early 1950s. They were active in church and civic affairs; he worked for 25 years as a gardener; she produced many award-winning quilts for various specialty shops in the county.

The couple was last seen three days ago leaving their home on Butternut Tree Lane. It is believed by Constable Sears that they were on their way to Laufer's Woods, and a search has been mounted there.

The couple also . . .

From *The Leeds Gazette:* September 25th:

SCARF ONLY CLUE IN CASE OF MISSING WOMAN

A red silk scarf apparently belonging to 41-year-old Josephine Alesi, of Burlow Street, Leeds, is so far the only clue to her mysterious disappearance two days ago.

The subject of a massive search by local volunteers and a dozen state troopers, Mrs. Alesi was last seen walking alone near the Green's Bird Sanctuary, off Route 87, a half mile outside the Leeds town limits.

Although the search is continuing, a spokesman for the search team expressed pessimism that the woman would be found.

In an incident which may be related, two twelve-year-old boys from Rhinebeck, forty miles south, have also been reported missing near the Green's Bird Sanctuary, and the search has been expanded to include them. The boys were reported missing by their mother when they failed to return home after a nature hike to the Sanctuary yesterday. It was not immediately determined if the boys got to the Sanctuary, and the investigation is continuing . . .

Chapter 40

In the Basement of an Abandoned Apartment Building in the South Bronx

Joe Washington grumbled, "Shee*it*!" *You gotta wake up, Joe Washington!* he told himself. *Maybe this is the* day, *man!* And he thought he'd called that last voice up from his distant past, that he was trying to give himself *hope*, or something. "Shee*it*!" He put his hands palm down on the concrete floor to push himself to a standing position. He became dimly aware that he'd wet himself in the night, and then that his bottle of Thunderbird was empty. He cursed again. And heard the curse repeated—in his voice—from somewhere close by. He looked about confusedly. He saw the child only for a moment. Then he felt soft pressure at his throat. The pressure increased; he hacked once, a smile broke through his agony, and he died.

In Another Part of the South Bronx

Doris Hall awoke feeling very, very good. Great, in fact. As if, she thought, she'd just spent the night involved in the most exquisite lovemaking of her young life and was basking in the afterglow. Then she remembered that a series of amazingly erotic dreams had carried her through the night. She lingered in bed a long while. She hoped the day wouldn't be a long one.

Something in a corner of the dimly lighted room caught her eye. She looked. The corner was empty. She got out of bed, went to the corner. She felt something brush past her, felt something like a hand touch her bare belly.

She heard a scream from below, from the building's first floor. A quick, abrupt scream, as if it had been broken off midway. And then, from another part of the building, she heard what she knew was gunfire—a handgun, she guessed. Small calibre. It sounded again, and again. Then there was silence.

Several Hundred Yards North

He was an old man, and his eyes were bad, his hearing worse. But his memory was good, and he could not remember seeing anything quite like what he was seeing now.

He rubbed his eyes. He squinted. The image remained. He murmured to himself, *"Que pasa?"*

It was a bleak landscape he was looking at; one man, a politician, had once compared it to the surface of the moon. The comparison was as much true as poetic.

The rubble of decades of neglect lay here, stretched out over a thousand acres or more. It was normally as still and as motionless as it was bleak.

This morning, it was alive. It moved. The rubble itself seemed to rise up, split into twos and threes, and walk about. Then fall back. Only to rise up again in another place.

But that is what the old man saw. And his eyes were bad. He heard this: ". . . the others, the ones who stayed . . ." And, ". . . survivors, Elena . . ."

And ". . . our island . . ."

He heard more, but thought nothing of it. He spoke no English.

From *The Rhinebeck Post*: September 27th:

NOSTALGIA CORNER
REMEMBER THE STREAKERS
It's the late 70's, you're walking to the library or to your favorite restaurant, you're minding your own business when—whoosh!—from out of nowhere come

a half dozen bare bottoms. You gasp. And it's over.
The bare bottoms (and God knows what else) are
just a memory. "Lord," you say to yourself, "I've
just been streaked!"

Remember that?

The good ole days, right?!

Well, they're back!

And they're back with a vengeance!

At least a dozen of the little heathens, all in a line,
were reported a week ago on Route 87, just north of
Purling, New York—a small town 75 miles north of
here—and, in Leeds, several more were spotted in
front of the Town Hall, of all places.

Of course, these "sightings" took place in the
dead of night, so apparently these streakers are, alas,
somewhat less than courageous . . .

From *The New York Times*, September 29th:

BODY FOUND IN NEW CROTON RESERVOIR A MYSTERY

The nude body of a boy apparently aged twelve or
thirteen found floating in the New Croton Reservoir,
near Westchester, twenty-five miles north of Manhattan,
is baffling investigators. Initial efforts at identifying the
boy—who is described as a dark-skinned Caucasian
with light blue eyes and very dark, shoulder-length
hair—proved futile, and an autopsy performed at
Bellevue Hospital by Dr. Urey C. Birnbaum, Chief
Pathologist, was, sources say, "inconclusive." The
same sources also explained that according to certain
confidential documents, the boy's "physiology" is,
in several ways, unusual. The sources could not
elaborate further.

Asked about the cause of the boy's death, a spokesman for the Coroner's Office explained that the boy
"probably drowned," although he would not rule
out the possibility that the boy may have been a
victim of child abuse.

Dr. Birnbaum . . .

Chapter 41

A thousand deaths happened that day. Most of the deaths went unnoticed, except by those that killed and those that died. The city survived because of the dead; the dead made room for the living, and the children and grandchildren of the living.

Near the edge of the city, at the perimeter of a landfill, in a place where they would not be seen, two brothers laboriously dug a deep hole and then dumped the body of a going-on-middle-aged hooker into it. The hooker had died at their hands; the reasons didn't matter.

In Harlem, a man barely in his twenties leaped from the top floor of his tenement house and died instantly when he hit the pavement, fifteen floors below.

On East Houston Street, in The Bowery, a sanitation engineer standing too far out in the street, waiting for his co-worker to return with a load of garbage, was clipped by a passing taxi and sent sprawling head first into a street sign. He broke his neck.

In the Holland Tunnel, a woman on her way out of Manhattan to visit her daughter in New Jersey, began swiping furiously at a bee on the inside of her windshield and hit another car head-on. A gasoline tanker, just behind her, jackknifed into the wreckage and exploded within seconds. The resulting inferno killed a dozen people, and sent another dozen to various hospitals in Manhattan.

In Greenwich Village, a four-year-old boy playing with his father's .38 pointed the weapon at his mother, said

"Bang!" and pulled the trigger. The bullet lodged in his mother's lung; she died four hours later of massive hemorrhaging.

These were the kinds of deaths that happened regularly in Manhattan. And those who paid attention to them would merely shake their heads and cluck that accidents happened all the time, there was really nothing anybody could do about it, or they'd whisper that the Mafia had its hands into everything, or proclaim that they'd never have a gun in *their* house.

These were the kinds of deaths that people could deal with.

In a sense, they were a form of entertainment. They were, at least, understandable. And they were mundane.

So they frightened no one.

Part Two

ASSAULT ON MANHATTAN

Chapter 42

Approximately one-and-one-half million people live on the island of Manhattan. It is shaped roughly like a heelless shoe, viewed from above, with the ankle at its northern end, and covers about thirty-one square miles, eight of which are inland waterways.

Manhattan is the smallest of New York City's five boroughs—Queens, Brooklyn, Manhattan, The Bronx, and Staten Island. Several ethnic and cultural areas have sprung up on the island, including—looking south to north—Chinatown, near the island's southern tip; Greenwich Village, about a mile north; Stuyvesant, a half mile east of Greenwich Village; and, a mile and a half northwest, the Garment District, then the Theater District. East of Central Park, there is the Upper East Side and Yorkville. Northwest of Central Park, there is Morningside Heights, home of Columbia University. And east of Morningside Heights, Harlem. East of Harlem is East Harlem.

The Harlem River cuts the island off from land at its northern end. On the west, it is separated from land by the Hudson River, and on the east by the East River. Upper New York Bay is at its southern end.

Peter Minuet purchased the island from the Manhattan Indians in 1624, for twenty-eight dollars worth of trinkets.

A first-time visitor to the island is struck first by the very *pace* of things. *Business* is the business of Manhattan, and it is accomplished with all possible speed. If you are walking, you walk fast, with your head down, and you talk to no one. If you are driving, you drive fast and, of necessity, view other drivers with a cool, if not always quiet, disdain. The rule of thumb that applies in Manhattan—both to pedestrians and to drivers alike—is: If you get there first, you have the right of way.

The first-time visitor to Manhattan also is struck by the attitude of New Yorkers. Publicly, it is a thin-lipped, stiff-legged stoicism that says very loudly, *I'm minding my own business, you mind yours. If you want to run around naked, for Christ's sake, it's okay with me, as long as you don't invade my space.* It is an attitude which first-time visitors often mistake for rudeness. It is not rudeness. It is survival. In a city the size and complexity of Manhattan, no one can afford to mind anyone's business but his own. To do otherwise would be to risk one's sanity.

The first-time visitor is also struck by the *order* of things. The drivers drive like maniacs, sure, and the pedestrians are not much better, and there's nothing but foul air to breathe, and thousands of miles of pavement, and millions of square yards of buildings to look at, and a constant din of cars, and people . . . But still everything looks as if it's preordained. Everything seems to work! There is order to the chaos! For some first-time visitors, it is a very, very disconcerting experience. There cannot *be* such order in a place like this. It's not natural. But, of course, there has to be order in a place like this because if there wasn't, it would fall apart.

Chapter 43

Winifred Haritson leaned forward slightly in the bold aluminum-and-blue vinyl kitchen chair. She sipped delicately at the soup Georgie MacPhail had prepared for her, then looked up at him and smiled an anemic little smile. "Thank you, Georgie. You're a good boy."

Georgie wasn't at all sure he liked being called "a good boy," but he smiled back. "It's all right, Mrs. Haritson," he said. "I cook for my mom and my little brothers a lot, too."

"You'll get back to 'em, Georgie. Don't worry."

He shrugged. "Yeah, they'll be okay for a couple more days, I guess. I sure wish I could call 'em up, though."

"Just go on out and use a pay phone, Georgie. Just go on out the way you come in. That bunch"—Snipe and his lieutenants—"won't see ya."

"We don't have no phone, Mrs. Haritson. We used to . . ."

"Maybe you can write her a letter. Nothin' says you can't write her a letter, Georgie."

He grinned a strange, lopsided grin. "I can't write, Mrs. Haritson."

She looked vaguely puzzled. "You can't write, Georgie?— twelve years old and you can't write?"

His grin grew more lopsided. "I never had no time to go to school, Mrs. Haritson."

She thought a moment, then said, "I'll write it for you, Georgie. How's that sound?"

Georgie considered it. "No," he answered. "Thanks anyway, but for sure I'll be back before a letter could reach her."

Mrs. Haritson touched his hand lightly, as if to comfort him. She lowered her head. When she looked up, there was a look of grim resignation on her face. "Georgie, you know . . . the elevator shaft . . . I mean . . ." She could not ask the question point-blank.

He did not want to answer her, but realized that if he'd learned anything in the last day and a half, ever since taking shelter in The Stone, it was that this old woman could easily spot a lie. "Yeah," he said. "Yeah. A woman. Some old woman. She looked like a bag lady."

Mrs. Haritson sighed. "That'd be Ms. Ida Cooper. She probably didn't have nothing to give 'em so . . ." She stopped; her lower lip started quivering. "What am I going to do, Georgie? What am I going to do?" It was a question she'd asked more than once in the last day and a half and it made Georgie very uncomfortable, because he had no idea how to answer it.

Chapter 44

It is unsettling to wake up in a place you don't recognize. It is unsettling, as well, to realize that you've misplaced several days of your life, that no matter how hard you try, the details and even the very substance of those days will not come back. As if the memory itself, in panic, has pushed them away.

That was the position that Jim Hart found himself in on the morning of September 30th, and it scared the hell out of him. It was clear that he was in a hospital room. A private room—small, and cluttered with equipment. Two plastic tubes snaked into his nose from a large, cream-colored, rectangular device beside the bed. Several monitors just above the bed beeped and hummed rhythmically. His sheets were very clean and crisp.

He had no feeling of pain. He felt, in fact, quite buoyant, and free of physical sensation, as if he had taken an overdose of Valium. He guessed, correctly, that he had been sedated. And he guessed, also correctly, that without the sedation he would probably be experiencing a very great deal of pain now. That scared him. He supposed that he had awakened because the sedative was wearing off.

He watched as a male nurse entered the room, checked the tube connections, went to a closet, rummaged around in it a moment, turned and looked at him a second. A scowl appeared on the nurse's face. He hurried from the room. Jim had read the name on the man's name tag; Mr. Searles. And, just above it, in small, light-blue block

144

letters, the words, *Bellevue Hospital*. He thought, *What in the hell am I doing in Bellevue?* And, as if sent specifically to answer that question, a doctor came into the room. She was tall, thin, sallow-complexioned, and looked extremely efficient. She smiled pleasantly. "So, you're back with us?" she said.

Jim supposed that he nodded slightly.

"You gave us all a bit of a scare, you know." Jim heard what sounded vaguely like a British accent, though it could just as well, he thought, have been an affectation. "That bullet lodged very close to your spinal cord, Mr. Hart, and if you have to have a bullet lodge somewhere, that is *not* the best place in the world to have it lodge."

Jim opened his mouth a half inch, then closed it.

"No, no," the doctor warned, "don't try to talk just yet. There's plenty of time for that. There are lots of people waiting to ask you lots of questions."

Jim breathed a name. "Marie."

"Marie?" the doctor asked. "Is that your wife? Your girlfriend?"

Jim felt himself nod once. Then he closed his eyes tightly against the pain that shot through him.

"Mr. Hart?" the doctor asked urgently. "Do you have pain, Mr. Hart?"

The pain dissipated. He shook his head slightly.

"Mr. Hart, can you point to where you experienced the pain? Can you do that for me?"

Jim shook his head again, more vigorously, straining at the plastic tubes snaking into his nostrils. The doctor put her hands on the sides of his head: "Try to lie still, Mr. Hart. We'll get these things out of you before long, but in the meantime you must lie still. Please point to the area where you experienced the pain."

"My head," Jim whispered huskily.

This seemed to upset the doctor. "Christ!" she murmured. Jim shook his head again. "Where are they?" he whispered.

"Who, Mr. Hart? Where are who?"

"No," he whispered. "Them. The children."

The doctor pursed her lips in annoyance. "Christ!" she

said again. "Mr. Hart," she went on, pressing a button above the bed, "we're going to sedate you again."

Preliminary Physician's Report:

Patient: James T. Hart, age 32
Admitted: Sept. 26
Gunshot wound; small calibre bullet lodged close to Thoracic duct; microsurgery performed:
Prognosis: Good

   Patient appears to be suffering recurrent delusions. He speaks of a woman named "Marie" and of others he refers to only as "the children." Attempts at finding out who these "children" are and who the woman "Marie" is have proved largely unsuccessful.
   He seems to ascribe certain magical powers to the "children." He indicates strongly that they have the ability to "appear" and "disappear" at will. He also indicates that they eat human flesh, though he has not said this in so many words.
   I strongly suggest he be interviewed by a psychiatrist, as his delusions may effect his physical well-being and may impede his recovery from surgery, though his recovery appears to be progressing well.

Submitted, _____

                              Dr. Constance Wellaway, M.D.
                                          Bellevue Hospital

Distribution: Normal

Chapter 45

Snipe was getting bored. He liked the money he collected from these people. He liked being the boss. He very much liked tossing the damned bag lady down the elevator shaft (because, hell, what good was she? Everything she owned was crap she'd picked up off the goddamned street!), but still he was bored. There was Winifred Haritson's apartment still to get into, and for sure someone was hiding in the building somewhere—Snipe had *heard* him. But shit, he'd take care of those little problems soon enough, and that would be that. Big fucking deal! Because then where would he be? Same place he was now—stuck with eight old farts who shivered and shook whenever he got close to them (except for "Mr. Klaus." But that was okay. It was neat to watch him suffer without letting on that he was suffering. The guy was tough, that was for sure).

And there was the time problem to think about, too. Because he had another month, anyway, to keep these people in line. Another month until their checks came through again. Another month to wait around in this damned stink-hole.

He shoved a forkful of overdone Kraft Macaroni-and-Cheese Dinner into his mouth, swallowed it without chewing—to avoid the pain that chewing would cause—and barked toward the open door of his makeshift "office" (which had once been Lou's apartment), "Hey, c'mon in here, we gotta talk!"

One of his lieutenants appeared immediately and goose-

147

stepped over to the small, banged-up wooden table where Snipe was eating. Snipe inhaled another forkful of macaroni and cheese. "Why you walking like that?" he asked.

The boy answered proudly, "It's the way the Nazis used to walk, Snipe!"

"Are you tellin' me yer a fuckin' Nazi?!"

"No, Snipe, I ain't tellin' you that, I just thought you'd like it if I—"

"I don't like it. It looks like you got a broom up yer ass."

"Sorry, Snipe."

Snipe nodded at his plate, which was nearly empty. "We got any more of this stuff?"

"Sure, Snipe. I'll tell Ding to fix you some."

"Good. Tell him to make it quick. Tell him I got big plans for later on."

"Oh yeah? Like what, Snipe?"

"I don't know. I gotta think about it first."

"We gonna throw someone else down the elevator shaft, Snipe?" The boy was clearly excited. "Maybe that big guy, Mr. Klaus?"

Snipe looked annoyed. "Like I said, I gotta *think* about it first. I wanta do somethin' more *creative* than that, know what I mean? And how am I gonna be *creative* when my stomach's fuckin' empty?!"

"Oh," the boy said. "Yeah. Good, Snipe." He reached for the plate, glanced questioningly at Snipe, who nodded, took the plate, and quickly left the room.

On Staten Island

"How about a week from now, Joyce?" Sam Campbell asked. "A week from yesterday."

"For what, Sam?"

"To visit Marsha. Are you planning anything?"

Joyce thought a moment; "Next week?" She grinned. "No, Sam, I'm not planning anything."

Sam grinned back. "Good. It'll be around 6:30. Visiting hours start at 7:00—she knows all about you, Joyce. I think she'll like you. She makes attachments easily."

"Yes, I hope so, Sam."

"She became attached to Lynn"—Sam's late wife; he snapped his fingers—"just like that."

Again Joyce grinned. "Well, of course, Sam, a mother-daughter relationship–"

"She's adopted, Joyce. I thought I'd told you that."

A moment's pause. "No, you hadn't told me, Sam."

Sam nodded. "When she was ten years old. She's been with me only a couple years, now."

Joyce reached across the table and touched his hand. "I like that, Sam. I like that about you."

He said nothing.

BELLEVUE HOSPITAL
INTERNAL MEMORANDUM: CONFIDENTIAL
Addendum to post mortem performed Sept. 27 on body of John Doe, age 12-14 years, admitted DOA: *Apparent* drowning victim:
File reference: 243546

NOTE: Anomaly in the digestive system of this subject suggests an abnormal or hypernormal function. Very high levels of pepsin and hydrochloric acid plus extremely high levels of bile and pancreatic fluids: Inner walls of colon and small intestine display abnormalities—i.e., *hypernormal functioning:*

NOTE: Dentition is that of an adult. All the subject's wisdom teeth are in place. Molars and premolars show abnormal wear for a child this age.

Jaw muscles, particularly the orbicularis oris muscle and the masseter muscle, display a very high degree of flexibility and strength.

Melanin levels in the epidermis: Melanin appears to be produced, also, within the *sebaceous glands* themselves, and although testing was difficult in this subject—due to the fact that the child had been dead for two days or more—it appears that the melanin was *nearly fluid*, which would lead one to speculate that the specimen's skin color could change dramatically, or at least appear to.

150 T. M. WRIGHT

Strongly suggest further investigation and testing of this individual.
Please advise.

Submitted _____

Dr. Urey C. Birnbaum
Chief Pathologist

Distribution:
Sears
Linholst
Massane

Chapter 46

He was forty-two years old, married, with three kids—a boy, two girls. He worked days as a pastry chef in a restaurant on West 150th Street, and nights as a bartender closer to his home in the North Bronx. He loved his wife and children deeply; he liked his mother-in-law and wished she'd visit more often.

He left the restaurant where he worked every day at precisely 4:05. The restaurant, called Peter's, was located a good distance from a subway station, and leaving at 4:05 gave him more than enough time to get home by 4:30.

He walked quickly, as most New Yorkers do, and he paid little attention to what was going on around him, unless it was an obstruction to his course of travel—a car, or a delivery truck, or someone passing out pamphlets of one kind or another. He usually detoured around such obstructions, if possible, or waited for them to clear.

At 4:10, he was two blocks from his subway entrance. To his left, on West 150th Street, the traffic was heavy, noisy, and fast-moving—New York City traffic. The air was cool, in the high forties, and smelled vaguely of bagels and fresh ironing, as it always did in this part of West 150th Street. Ahead, about ten yards, a young man was asking directions from the owner of a newsstand. To the right, several old people were looking at a display of expensive cameras in a shop window. ''I got an old Kodak at home, and I bet–'' he heard as he moved past them, and wondered for the barest fraction of a second what the point of the sentence had been.

Other than the old people, the young man asking directions, and two women just behind him—they looked like models—he wondered what they were doing around this part of the city—the sidewalk in his general vicinity was not particularly crowded. Fifty yards ahead there were little knots of people either waiting to cross the street, or waiting for taxis and buses.

When he heard one of the women behind him scream suddenly, he didn't turn to look. The woman's scream had been low, harsh, and abrupt, much like a man's, and the quick mental image he got was of a transvestite having a seizure or a heart attack, and it made him very uncomfortable.

He noticed then that his pant legs were fluttering, as if in a stiff wind, and his brow creased in puzzlement because the warm air was very still.

"Tanya?" he heard then, from one of the women behind him, and he noted that there was the hint of panic in her voice. He turned his head slightly, until he caught sight of the two women out of the corner of his eye. He supposed that they had stopped walking because he could see that he was pulling away from them as he walked. He turned his head further toward them.

"Tanya?" he heard again.

He thought at first that he was seeing a dim reflection of the women in a small, dark shop window, but realized at once that the impression was false, because the women were in the middle of the sidewalk.

He heard a scream again, much like the first, and he noted that the old people looking at cameras in the store window glanced over to see what the trouble was. One of them, a distinguished-looking man with a fine head of bright, white hair, stepped forward and said, "Can I help?"

The man on his way to catch a subway train glanced at his watch: 4:12. He quickened his pace.

After a few moments, when he heard another scream— louder and more shrill and extended than the first—he craned his head around again. He saw that the women, apparently, were gone. Several of the old people were standing near the spot where the women had been, and though it was difficult to judge at that distance, the man supposed that the look on the faces of the old people was one of awe, or shock, or revulsion.

He turned back, glanced at his watch, and quickened his pace again. He caught his train at 4:20, and by the time he was halfway to the Bronx the incident on West 150th Street had faded far back into his memory.

Transcript of a Portion of a Special News Bulletin Aired on Channel Three TV at 5:20 P.M. the Same Day

A bizarre and grisly double murder occurred on West 150th Street this afternoon. At around 4:15, two female employees of the Welco Advertising Agency, on West 110th Street, were brutally knifed by as yet unknown assailants. The women, whose identities are being withheld pending notification of next of kin, were, according to investigators, knifed repeatedly and then dragged into an alley, where the brutalization continued.

Witnesses to the crime have given police investigators conflicting accounts of what actually took place. One apparent eyewitness claims that "a very tall man in a dark blue suit" committed the murders, while another eyewitness, who watched from a restaurant across the street, says that she saw a man of medium height—in his early to middle forties—hurrying away from the scene . . .

Thirty Years Earlier: On a Small Farm near Penn Yann, New York

Rachel Griffin set the box of matches on top of the stove, went over and peered out the kitchen's small back window.

Well, she thought after her eyes had adjusted to the sunlight, it was all rather pleasant, wasn't it? Something like Central Park, though, of course, a great deal larger. Larger, and far more colorful, and obviously wilder. Much wilder.

She reconsidered. There was, she sensed, a kind of order, a kind of symmetry here. It was difficult to pin-

point, almost subliminal, but present nonetheless. A curious. thing.

She frowned. Take me back, *she thought,* Paul, come home and take me back to what I know. *She realized— though she would not have admitted it—that the words formed a very gentle, unimpassioned plea. That she was vulnerable.*

This place, the land around the farmhouse, was moist with life. Life had been allowed to run rampant, unchecked, and it had sought its own level. There was a certain frantic harmony to it, understandably discomforting, she reasoned, to a person like herself, whose only previous acquaintance with harmony had been at Carnegie Hall, at the Metropolitan Opera, and in poetry. But those were imitations. The harmony of fields and forest and color had been their model. But, understanding this—albeit in a vague, oblique way—didn't make it any less discomforting. The frantic harmony she sensed here—had sensed, she knew, from her first moment at the house—was at odds with what she'd grown accustomed to.

Chapter 47

Snipe said to one of his lieutenants, the one nicknamed "Cheese," "They all in their apartments; they all tucked in good and tight?"

Cheese nodded. "Uh-huh." He came over and glanced at the TV Snipe had pulled his chair in front of. "What'cha watchin', Snipe?"

"Nothin'," Snipe grumbled. "Just some show about predators, that's all. I'm thinkin'."

Cheese pulled another chair over and set it next to Snipe's. "Oh, yeah? What're you thinkin' about? What're predators, anyway?"

"I'm thinkin' that I'm bored. I been thinkin' about it since yesterday. Predators are like lions and tigers and wolves. Coyotes, too. Coyotes are predators."

"You mean, like animals that kill other animals. Is that what'cha mean?"

"Yeah, sure," Snipe answered, making a show of impatience with his lieutenant's ignorance. "Like lions and tigers. Like I said."

Cheese thought a moment, then asked, "You think we're predators, Snipe? You and me and Tramp and Ding and the rest? You think that's what they'd call us?—predators?"

Snipe harrumphed. "No, dumb shit, 'cuz we don't *eat* what we kill. Predators *eat* what they kill. That's what they kill for. Christ, you're dumber than used gum."

155

Cheese sulked. "It was just an idea, Snipe."

Snipe harrumphed again.

Cheese shrugged. "I heard Mrs. Haritson movin' around inside her apartment today. I heard her banging some pots and pans around. I yelled through the door at her, 'You old slime bag,' I yelled. 'You come on outa dere!' Then I said if she didn't come out we were comin' in to fry her brains up and have 'em for our fuckin' supper, Snipe." He chuckled. "That's pretty good, huh?—'Fry her brains up and have 'em for our fuckin' supper!' Pretty damned good!"

Snipe grinned at him. "You wouldn't eat no scuzzy old lady's brains. You're fulla shit!"

Cheese seemed momentarily surprised by the observation. Then he shrugged; "Sure I would. Why not? I ate a pig's brain once. And a cow's tongue, too."

Snipe continued grinning. He reached over, shut the TV off, and turned his chair around so he was facing his lieutenant. He whispered huskily, conspiratorially, "Yeah, and I still say yer fulla shit, and I'm gonna prove it, too." He paused; Cheese looked suddenly uncomfortable.

"How you gonna prove it, Snipe?" he asked, conjuring up a little grin of his own that quivered with nervousness.

Snipe chuckled shortly, silently, in the middle of his chest. He lowered his head and shook it slowly, as if in condemnation.

His lieutenant said, "You want me to eat some old lady's brains, Snipe?" He considered a moment, then continued, "Which . . . which old lady's brains?"

Snipe looked up slowly; his timing and delivery were perfect—under vastly different circumstances he might have been a comedian. "The bag lady's," he said.

Cheese's nervous grin faded at once, then reappeared, quivering mightily. "But she's down at the bottom of the elevator shaft, with the super." Actually, she lay on top of the elevator itself, which was stuck almost at the sub-basement level. The two sets of doors above it had locked themselves shut years before. "How I gonna get at her, Snipe?"

"How do you *think* yer gonna get at her?" Snipe said.

"Climb?" his lieutenant guessed. "I'm gonna climb down there to her, Snipe? Is that what I'm gonna do?"

Snipe's grin broadened. He said nothing.

"Jees, Snipe—you know I'm scared of heights. Jees, they make me wanta puke, Snipe! I get up on top of a building or I look out a window, and shit!—I wanta puke! And I can't do *nothin'* about it—"

"Pussy meat!" Snipe growled.

"No," Cheese protested, "I ain't pussy meat, Snipe." He looked away in search of some other excuse that would keep him from having to climb down the elevator shaft. He looked back suddenly. "And besides, Snipe—that woman, she's been lyin' down there for a week now. She's probably all rotten, Snipe, and if . . . I . . . I mean, she's probably full of food poisoning or something."

"You are pussy meat, and I don't need pussy meat hangin' around me!"

"Jees, Snipe, Jees—"

"You understand what I'm sayin' to you?"

"Sure I do, Snipe, but, Jees, it's like asking some guy with two broken arms to go and have a boxing match or somethin' . . . I mean, I gotta get ready for it, I gotta think about it—"

"Think about it? You wanta *think* about it?"

"Yeah, Snipe. Just for a day or so. I mean—I'm gonna do it and everything, I just gotta—"

"You got till Saturday. After that, I don't want you around me. Okay?"

"Okay, Snipe."

Chapter 48

At Bellevue

Lenny Wingate was waiting. It had been two weeks now since she'd started working at Bellevue and she had been told, by practically every other employee she'd talked to, that the job would become pretty routine sooner or later. "If it doesn't," one nurse had told her, "let us know and we'll set you up in B Ward," which was the ward that took care of the very worst of "the crazies."

But she was still waiting. Waiting for the job to become routine, waiting for the hour when the next patient who was brought in, no matter what his problem—a gunshot wound to the head, or delusions, or psychoses of one awful kind or another—would be nothing more than a crisp notation on the admittance sheet. She was waiting for that hour, and hoping that it never came. Because, as much as it drained her—and there were nights when she went home unable to do anything more than sleep fitfully— she did not really want to lose that ability to *feel* the pain and the panic that these poor people felt.

"You've got to forget about empathizing, Lenny," one of the doctors had told her. "It may seem noble to you, and kind, and good, but in the end it's self-destructive. Sympathize, yes, but don't try to empathize. Because it's impossible. There's a man up on the fourth floor—he underwent some pretty intensive microsurgery a couple days ago—who was there when that . . . accident (I don't know, are they still calling it that?), the one up in the Adirondacks, happened. I guess he saw the whole thing, but apparently remembers nothing at all. He just gives us some gibberish about monstrous children, and it's clear that his brain is turning into mush. Try to empathize with *that*, and you'll end up in the same boat.''

''Yes, you're right,'' Lenny had answered dutifully.

''Good,'' said the doctor. ''I like you, Lenny. I hope you can tough it out.''

But Lenny was rapidly beginning to believe that she wouldn't be able to ''tough it out.'' Even the air itself, here, seemed oppressive with desperation and panic. She thought that if she could actually see the air she would see miniature storms swirling through the corridors—tight, little currents of darkness moving in and out of the rooms, wrapping themselves around everyone and everything in the hospital.

It was an awful thought, and she shook her head briskly to get rid of it.

She looked up suddenly, startled out of her reverie by the whirring sound of the double automatic doors sliding open. Two attendants wheeled a man in; the man was in a wheelchair; his head was bandaged heavily from beneath his jaw to around his skull—as if to keep the jaw in place—and his left leg was pointing out straight. He was dressed in blue hospital clothes, though not Bellevue's, Lenny realized.

The attendants wheeled the man over. One of them said, ''This is the transfer from Fort Lee. His name's William Devine—you should have a note on it.''

Lenny nodded. She remembered the name. ''Park him over there, please.'' She nodded to her left, toward a corridor leading to a restricted area of the hospital. ''Mr. Devine,'' she went on, ''I'm afraid we're going to have to put you in a Psych ward for the time being; we don't have a bed for you on any regular ward. The doctors tell me, however, that it'll just be for a day or two at most.''

She thought the man nodded resignedly.

Chapter 49

The couple walking together on West Drive on Central Park, just east of a huge open area called the Sheep Meadow, drew many admiring glances. They were a beautiful couple, as beautiful as anything the earth can produce, and they walked with the smooth, sure grace of wild creatures.

It was a bright, warm day, but the Sheep Meadow was not quite as filled with people as it normally should have been. Many who had planned to go to the park today were understandably nervous about the grisly double murders that had been committed on West 150th Street just two days before. One group, from a Christian school in Hempstead, Long Island, had cancelled an outing at the park not because of the murders—which, of course, they thought were bad enough—but because "streakers" had been reported in the area, and if anything would forever spoil the memory of a day at the park it would, of course, be the sight of a bunch of naked people running about, their private parts flapping in the breeze.

The couple walking on West Drive, east of the Sheep Meadow, walked very close together, their hands touching lightly.

Many of the children are going to die, Seth, when winter comes.

Most passersby would have said the couple wore slight, pleasant smiles, though the more astute would have seen a whisper of pain, or even desperation on their faces, but

160

would have dismissed the idea almost immediately. What could such a marvelous young couple, obviously very much in love, have on their minds but the very beauty of being alive, and being together?

Seth's big, powder-blue eyes followed the long, slowly merging vertical lines and the contours of the great buildings surrounding the park.

This city was a place of death.

"The children will fend for themselves, Elena." And they did. "Those that will die, must die!"

She understood that. Years before, she had watched her own "brothers" and "sisters" rise up from the earth with her, and wither and die in a season. Except for a few.

If there was the hint of pain, it was from something romantic, passersby would believe, something timeless, a lover's quarrel, perhaps.

"I can see the desperation all around us, in this city, Elena. It's like rain."

Passersby might have noted that the couple was dressed perhaps a bit too warmly for the day—he in blue jeans, a bulky, white, pullover sweater and jacket, and she also in blue jeans, white sweater, and jacket—but would have thought it was precious that people in love still occasionally dressed alike.

Which was the reason he walked here. Because the rain that fell outside the park was heavy and confusing. He was an imperfect creature who had done an imperfect thing. He had allowed his perceptions to grow until he could not control them. And now this place, Central Park, 864 acres of his mother, the Earth, was where he had to stay. While the children moved freely in the city all around him.

"Those that will die, must die!" he repeated, as if to convince himself. "And there are the others, too." She knew this. "There are the survivors; and they will come to know who they are. This place will be ours once again, Elena." She believed him. "The desperation here is like a sickness, Elena. It will turn inward." She understood; her perceptions were not nearly as strong as his—she did not see the rain, she could not reach out and "touch" the

*ones he called "the survivors," and know they were there,
but she understood.*

The beautiful young couple turned left off West Drive
and into an area of the park called the Ramble. A jogger
passed them and noted dimly that although the day was
warm, and the couple dressed for autumn, they huddled
close together, shoulders up slightly, as if the air were
brisk, and winter approaching.

John Marsh fished his wallet from his back pocket, took
his driver's license out and handed it through the open
truck window to the cop.

"What's the problem, officer?"

The cop nodded toward the back of the truck. "Your
brake lights aren't working."

"They were when I left Penn Yann."

"Penn Yann?" The cop handed the license back.
"Where's that?"

"In the southern tier."

"Uh-huh. You wanta give me your registration, please."

Marsh took it from the wallet and handed it over. "I had
the whole truck checked, as a matter of fact."

The cop glanced at the registration and handed it back. "I
won't cite you this time, Mr. Marsh, but I want you to go
get those brake lights fixed today."

"Thank you. I will."

"You got some reason for being in Central Park? You
sightseeing or what?"

Marsh paused only a moment. "That's right, officer—
just sightseeing."

"Okay, then"—he stepped away from the truck—"you
go get those brake lights fixed. And"—he added as an
afterthought—"enjoy your visit."

Marsh pulled away. At an intersection fifty yards ahead
he turned left, and headed for the Sheep Meadow.

He reached over and scratched Joe's ears. "We sightseeing,
Joe?"

The dog panted in the heat.

"He's here, ain't he, Joe?"

The dog continued panting. Marsh pulled into one of the

park's many parking areas. He shut the ignition off. "What's he think, Joe—does he think we can't read or something?" He looked through the windshield at an area of the park called the Great Lawn, a name that fit it well. "He's in this city, Joe. I *know* he's in this city." He watched a jogger pass by. "Maybe he thinks he can hide here, Joe. Maybe that's what he thinks."

Joe growled very low in his throat, and Marsh glanced quizzically at him. He saw that the dog was looking out Marsh's window; he followed the dog's gaze. Fifty yards away, the path that the jogger had been on sloped at a casual angle, and curved slightly to the right, where a small, picturesque stone bridge had been built over it. The area beneath the bridge was in shadow, and Marsh could make out, vaguely, the form of a child standing motionless there. "Just some kid, Joe–" Marsh began. And the child was gone.

Marsh cursed. His head darted from right to left in a frantic and futile search for the child. He leaped from the truck, slammed the door shut—closing Joe inside—and moved as quickly as his old legs would allow to where the path and bridge met.

He moved slowly to the area beneath the bridge. He stood quietly in the shadow of the bridge for several minutes. Finally he murmured, "God, no!" then turned and started quickly for the truck.

He stopped at once.

Heading for him, on the path, about a hundred feet away, were Seth and Elena. Their heads were down slightly, as if they were in secret conversation. He could not see their lips moving.

Spontaneously, he backed away, realized what he was doing, stopped, and waited.

The couple turned right suddenly, off the path, and onto the Great Lawn.

This island is ours, John!

Marsh felt his mouth fall open dramatically. He watched the couple moving away from him, their pace quickening with each step.

It has always been ours! We have only to take it back!

A white hot pain seared through Marsh's head. He put his hands hard to his ears. "My God!" he screamed, "My God, My God!"

His hands fell away; his jaw slackened again. For a moment he stood motionless and dazed; another jogger, coming toward him as he crumbled to the path, turned around quickly and jogged in the opposite direction.

BELLEVUE HOSPITAL
RECORD OF ADMISSION

NAME Marsh, John   HOSPITAL # 087565 UNIT:AIT
_____   _____
     last   first

DATE 10/3   TIME 7:45 p.m.
_____   _____

I.   *IDENTIFYING DATA:* This 73-year-old single, white male was admitted on an HOC from Surgical Unit 5-1400.

II. *CHIEF COMPLAINT:* "There is a 'being' in Manhattan that has powers we don't have. This being looks like us, and acts like us, but he is not one of us. He is a creature of the earth. The earth produced him, and I'm the only one who knows."

III. *HISTORY OF PRESENT ILLNESS:* Patient was transferred from Bellevue 5-1400 where he was agitated, exhibiting delusions, and attempting to leave against medical advice. Patient was brought to Bellevue via ambulance after suffering collapse at Central Park resulting in possible brain trauma due to subdural hematoma noticed on left side of head. Patient was sedated en route due to agitation and pain. Admitted to 5-1400 for observation.

     This is the first known psychiatric hospitalization for this patient.

IV. *PAST AND FAMILY HISTORY:* Patient was born in 1922 in Elmira, New York. Only child with no surviving relatives. Patient claims there was no mental illness in the family. Patient never married.

     Patient states that he worked until the past few years as an electrical subcontractor and handyman in the New York State Finger Lakes region.

The reason for this patient being in Manhattan at this time is unclear. He claims to have come here following this "being" that only he can see and only he knows about, and further claims to have found this being in Central Park.

Patient spoke additionally of a dog named "Joe," which he apparently left in a pickup truck at Central Park.

V.   *INITIAL MENTAL EXAMINATION:* This elderly white male was cooperative during interview and reasonably neat and clean in his appearance. Oriented as to person, place, and time. Memory appears good. Affect is appropriate. Speech is coherent and without flights of ideation though clearly delusional and paranoid.

Patient is preoccupied with paranoid delusions concerning someone he saw in Central Park, referring to said person as a "being." Claims to have been in pursuit of this being from the Finger Lakes Region to Manhattan over a period of many years.

VI.   *INITIAL PHYSICAL IMPRESSION:* Patient appears to be his stated age. Well-built, healthy for his age. Subdural hematoma left side of head, some minor bruising on left arm and thigh.

VII.   *INITIAL DIAGNOSTIC IMPRESSION:* 293.5 Organic Brain Syndrome, Brain trauma.

VIII.   *INITIAL TREATMENT PLAN:* 1. Admission to 5M. 2. CAT Scan and EEG. 3. Start Mellaril 25mg.

IX.   *JUSTIFICATION FOR ADMISSION*

1) Diagnosis (at least provisional) of a mental illness and at least one of the following in addition:

2) Aggressive violent behavior toward self or others.

3) Incompetence to extent, unable to care for self.

4) Physical condition hazardous to health.

5) Toxic condition hazardous to health.

6) Delusions, hallucinations, confusion, or impaired reality testing to the extent the individual is rendered incapable of caring for self or in personal affairs.

7) Uncontrollable behavior requiring inpatient

patient observation for diagnostic treatment or assessment.

8) Need for more evidence on which to base assessment and diagnosis. A brief interview does not allow proper determination to be made.

Submitted: _____ 10/3

Kashmar Nerval

Referred: *Halloway*

Chapter 50

Riverside Drive, on the Upper West Side of Manhattan, is an area of nicely kept brownstones, large apartment buildings, and carefully maintained trees and gardens. It parallels the Hudson River for all of its sixty-five-block length.

The woman walking on West 95th Street on October 4th, at about 2:00 P.M., was new to Manhattan; she had found no job yet, but had enough savings to last her in her small efficiency apartment for at least a couple of months.

She walked almost jauntily in the bright, early autumn heat, her head moving quickly from side to side because she was very interested in her surroundings. She had been raised in a small Midwestern farming town and still held the smiling, inquisitive optimism about all things which had been instilled in her there.

She liked the way the brownstones rose up out of the steeply angled, grassy plateaus around her, as if each had risen out of the earth through the sheer force of its own will. She liked, especially, the little gardens that people planted at the tops of some of the brownstones, and on some of the balconies, and her gaze was constantly wandering up the sides of the buildings to those gardens, and lingering there for a moment.

It lingered an extra moment on what she supposed was a small group of children, standing side by side on a balcony ten floors up one of the brownstones. The early afternoon sunlight was on the children and their lower bodies were obscured by the solid balcony wall. She raised her hand to wave, but hesitated, uncertain of her first impression that the children were watching her. She guessed now that their gaze was on the Hudson River, a hundred yards to her right, and she turned her head to see what they were looking at—a scow on its way to dump its daily load of garbage ten miles out in New York Harbor. She turned her head back and looked at the balcony again. It was empty.

The stocky, middle-aged man had been the maintenance supervisor at the Wellsley Apartments for twenty-five years. He liked his work—it was secure, the pay was okay, and he could keep pretty much to himself.

It was 2:15. The young woman from the Midwestern farming town was walking past outside, on the sidewalk, and the maintenance supervisor could see her through the building's front doors.

He thought, *Good looking babe!*, smiled nostalgically for his own younger years, and then continued with his work—the rewiring of an EXIT sign over the doors.

He noted obliquely that the building was unusually calm this afternoon. It was never noisy, of course—most of the people that lived in it liked their privacy, their peace and quiet. Consequently, the owners of the building rarely rented to couples with children. But still, in the afternoons, there was usually the distant, tinny whisper of TVs, the low hum of vacuum cleaners, and occasionally someone took the clackety service elevator into the basement to do laundry.

The maintenance supervisor stopped working again, to listen. He heard a TV, from several apartments down near the middle of the long, wide corridor that led to the building's rear exit. He heard traffic from outside, on Riverside Drive. He heard a phone ring, distantly, from an apartment on the opposite side of the corridor, he supposed. He heard little else; someone humming from above, near the stairway landing, and, very distantly, like a bee buzzing intermittently from the opposite end of the second floor, someone's small dog yip-yipping frantically. The maintenance supervisor catalogued these sounds mentally and concluded, with pride at his intellectual feat, that silence is not always what it seems, and that complete silence, the total lack of sound, would probably be very disconcerting.

He heard the man who was humming start down the stairs, and wondered a moment why the man hadn't used the elevator. As he thought this, the man stopped humming abruptly; and a short, quick series of grunts came from the stairway, followed by a monosyllabic belching sound. And then silence.

The maintenance supervisor leaned slightly to the left on the tall stepladder he was using so he could see the bottom half of the stairway. He called, "Is something wrong up there?" He got no answer. He got down quickly from the stepladder and turned his body around toward the stairway. "I said, is something wrong up there?" And then heard, from the top of the stairway, in his voice, "I said, is something wrong up there?"

"Jesus!" he breathed.

"Jesus!" he heard, from farther down the stairway.

He felt himself backing away from it, toward the front doors; his hand touched the side of the stepladder behind him; he detoured around the ladder. "Listen," he called nervously as he backed toward the doors, "you ain't supposed to be in here unless you got some business in here."

He heard a woman call, "Who in the Sam Hill are you?" He recognized the voice; it belonged to the tenant in 2F. "Mrs. Petersak?" he yelled, and stopped backing toward the doors. A little quivering smile of relief creased his lips. "What's going on, Mrs. Petersak?" he asked, slowly moving toward the stairway. He got a ludicrous, mental image of old, dowdy Mrs. Petersak indulging herself in impressions or ventriloquism, and it made his smile broaden.

"What's going on, Mrs. Petersak?" he heard from the stairway. He stopped walking at once. The area just above his upper lip moistened with nervous sweat.

"Mrs. Petersak?" he called.

"Jesus!" he heard, and, at the same time, from just

above the first voice, "I said, is something wrong up there?"

He started backing toward the doors again. He found that he was still smiling.

He called shrilly, "You're scarin' the holy crap right out of me, Mrs. Petersak!" And he saw a pair of small, dark, naked feet and calves appear on the stairway. He stopped again. He thought, *It's some damned kid!*

"Mrs. Petersak!" he called. "It's some goddamned kid, begging your pardon!"

". . . begging your pardon!" he heard from the stairway. And the creature there took another step down, so its smooth, well-developed thighs and genitals appeared.

The maintenance supervisor felt righteous anger boil up quickly within him. "God*damn* you!" he shouted. "You get your fucking clothes on"—he ran toward the stairway as he shouted—"and you get back to your goddamned apartment . . ." He got to the bottom of the stairway. He stopped. His arms and belly and lower lip quivered with fear and confusion. "Who in . . . the hell are you?" he blubbered, and found instantly that he could say no more, that the ten exquisite faces looking down at him were not the faces of children—that was clear; they were faces he had seen in still ponds, and in bright blue skies; they were faces and bodies and brains that the earth had called up from itself. And they were in need of him.

They swarmed hungrily over him. In fifteen seconds they had reduced him to his vitals. Soon, they had reduced him to his bones. They left them scattered at the bottom of the stairway and, as one, moved to the doors, through them, to Riverside Drive itself.

The woman walking there had enough time to turn and look wonderingly toward the sound of the doors exploding outward. She thought for a moment that there had indeed been an explosion, because she saw movement, and darkness, and she put her hand to her mouth and murmured a tiny "Oh no!" because she had once seen the explosion of a grain elevator in her Midwestern farming town, and its aftermath had been nightmarish.

But then the movement and the darkness ended, and she

convinced herself that the early autumn heat had somehow caused the glass doors to explode—it happened to cars that were left locked up, she knew—and she was thankful.

It was with that thankfulness in her mind that she died.

Transcript of a Special News Bulletin, Channel Three: 6:45 A.M.:

We interrupt our regularly scheduled program to bring you this news bulletin from Gwen McDonald, Channel Three's Roving Eye, reporting on the scene at 1220 Riverside Drive:

GWEN: *Doug, I have just talked to Chief Inspector Dale Simon, N.Y.P.D. Violent Crimes Division, and he has informed me that there are at least fifteen, and possibly as many as twenty-five victims here in one of the most spectacular and gruesome mass murders in New York City's history. I am standing in front of the Wellsley Apartments, on Riverside Drive near West 95th Street, and as you can see, Doug, it is a scene of almost complete chaos . . .*

DOUG INTERRUPTS: *Gwen, Gwen, can you tell us if there are any suspects as of yet—are there any suspects, Gwen?*

GWEN: *No, Doug, though according to Chief Inspector Simon, the modus operandi appears to be very much the same as in the murders, two days ago, of two young women on West 150th . . . Hold it, Doug: Doug, this is Chief Inspector Simon. Chief Inspector, I'd like to ask you just one or two more questions if I–*

CHIEF INSPECTOR SIMON INTERRUPTS BRUSQUELY: *"No, I'm sorry, please, just stand aside, give us a little room."*

GWEN: *Chief Inspector Simon, of the NYPD Violent Crimes Division. Doug, I have been informed also that robbery does not appear to have been a motive here. The victims apparently range in age from eighteen years to seventy, and I have learned that a good many of them were found in or near their apartments–*

DOUG INTERRUPTS: Gwen, is there any indication whatsoever that this is a mob-style, gangland execution? Do you see any of that–

GWEN: No, none at all, Doug, though, of course, the NYPD is just beginning its investigation and I would guess that leads are being turned up by the moment– ·

Chapter 51

At Bellevue

Lenny Wingate noted the time on the admissions sheet, stood, and looked over the desk at the gurney. "Name?"

"Marsh," said the attendant, and spelled it. "First name's John."

A doctor appeared. "Is this the one from Central Park?"

"Yes," the attendant answered.

"Get him to OR 3; we'll have a look at him."

The attendant nodded; "He's been babbling. Something about his dog."

The doctor looked annoyed; "I don't care about his damned dog—get him to OR 3."

Lenny said, "He's waking up." A short pause, then, "Mr. Marsh?" she continued. "Can you hear me?"

"Of course he can't, Miss Wingate," the doctor cut in. "He's sedated."

"My dog," Marsh whispered. "In the truck, my pickup—"

The attendants wheeled him away; Lenny called after them, "Where'd you find him? What part of the Park?"

"West Side," they called back. "Near the Amphitheatre. And he didn't have no dog, and he didn't have no truck." And they were gone.

At The Stone

Georgie MacPhail thought that maybe the ghost in the back room where he lived had followed him here. He was surely seeing something in this big, dreary place. Some-

173

thing that moved quicker than the eye could move; something that was as quiet as a cat sleeping; something that was dark, and blue-eyed.

A ghost for sure.

Maybe Hiram, or Handy.

Maybe the ghost of some little kid that used to live in this building. And then died in it.

Georgie thought that if there was such a ghost, it would make staying in The Stone a couple of days longer a lot more interesting. (And he thought that now that he had Mrs. Winifred Haritson to take care of—who'd begun complaining now and again about a pain in her belly—he wasn't really sure *how* long he'd have to stay here.)

He came to the junction of two hallways; he stopped, put his back to the wall, and took a small, frameless mirror out of his shirt pocket. (He was on the fifth floor of The Stone. He was doing little more than getting to know the building, because all buildings had their own secrets, and their own stories to tell. So far, The Stone's had been dreary stories that smelled vaguely of decay. And now with those creeps below taking over . . . but there was the ghost, too. And the ghost was promising, indeed.) He stuck the mirror around the corner—it had four inches of pencil taped to the back of it—studied the reflection critically a moment, and decided that the hallway was clear. He had found that the people who'd taken over here usually went no farther than the third floor, because that was the highest floor on which any of the old people had chosen to live. But he knew they were looking for him and so he was especially cautious.

He turned the corner and started for Apartment 5F, three doors down. There were no lights here. The only light was morning sunlight streaming in through bare apartment windows and then filtering into the hallway through opened apartment doors on the right hand side of the corridor. Consequently, the corridor had a subdued, vaguely reddish blue and shimmering glow to it, as if the Northern Lights had been set loose within it. Georgie supposed briefly that the ghost he'd been seeing in The Stone in the last two days was probably just the result of the weird lighting, his anxiety, and his "bounteous 'magination,'' as his Uncle Nate put it.

When he got to Apartment 5E, he stopped. He had heard someone talking at the opposite end of the corridor, near the opened elevator doors. He stiffened up, listened. The talking seemed to be coming from a distance, and there was a hollow, echoing quality to it, as if whoever was talking was doing it through a long, hollow tube. Georgie realized at once that the talking was coming from *within* the elevator shaft. He grimaced. For sure they were throwing someone else down it, maybe the big guy, Mr. Klaus, because he wouldn't knuckle under to them.

Georgie made his way very quickly and very quietly to a spot just to the right of the opened elevator doors and stood with his back against the wall. He listened again. He heard someone cursing desperately, and someone else—Snipe, he realized—cursing back. He got down on his belly. He peered very cautiously over the edge of the shaft.

He saw very little. It was an eighty-foot drop to the sub-basement level, where the bodies of Lou and the bag lady, Ms. Ida Cooper, languished. He could see them very dimly. He thought they were throwing off a strange, weak, yellowish-orange glow all their own, and realized at once that it was merely the morning sunlight making its way through a hundred bare windows, and half a hundred opened apartment doors, through a dozen opened elevator doors, and finally focusing down the shaft.

He could also see that someone with a flashlight was making his way down the shaft wall. He imagined that whoever it was was using a rope, but he could see no rope, only the narrow, anemic yellow beam of the flashlight, and the suggestion of a large, dark form behind it. He heard then: "I'm gonna puke, Snipe. Really, I'm gonna puke!"

Then someone laughed shortly—Snipe, Georgie thought— and shouted back, "Go ahead—puke! It won't matter none to *them*, will it?!" Then he laughed again, louder.

The flashlight shifted around, and for just a moment Georgie saw that the guy repelling down the shaft wall—or attempting to—had something thin and metallic sticking out of his back pocket.

"Snipe, Jees," the guy pleaded, "I'm gonna fall if I puke. Jees, I'm gonna fall!"

"You ain't gonna fall, pussy meat. We got hold of ya."

Georgie moved back from the lip of the shaft. He saw the elongated beam of the flashlight play on the walls; "Hey, Snipe," he heard, "I saw somethin' up there. Hey Snipe . . ." And Georgie grimaced as the guy stopped talking in midsentence and vomited down the shaft.

Chapter 52

At Bellevue

Jim Hart stared disconsolately at the man in the bed to his right. The bed had been empty just an hour before (the guy using it had been carted off mumbling something about Ba'al taking his pillow away), and Jim had thought it was too bad—the guy had been good company.

This new guy, though, didn't look like he'd be good company at all. He was old, and flushed, and he looked very tired.

The man's eyes fluttered open. Jim watched as he stared silently at the ceiling for a few moments, then turn his head toward Jim, blink twice, and say, "What is this?—Is this a hospital?"

Jim nodded. "It's Bellevue."

The man sighed. "That's where they put crazy people. I want my dog. I gotta have my dog."

"We all have our little crosses to bear," Jim said, and grinned.

The other man did not grin. "And what about Seth?" he said.

"Is that your dog?"

The man shook his head violently. "Seth is here! In New York."

"And Rita Hayworth, too," Jim said.

The man looked very annoyed: "You don't understand. Seth is *here*, Seth is in Manhattan . . ."

An attendant came in; "You're awake, Mr. Marsh—

177

good," he said. "Our Dr. Halloway would like to have a few words with you after breakfast, please."

"Dr. Halloway?"

"The head shrink," Jim said.

"Just a few words," the attendant reiterated. "Then you'll be able to come back here and rest. You'll be pleased to know that we found nothing physically wrong with you, Mr. Marsh—"

"He wants his dog," Jim interrupted.

"Seth," Marsh murmured, "is here. In Manhattan."

"Seth?" the attendant asked.

"That's his dog," Jim said. "He can't live without him. I told him—"

"Is Seth your dog, Mr. Marsh?" the attendant asked.

"No, it's not my dog—"

"I told him, no one *dies* in Manhattan. They die in Queens, and in Brooklyn, and The Bronx, and on Staten Island. But not here. Not here in Manhattan."

"Yes," the attendant said, "we've heard all that, Mr. Hart."

At Central Park: Near the Sheep Meadow

Lenny Wingate had hoped there would be joggers here. She'd heard that the park was usually packed with them, even early in the morning. But not, she realized, this early, and she was nervous.

The morning air was crisp and still. Occasionally she could hear the distant blare of a truck's horn from outside the park, but beyond that there was silence, and it added to her nervousness. She'd grown to mistrust silence in Manhattan. She'd grown comfortable with noise. She'd adapted.

Her shift in Admissions at Bellevue had ended forty-five minutes earlier, and she had caught a taxi to the park immediately. The driver had almost refused to let her off—"You're not goin' in there *now*, lady!"—but she had insisted, and now was rapidly beginning to feel that it was a big mistake. The ambulance attendant had been right, of

course. There was no pickup truck. And no dog. The guy
they'd brought in merely had been reacting to the sedative.
What could be simpler?

She saw the pickup truck then, at the opposite end of the
parking lot, a good hundred and fifty yards off. She saw it
only dimly because it was roughly the same color as the
trees behind it. She started for it. It was the only vehicle in
the lot.

At the Channel Three Newsroom

Gwen McDonald said, "Hey, Al, look what Garvey sent
down from the Tenth Precinct." She handed a sheet of
yellow legal-size paper across her desk to Al Borlund,
Assistant Producer. He glanced the sheet over, shrugged,
and handed it back. "I always said jogging was dumb."
He grinned.

Gwen set to work on a rewrite of the piece. She looked
up after a moment. "But *three* of them, Al? I know a lot
of people turn up missing on this island every year, but–"

"A couple thousand, Gwen."

"Uh-huh. Still, this is pretty weird stuff, wouldn't you
say?"

He shrugged. "Lots of weird stuff goes on in Manhattan.
And it's our job to sort it out."

She rolled her eyes. "Sure, Al, whatever you say, Al."
He grinned again.

Lenny tried not to listen to the soft, scraping noise of
her crepe-soled shoes on the parking lot surface because it
seemed to echo slightly, and set her to thinking that someone was just behind her, or just to her right or her left, and
was following her. She reached into her handbag and
pulled out a long stickpin with the figure of a cat in yellow
gold at one end. She clutched the pin as she walked.

Her shadow, silhouetted in red, appeared to her left
suddenly. The sun had risen at last. She sighed, relieved,
and felt her pace quicken. She stopped. She was certain
she'd seen movement near the pickup truck, beyond the line

of trees in back of it, she guessed. *Joggers*, she told
herself, and continued walking. She clutched the stickpin
more tightly, and began thinking that what the doctor had
told her about empathizing with the patients was true—it
got you into trouble. She discarded the idea at once. She
wasn't in trouble. She was nervous. A little scared, maybe.
But she wasn't in trouble.

She saw movement again near the trees in back of the
pickup truck. She stopped, took a deep breath, then focused on the area where the movement had been. She saw
the foliage move slightly in the whisper of a breeze that
came up and died.

She saw what she supposed was a bird hopping about on
one of the branches—it was still too dark to be sure—and
what looked like a tall man walking on a path beyond the
line of trees. She sighed again. "Christ!" she breathed,
and she got a sudden urge to yell "Hi!" to the man
because he was obviously as crazy as she was. She con-
trolled the urge. She kept walking.

When she got to within fifteen feet of the pickup, she
stopped again. She could see no dog. The truck looked
empty. And if there was a dog, she asked herself, how
could she be sure if it was friendly? What if it was some
kind of trained guard dog? What if she opened the door
and said her hellos and it leaped at her and sunk its teeth
into her throat. What then?

She'd talk to it first, of course. Through the closed
window (she looked; yes, the window was closed); she
smiled slightly. She'd talk to the dog, she'd soothe it, and
then, when she'd assured it that she was a friend, she'd
open the door. She'd owned dogs. She knew how to talk
to them and how to size them up . . .

She covered the remaining fifteen feet to the pickup
very quickly and, surprising herself, put her hand on the
door handle. She stopped, grinned self-critically, shook
her head; "Oh no you don't," she whispered. She let her
hand fall. She peered into the cab of the truck.

It was empty.

"Oh for God's sake!" she whispered. "Lord, lord . . ."

And she heard a low, continuous growling sound from the line of trees just behind the truck.

At the Channel Three Newsroom

Al Borlund leaned over his desk and put the sheet of yellow legal paper back on Gwen McDonald's desk. "I've seen this, Gwen."

She shook her head and held up another piece of yellow legal paper. "No, you haven't. You've seen this. This"— she fingered the other piece of stationery—"is brand new. It just came in."

His brow furrowed. "Three more? Jesus!"

"Not three more joggers, Al. Three gays. Over in The Ramble. Here, read it." She handed the sheet back to him.

He read it. "Lover's quarrel," he quipped.

"I'm going to use both these items, Al."

He looked ill at ease. "Why don't we wait on it, Gwen? On the second one, anyway. How long have these people been missing?" he asked himself, then checked the piece about the gays. "Not even twenty-four hours," he answered. "Let's wait a while, Gwen. Another twenty-four hours. Okay?"

Lenny climbed quickly into the pickup truck and locked both its doors.

She began cursing herself immediately, in low, nearly inaudible whispers—her eyes darting from right to left but seeing nothing out of the ordinary. "Damn stupid airhead! Why the *hell* can't you mind your own business?! Damn stupid airhead!"

She sat very stiffly in the middle of the bench seat, her arms straight and the palms of her hands pressed hard into the seat fabric. She noted that the seat felt gritty, and that she suddenly needed to get to a bathroom. She noted that the sun surely should be rising faster than it was, and she said to herself, "Why isn't it rising faster?"

A sudden, sharp tapping at the driver's window caused her to scream shrilly. She turned her head sharply. The cop peering in looked very concerned. ''Miss, can I help you, Miss? Is this your . . .''

In one swift motion she reached over and unlocked the door. The cop opened it. ''Is this your dog?'' he said, and Joe leaped into the cab and began smothering her with wide, very sloppy kisses.

She laughed joyously through them.

Chapter 53

At The Stone

"You've been setting there like that for half a fuckin' hour!" Snipe called to Cheese, who was dangling halfway down the elevator shaft from a strong length of rope. The other end of the rope was being held by several of Snipe's other lieutenants; they were beginning to weaken noticeably. "So get a move on! You done your puking! What're you gonna do now, take a crap?"

"It ain't been no half hour, Snipe. And I really did see someone up there." He shone the flashlight up the shaft again. "Way up there, Snipe. Near the top."

"You get down there right now, pussy meat," Snipe growled, "or I'm gonna tell these guys here to let go; they're just about to, anyway, I hate to tell ya." He nodded at the guys holding the rope; they let it slip several inches. Immediately, a low-pitched screech rose out of the elevator shaft. Snipe looked down it again. "Okay, pussy meat?"

Cheese began lowering himself once more, very slowly, with the utmost care. "It's goddamn dark down here, Snipe."

"Well, you got the freakin' flashlight."

"It ain't no good, Snipe."

"Stop complaining. You're the one wanted to eat old lady's brains, so now you got your chance. And I'll tell ya, I hear one more word out of you . . ." He didn't need to say more.

It was still a good fifteen feet to the bottom of the shaft.

Cheese thought he could see better without the flashlight, so he turned it off. He looked up—though something inside him said that that was a stupid thing to do—and the long, ever-brightening shaft rising above him made him queasy again. He closed his eyes, lowered himself a few more feet, then looked down. He could see Lou and the bag lady clearly. Lou had apparently hit head first because the side of his head was nearly parallel with his shoulders and his entire body lay crumpled in a roughly upside-down position in a corner of the shaft. His face wasn't visible; it was still too dark for that, and Cheese was thankful.

The bag lady, Ms. Ida Cooper, lay in a more natural position, almost as if she were sleeping. She was on her side, her arms extended, so her upper arms covered her face. Her hands were clasped, and her legs were apart, as if she were walking and praying at the same time.

Cheese chuckled nervously at the thought; his queasiness cleared slightly.

And then the smell hit him. His queasiness returned with a vengeance.

Death was nothing new to him, nor was its smell. He'd lived in the seamier sections of Manhattan all his life. He had seen people die. He had caused people to die. He had happened upon people who'd been dead a good length of time. But he had never gotten used to the smell. No one does. It is an overwhelming, nearly toxic, smothering *presence* that all but shouts that it is more than merely the smell of rotting meat, that it is a piece of Death itself floating about, getting into everything.

Cheese could not help himself. He vomited again. The dry heaves. And he kept it up for several minutes, until exhaustion overtook him and he dangled at the end of the rope breathless and shaking and fully ready to let Snipe do to him whatever he wanted to do. It was then that he heard Snipe calling to him and he realized that he'd been calling for a long while.

"I said, 'What the fuck are you puking for again?' Jesus, Mary and Joseph, you could jump on 'em from where you are."

Cheese managed, "The *smell*, Snipe, Christ—"

" 'Course they smell. They been dead for a couple days, now–"

"Snipe, please–" He paused quizzically, turned his flashlight on, and shone it up the shaft again. "Snipe," he continued, "there's something up there, I *know* there's somethin' up there!"

At Film Planning Associates: The fourth floor: 38 West 20th Street

Like many similar businesses in Manhattan, Film Planning Associates was struggling mightily to stay afloat. It owed much more than it was bringing in; its equipment—cameras and editors and splicers, plus a small but expensive computer—was quite serviceable, though a lot of it was getting old. The business itself had moved, three years before, from a nice location on the Upper West Side, to its present location on the fringes of midtown. The buildings here were old, crumbling, cavernous, but the rent was cheap.

The owner of the business, a small, friendly, gray-haired man named Francis, got to work every morning just before 7:00. He took the noisy elevator four flights up to his work area, got off, made himself some instant coffee, and relaxed until 7:30, when his three employees began arriving.

He had no office, per se. He had a desk, a couple of new, Mediterranean-style couches—which looked very much at odds with their gritty surroundings—and several drafting tables where preliminary artwork was done. He'd set up several black Oriental screens between this makeshift office and the work area.

It was from the work area, as he prepared his coffee and looked forward to a half hour's relaxation before the start of yet another work day, that he heard low, conspiratorial giggling. He looked; he saw the vague outlines of projectors, and the huge, computer-driven Oxberry animation camera—where much of the business's work was done—as well as editing tables and movie screens set up here and there. But mostly he saw darkness, because the work area was very

large—two thousand square feet of open space, uninter-
rupted by walls, and very difficult to light, anyway.

The soft, conspiratorial giggling continued. "Betsy?"
he said, thinking momentarily that it was one of his more
playful female employees back there, and discarding the
idea immediately.

He saw movement in the darkness.

"Who's there, please?" he said, and found that he was
smiling nervously. He picked up his coffee cup—it was
empty—and started toward the work area. It occurred to
him that he should probably turn on the lights, then decided no, that that would be admitting his nervousness.
Like many New Yorkers, he had for a long while harbored
a deep-seated fear of his city; a fear he had sublimated
because Manhattan was, after all, where he made his home
and carried on his business. To live in constant fear of it
would be stupid and self-destructive. He did not want to
admit that fear now.

The giggling altered abruptly. It became laughter—loud,
raucous laughter—the laughter of drunken men. And he
remembered that the previous evening the people on the
floor just below had had some kind of party that had gone
on at least until he'd left the building at 8:15.

"Who's there, please?" he said again, trying to conjure
up the idea that a couple of the men from that party had
found their way up here somehow, had fallen asleep, and
now had awakened, still drunk. "This is a private office,
you . . . you know," he said, and found, to his dismay,
that his stutter—which he had supposed he'd cured himself
of years before—had returned.

He saw movement again in the darkness, as if the
darkness itself had liquified and was flowing gracefully
right and left.

He heard then, in the voice of a man obviously drunk,
"Another, another, and still another!" And his patience
ended.

"For Christ's sake, don't you know . . . don't you know
that . . . that this is a private . . . a private office!" And he
stalked into the work area.

He stopped after a few steps. He glanced about. "Hello?" he said.

He felt pressure at the side of his neck. Soft, at first. And then much harder. He put his hand there, held the hand up to his face. In the semidarkness he could see that it was layered with blood. "What . . . what's this?" he said, and he was grinning incredulously.

At the Channel Three Newsroom

"Airtime in ten minutes, Gwen. How's it going?"

"It's going okay. I've just got to polish up some of this new stuff Garvey sent over."

"The stuff about the joggers? You're going to use that?"

"Not the joggers, Al. He just phoned in something else—another streakers story. And yes, I'm going to use the jogging story. You said to shelve the one about the gays, remember?"

"Streakers? Where?"

"West Seventy-ninth Street. And get that lascivious grin off your face; it was just a bunch of kids, naked as jaybirds."

"And you're going to use it? It sounds pretty ho hum to me."

"Sure I'm going to use it. It'll perk people up."

Cheese realized that he could indeed jump to the floor of the elevator shaft from where he was; it was only eight or nine feet. His problem was letting go of the rope. It was tied securely around his stomach and then under his arms, and wriggling free of it required that he let go and maneuver out of it. He realized that he could not let go of it.

"Lower me all the way down, Snipe!" he shouted.

Snipe shouted back, "Can't do that, my man. This is all the rope we got, so it looks like you *have* to jump." He laughed.

In horror, Cheese realized that his eyes were beginning to water and that he was going to cry. "Jesus!" he whispered.

He heard, "Can't do that, my man. This is all the rope we got, so it looks like you *have* to jump."

His tears started.

"Listen, pussy meat," Snipe called, "I don't take that kind of shit from no one, so can it!"

"I can't help it, Snipe, Jees—"

"Listen, pussy meat," he heard, "I don't take that kind of shit from no one, so can it!"

He looked quizzically up the shaft. He heard, "I can't help it, Snipe, Jees—"

"Snipe?" he called. He shone the flashlight up the shaft. He saw movement about two floors up, and, three floors above that, what looked like someone's head sticking out over the lip of the shaft. "Snipe," he called, "there's someone . . ."

He became aware of a presence, just behind him, on a little niche in the shaft wall; he maneuvered around, shone the flashlight on it:

He saw a pair of pale blue eyes shining back. A wide open mouth—two rows of exquisite and perfectly developed teeth. He screeched in surprise. A moment later, the flashlight clattered to the floor of the shaft. His hand, raggedly severed at the wrist, was still clutching it.

Two floors above, Snipe heard him scream, "Mama, oh mama—" And turned to the guys holding the rope, "Haul him up. Quick!" They did as they were ordered.

On the fifth floor Georgie MacPhail wasn't at all certain of what he was seeing. Some kid, he realized—a kid his age, and his size, moving rapidly up the elevator shaft wall toward him. And below . . .

He had seen the flashlight fall and had heard the scream. But in the dark green morning light there he could make out very little.

He could see the kid climbing hand over hand on the inch or so of brick edge that stuck out into the shaft; he could see the kid's long dark hair, the dark skin; he caught a hint of pale blue eyes; he knew that the kid was naked:

Georgie scrambled to his feet. He looked down the shaft again quickly. The kid was at the fourth-floor level.

"Who are you?" Georgie called, and realized at once that someone below, on the first floor, stuck his head into the shaft immediately and looked up at him.

"Hey, there he is!"

Georgie ran. When he got to the fire exit door, he looked back.

The 7:45 A.M. Channel Three Report: A Transcript of a Portion Thereof:

GWEN MCDONALD REPORTING: . . . and in this late-breaking news development: Tragedy this morning on West 20th Street: Details are still sketchy, but according to our Live Eye reporter Paul Garvey, on the scene now, there seems to have been another mass murder similar to the one that hit an apartment house on Riverside Drive several days ago. We will take you now to Paul Garvey, at the scene; Paul?

PAUL GARVEY: Gwen (he looks away from the mike, toward the front of the building on West 20th Street, then looks back) . . . Gwen, this does indeed look like a repeat of the tragedy on Riverside Drive. We have learned very little about what actually happened here, only that there appears to be a number of victims, perhaps as many as ten, at this point we can't be sure. The police are naturally reluctant to tell us anything, since the first bodies were found only a half hour ago . . .

Chapter 54

Seth had reached out to the others. The ones who had stayed, and survived. The ones who had risen up here two hundred, three hundred, four hundred years before. These who had learned quickly what the winters could do, and how to protect themselves from it. Those who waited, and watched, and had seen their island overcome.

Seth had reached out to each of them, in his way. *We are here!* he had told them. *This island is ours, once again. Look around you. See the little ones; the new survivors.* And he had listened. And what he heard in response had brought him as close to fear as he had ever been.

He heard silence.

Chapter 55

John Marsh was angry. "Who'd you say's got my dog?" he demanded.

The doctor inclined her head toward the door to indicate the Admissions area. "Lenny Wingate, in Admitting. Apparently she's taking good care of it, Mr. Marsh. You should be thankful. The other alternative is the city pound."

"Sure I'm thankful," he harrumphed. "And as soon as you tell me where my clothes are I'll go and thank her personally, on my way out." He swung his feet off the bed to the floor.

The doctor put a firm hand on his shoulder. "I'm afraid you're going to be staying with us a few days, Mr. Marsh."

He stood abruptly. "The hell I am!"

She leaned quickly to one side and pushed a button above the bed. Seconds later, two beefy attendants appeared in the doorway. "Yes, Ma'am?" one of them said.

"Please stand by," she told them.

Marsh looked incredulously at her.

"It's for your own protection," she told him.

He sat heavily on the bed, first looked quizzically at the attendants, then at the doctor. "My own protection?—I'm not crazy!"

"I know you're not crazy, Mr. Marsh. Few of the people in this hospital are. Mostly, they're troubled. We think that is a category you might fit into, we're not sure. And that's why we're going to hold you here for a few days.'' She smiled benignly. ''Another forty-eight hours, to be precise.''

''Could I ask why?''

''Why we think you might be 'troubled,' Mr. Marsh?— Because you've been saying things to people—the other patients and the nurses—that don't make very much sense. At least not at first blush. And so we would like to give you the chance–''

''Doctor,'' he interrupted, ''have you ever heard of a place called Granada.''

''Yes, Mr. Marsh,'' she answered at once, ''it's a city in Spain, if I'm not mistaken.''

He shook his head. ''No. I'm talking about a little development in the southern tier. About fifteen years ago, twenty people died there.''

She thought a moment, then nodded slightly. ''Yes, I think I recall something–''

''Do you know why those people died? Do you know *what* killed them, Doctor?''

She shook her head. ''No. Perhaps you can tell me, Mr. Marsh?''

He didn't answer at once, and the doctor coaxed, ''You were saying, Mr. Marsh?''

He shook his head again. ''No, I wasn't saying a thing, I'm sorry.'' He lay down, clasped his hands on his stomach, and focused on the white acoustical-tiled ceiling.

The doctor asked pointedly, ''Did the children do it, Mr. Marsh?''

He didn't answer.

''The children who—what is your phrase?—'popped up out of the earth'? Did they kill those people in Granada?''

He stayed silent.

''Who is the creature that leads them, Mr. Marsh?—Is his name 'Seth'? Is that his name? It's a nice name, Mr. Marsh. Have you ever known anyone–''

''Are you a psychiatrist, Doctor?'' he interrupted.

''No,'' she answered simply.

''Then stay the hell out of my head,'' he told her.

A nervous grin played across her mouth. She left the room quickly.

Chapter 56

At The Stone

"There's more than one," Snipe growled, as some of the Macaroni-and-Cheese Dinner slid from his mouth. One of his lieutenants, a chunky hispanic named Carlos, agreed enthusiastically.

"Yeah, Snipe," he said, his head bobbing, "the one up on the fifth floor, and the one who cut Cheese up. You are right, Snipe!"

"And we're gonna find 'em both, and we're gonna do to them what they done to Cheese."

Carlos grinned broadly. "Oh that would be *very* nice, Snipe."

"Whad'jew do with him, anyway?"

"Cheese, Snipe?—What'd we do with 'em?" He inclined his head to the right. "He's down in the incinerator, Snipe. Jees, he was a real mess, Snipe. How'djew think they done that to him? You think they had machetes or something? Machetes can do that, you know. They can cut your fuckin' head off, whoosh—clean as spit."

Snipe pushed a big forkful of macaroni and cheese into his mouth; he shook his head. "C'mon, shitface, can'tcha see I'm tryin' to eat, here?—Christ!"

Carlos looked properly apologetic. "Jees—sorry, Snipe."

"Yeah, sorry," Snipe grumbled, and stuck another forkful of food into his mouth. "Go on and find Ding—I got somethin' I wantcha to do."

"I think Ding took off, Snipe."

Snipe looked up, wiped his lips with the back of his

193

hand, wiped the back of his hand on his jeans. "What the fuck you mean he took off?"

Carlos shrugged; "I ain't seen him all day long, Snipe. Last time I seen him he was helping put Cheese in the incinerator."

Snipe slammed the table with his fist. "Goddammit, how we gonna keep all these old farts in line with just the guys we got now?! How we gonna do that?"

Carlos shrugged again. "Jees, Snipe, I dunno—"

"What we got?—five, we got five guys now?"

Carlos held his hand up and counted off on his fingers. "You, that's one, me, that's two—"

"Mars-Bar, J.D., and Tramp," Snipe interrupted. "Christ, yer dumber than a fuckin' stone, you know that, Carlos?!" He held five fingers up stiffly. "Five guys to look after eight old farts, Carlos. So there's only one solution. We gotta get rid of a couple more of those old farts."

Once again, Carlos shrugged. "Which ones, Snipe. Klaus? Maybe Aunt Sandy, too?"

Snipe waved him away. "I don't know. Jesus, I gotta think about it. Get outa here."

Carlos began backing out of the room. He stopped. "Who's gonna sign their checks, Snipe?"

Snipe answered at once, "*We're* gonna sign 'em, airhead!" He shoved a forkful of macaroni and cheese into his mouth, swallowed, thought a moment. "Jesus!" he breathed, and he hit himself in the forehead with his open hand. "Jesus, I must have shit for brains."

"Whatsamatter, Snipe?"

"Get Mars-Bar, J.D., and Tramp," Snipe ordered. "And the four of you round up all the old farts and take 'em over to the elevator shaft."

Carlos grinned. "Sure, Snipe." And he was gone.

Winifred Haritson didn't like the way she was feeling. She didn't like feeling that all she ever was, and ever would be, was behind her, that the future held nothing but pain and self-pity and constant futile attempts to call back moments that refused to be called back fully.

She had told Georgie about it. "I can't even remember

what my husband looked like, Georgie," she'd whimpered. "I remember his name. It was Samuel. Samuel Dobbs Haritson. And I remember that he was tall, but not if he was very tall. He might have been very tall, Georgie. It's hard to tell from the pictures I have of him. He always insisted that I sit if it was going to be a picture of the two of us. And if not, he always insisted on portraits. There now, you see, Georgie—I can remember that, but not so many of the other things. Our honeymoon. Our first house. Our first child." And then she began to weep and Georgie wondered if he should tell her, as she had told him, that she had never been married. "I'm a spinster, Georgie," she'd said. But he didn't tell her. He was a very understanding and compassionate boy. He did not want to tear apart the little world she'd created for herself. The world—he knew, as if by instinct—that she'd carry to her grave.

And she'd talked to him about that too. "Georgie," she'd said, "I ask for nothing more than peace and quiet when my life is done." Georgie said nothing; he felt very, very sad for her.

She lay quietly in the bed now. She tried to ignore the constant pain in her belly. She listened to the dull noise of doors opening, commands being given, and protests made, from other parts of the building.

Chapter 57

Whimsical Fatman was certain he should be thankful. For the first time in nearly a decade he got three square meals a day, a place to sleep that was safe, secure, and warm, and people were tending to his injuries. So of course he should be thankful. But he wasn't. He felt as if he were in limbo—halfway between what was and what could have been—and the off-white hospital walls, the quiet efficiency of the staff, the low chugga-chugga of the rollaway carts, the beeping and humming of monitors of one kind and another all merged into a world that was strange and uncomfortable. And he wanted desperately to be away from it.

He maneuvered his wheelchair around a corner and stopped. WARD R, the sign on the door read: ADMITTANCE ONLY TO AUTHORIZED PERSONNEL. He saw a man looking through a small square window in the door. The man, he thought, was the spitting image of W.C. Fields, but maybe a little thinner. The man stared at Whimsy for a moment. Whimsy nodded. The man turned away.

"It's locked, Mr. Marsh," the aide—a blond-haired man in his early twenties—said, and took hold of Marsh's arm.

"Yes," Marsh said. "I can see that it's locked."

"It's for your own protection," the aide said.

Marsh stepped away from the door. He chuckled softly. "Bullshit!" he whispered.

The aide nodded to his right and smiled benignly. "Could you come with me, please, Mr. Marsh? Dr. Halloway would like to talk with you."

"Is that the psychiatrist?"

"Yes, sir. One of them."

"Then I don't know why he wants to talk with me."

The aide's grip on Marsh's arm strengthened—Marsh was amazed at how strong the man was. "Please, Mr. Marsh, Dr. Halloway's time is very valuable."

Reluctantly, Marsh followed him.

Thirty Years Earlier on a Farm Near Penn Yann, New York:

Rachel Griffin saw the three dark figures seated around the fire behind the house; she sketched in her mind the geometry, the symmetry those still figures represented.

Her eyes lowered. Her gaze fell on the four remaining snow-covered piles of wood, the beehives, the lopsided pyramids Paul had asked her to build weeks before.

She glanced at him. His eyes were closed now. He seemed in pain, somehow, seemed to be undergoing some deep inner turmoil . . .

. . . She took a deep breath, held it a moment. "How soon will they die, Paul? Do you think that fire of theirs keeps them warm?"

Paul looked at her; out of the corner of her eye she saw that he was looking. She turned her head; their eyes met. She extended her hand; he took it. "Come here," she coaxed. He joined her at the window. "It's their last night, isn't it, Paul?"

He squeezed her hand; his eyes watered suddenly. "And our first night," he said. She leaned against him. "Rachel, they want us to stay."

"I know it."

"And I wish we could. But . . . I've . . . I've grown beyond them, I think. I've grown beyond them."

Rachel said nothing.

"I thought," Paul continued, "that I owed them something. And perhaps I do. But if I owe them anything, I owe them myself, not you."

Again Rachel was quiet.

"Do you understand what I'm saying, Rachel?"

And she did understand, had understood, she knew, for weeks, and only now—the evidence so clear—able to admit it, or begin to understand it.

Paul had been one of them. It was as simple as that. He had been one of the children. And then he had become "Paul Griffin." He had learned, had grown, had survived. He had been transformed. And now, two decades later, what he had been was coming back, was destroying him— had been destroying him since their first day at the house— because it (she didn't know what to call it, she knew so little about it, only what the boy had shown her) no longer recognized him, and could no longer trust him.

Just as Lumas had not recognized him. Or trusted him. Because the world outside the land and the farmhouse had done its awful work.

Dr. Halloway's cavernous office was at the end of the corridor, between another set of locked doors. It was festooned with exotic plants, and a dark Oriental rug graced the floor. There were two couches—one, an overstuffed rococo style, the other a white fabric on rattan, which had been placed beneath a pair of unlikely bay windows. The room was dimly lit.

The doctor, a man who had been described by one of his patients as "depressingly average-looking," sat behind a huge, dark oak desk, his back to the wall farthest from the door. He nodded at the rococo couch when Marsh came in. "You may sit or recline, Mr. Marsh. Whatever you wish."

Marsh disliked him at once, he wasn't sure why. He went over to the rococo couch and sat on its edge, with his arms folded in front of him. He supposed that he looked very uncomfortable, and he was happy for it.

"Relax," the doctor coaxed smilingly. "We're just going to talk."

Marsh put his palms flat on the couch to either side of himself.

"That's better, Mr. Marsh. Now could you tell me, please, how old you are."

"I'm seventy-three."

"And can you tell me who the President is?"

"Yes, I can."

"Who is it, please?"

Marsh named the President.

"Could you tell me what city this is?"

"It's New York."

"The borough?"

"Manhattan."

"That's excellent, Mr. Marsh. Really excellent."

Marsh leaned forward. "I want my dog. One of your . . . employees has got him, and I want him."

Halloway checked a thin file on his desk. "Yes, I see that it mentions something here about a dog. His name is Seth?"

Marsh shook his head. "No. His name is Joe."

"Then who is Seth, Mr. Marsh?"

Marsh was rapidly learning to dislike this man—he seemed like someone who set himself apart from everyone else; *aloof!*—Yes, that was the word. "Seth is no one," Marsh said.

Halloway smiled a thin, patient smile: "No one, Mr. Marsh?"

"No one at all."

"According to the admitting physician, you had quite a lot to say about him—about this being you call 'Seth.' "

"Oh?"

"Yes, you did. You even went so far as to talk about certain 'powers' this being possesses. Would you like to tell me what those powers are, Mr. Marsh?"

"I'd like to know why I'm being held here."

"Do you feel that you are being held against your will?"

"The doors are locked and no one will unlock them; you figure it out."

Again the doctor smiled a thin, patronizing smile. "Is it one of Seth's powers, Mr. Marsh, to walk through unlocked doors?"

"No."

"I see. Then what powers does he possess?"

"I don't know."

"You don't know? How can you not know about your own creation, Mr. Marsh?"

"He's not my creation."

"Oh. Whose is he?"

"The earth's."

"That would really apply to all of us, wouldn't it?"

"To some of us more than others."

Another thin smile. But now, Marsh saw something else, something uncertain in the man's eyes, as if he were vaguely troubled. "To Seth more than anyone else, Mr. Marsh?"

"No."

The doctor's smile faded. "Do you feel that you are a troubled man, Mr. Marsh?"

"No."

"Do you feel . . ." He paused, looked away as if in search of the correct thought. He looked back, attempted another thin smile. "Do you feel that we here at Bellevue . . . do you feel that I . . ." He looked away again.

Marsh asked, "Is something wrong?"

The doctor waved the question away. "No. Nothing's wrong. Don't concern yourself." He looked clearly troubled now, as if he were in pain. "Don't concern yourself," he repeated. "A migraine, I think. A migraine. That will be all for this . . . That will be all for this . . . Do you feel, Mr. Marsh, that we here at Bellevue . . . Do you feel that I . . ."

Marsh stood. "Can I get you something?" he asked, and felt foolish for it—he wasn't sure why.

"Irving C. Halloway. And of course, my father was a member of the profession, as well. . . . You may be excused, Mr. Marsh. You may be excused." He put his hands to his ears; he lowered his head.

Marsh went to the door, opened it, and went back to his room.

Chapter 58

In Central Park: Near Bethesda Fountain

Seth could hear them at last. A thousand different voices
murmuring, shouting, whispering a billion different things.
Mundane things. Romantic things. Profound things. Human things. "Yes, of course I'll throw a Tupperware
party," and "The lessons begin on Friday?—How much
are they, please?" and "The damned train is late again,"
and "That was nice; that was *very* nice," and "Cloudy
tomorrow, with a chance of rain," and "In our discussion
of phobias, we must first *define* the term," and "Why did
she do it, Daddy?" and "What is this?—A size twelve?—I
asked for size eleven," and "It's a Nikon, officer," and
"If you show me yours, I'll show you mine," and "It's
De*press*ion glass, that's why I'm charging twenty-five
dollars; you can understand, I'm sure," and "I'm gonna
cut you right up the middle, my man!"

Seth could not sort it all out; he did not even try.
Because, of course, it was merely the gloss of civilization.
And humanity. It was window dressing. It was adaptation,
and need, and survival. He had merely to find its weak
spots, pierce it, and watch it disintegrate around him. And
then, naked, free of their little costumes, and knowing
what they were once again, they would follow him. And
they would take their island back.

Chapter 59

At The Stone

They were standing with their backs to the wall to the right of the opened elevator doors; Mrs. Dyson was the first in line: she was dressed in a flower-print white house dress. She was trembling; a continuous string of high-pitched, whining sounds were coming from her. Next to her stood Dr. Wanamaker, who had been allowed to appear here with his pants on, as well as his best white shirt, and a wide, purple-satin tie that he'd tied very neatly and snugly; Carter Barefoot, nervously scratching his red hair, stood next to Wanamaker. Mr. Klaus was next, as stoical as ever in his tattered but clean gray pin-striped suit, with only a T-shirt on beneath. There were some bruises and lacerations visible around his face and neck from the beatings that Snipe and his lieutenant had given him. One of Snipe's lieutenants, Mars-Bar, stood very close to him; he was watching and hoping for some sign of fear in Klaus' eyes, and because he wasn't seeing it he was getting angrier by the moment. Skeletal Bill Meese stood several feet to the right of Klaus; like Mrs. Dyson, he was trembling; he feared that his bladder might let go, and he raised his hand. "Sir," he said to Mars-Bar, which made Mars-Bar smile, "I have to go to the bathroom; please–"

"Shut up!" Mars-Bar commanded, and Meese fell silent. His hands went to his crotch; if only he could hold it till they threw him in because he was sure that's what Snipe had in mind.

"Aunt Sandy" stood weeping beside him; every now

and then these words bubbled out of her: "Ain't *no* way for an old woman to die; ain't *no* way for an old woman to die!"

Connie Tams stood angrily next to her, her body stiff and her fists clenched. She was working up a giant wad of saliva to bathe Snipe in when he appeared.

He appeared. He had a small pad of white notepaper in hand, and several pens and pencils. He stood at the center of the line, and several feet out from it. He held the note pad up. He smiled broadly, which tended to cheer up several of the old people a little—a mouth full of rotted teeth is not particularly frightening.

He said, "You think I'm gonna throw you down there, like I done to Lou and the big lady; that's what you think, ain't it?"

Several of the old people nodded sullenly.

Snipe shook his head; "I ain't gonna do that. Yer my meal ticket. All I wantcha to do is write yer names down here on these sheets of paper." He held the pens and pencils up. "I even brought these along. And when yer done with 'em you can keep 'em." He glanced at Carlos, standing to the left of the opened elevator doors. Carlos grinned. He looked back at the line of old people. "Ya see, what I want to do is save you old farts some walkin' and some aggravation havin' to stand in line at the fuckin' bank. That's why yer gonna sign these sheets of paper. 'Cuz then I'll know what your signatures look like. And then when yer checks come, I'll just go an' collect 'em and sign 'em myself and you won't have to worry about a thing." He smiled again.

"Bullshit!" one of the old people said.

Snipe looked quickly from one face to another. "Who said that?" he demanded.

"Bullshit!" he heard again from the same voice.

He glanced from one face to another, once more, saw something that looked like puzzlement on Klaus' face, and stepped over to him. Mars-Bar stepped away. "Was that you, Klaus?" Snipe asked evenly.

Klaus said nothing; the puzzled look faded.

"I asked you a question, man—an' I want an answer. I want an answer *now*!"

"*Now*!" he heard, from somewhere to his right. He looked toward the source of the voice, but saw little—only Aunt Sandy, Bill Meese, and Connie Tams looking back at him blankly, and beyond them, the poorly lit corridor that branched at right angles to the left and right about twenty feet away. His senses told him that the voice had come from one of those directions; his brain told him otherwise.

He slapped Klaus very hard. Klaus flinched slightly.

Snipe grinned. He took hold of Klaus' left hand, stuck a piece of the notepaper in it, took his right hand, and put a pen in it. "Your name, my man—write your name!"

Klaus held the paper against the wall, wrote on it, and handed it back.

Snipe was amazed at Klaus' apparent cooperation, but tried not to let it show; he took the paper. "That's my man," he started. Then he read what Klaus had written: SANTA KLAUS in big, bold print.

Snipe angrily crumpled the paper in his fist.

Klaus grinned tightly at him. "We used to eat people like you for breakfast," he growled, "and then we'd feed the bones to our dogs!" And in the next moment, his mammoth right hand was around Snipe's throat.

Connie Tams saw her chance; she stepped over and let loose with her mouth full of saliva; it hit Snipe squarely between the eyes, then slid very slowly down toward his gaping mouth.

Mars-Bar pushed her to one side: she fell to the floor. Carlos came over quickly; together, he and Mars-Bar tried wrenching Klaus' hand from Snipe's throat. It was impossible. The man's strength was enormous.

Carlos pulled a knife from a sheath on his belt; it was a long knife, with a six inch blade. He sunk it deep into Klaus' chest. Klaus flinched.

Mars-Bar glanced at Snipe, whose face was turning blue, whose struggles were weakening.

"Jesus, get him again!" Mars-Bar said to Carlos.

Carlos sunk the knife into Klaus' chest once more. Once more Klaus flinched.

Connie Tams struggled to her feet. She screamed shrilly, then her teeth found Carlos' thigh, and she bit hard. Carlos screeched, pulled the knife from Klaus, lashed out at her, struck her a glancing blow on the shoulder. She kept biting. He lashed out again. He missed. He tried again. The knife slid into Connie Tam's neck, near her jugular. She screamed, staggered back, her hand pressed hard to the wound. She crumpled to the floor.

Snipe had stopped struggling altogether.

Carlos plunged the knife into Klaus' forearm, severing the muscle. Klaus' tight grip on Snipe ended at once. Snipe, like Connie Tams, collapsed.

Klaus' eyes rolled back in his head. He fell to his knees; he hit the floor, face down.

Carlos bent over Snipe while Mars-Bar watched the rest of the little group, who were looking on in various stages of shock and revulsion. Bill Meese's bladder had let go; Aunt Sandy was weeping openly and loudly; Carter Barefoot was bent over at the waist, his hands covered his face; he was trembling.

"Snipe?" Carlos whispered, and saw that color was coming back to Snipe's face. "C'mon, Snipe, c'mon!"

A few feet away, Connie Tams began moaning softly; the wound at her neck was oozing a thin line of blood. Carlos stood, stepped over to her. "Fuckin' old bitch!" he hissed, and kicked her very hard—the toe of his boot connected with the side of her head. She stopped moaning, at once. He went back to Snipe, stooped over him again. "Snipe?"

Snipe coughed feebly.

"Snipe?" Carlos repeated.

Snipe coughed again and again. The coughing quickly grew fitful and urgent, as if he were trying desperately to bring up a piece of meat that had gotten stuck in his throat. He pushed himself up on all fours, his head hanging. He continued coughing, even more fitfully. Carlos became very concerned. He stood, mounted Snipe, grabbed him around the chest and hugged him strongly.

Mars-Bar, looking on, was flabbergasted. "Jesus H., what in the hell you doin'—"

"It's what . . . you do . . . when someone's chokin'," Carlos stammered through the effort of hugging Snipe.

Suddenly, Snipe stood, Carlos still hanging on to him. Carlos jumped off. Snipe vomited. Twice. Again. And again. At last, he stopped, put one arm to the wall, the other to his throat. He whispered hoarsely, "Throw 'em both down the shaft. Now!"

Carlos went over to Connie Tams' limp body; he could see that she was still breathing. He lifted her by the armpits, took her over to the opened elevator doors, and tossed her through. Seconds later, a small whumping noise came back to him. He went over to where Klaus lay face down. He studied him for a moment, then said to Mars-Bar, "I'm gonna need a hand here." Mars-Bar came over, and together they began dragging Klaus over to the elevator doors. Snipe watched silently; every once in a while a small cough escaped him.

Without hesitation, Carlos and Mars-Bar pushed Klaus over the lip of the shaft. It was a forty foot drop, and the fall just under two seconds.

Klaus died instantly when he hit.

But in the two seconds before that moment, he saw much in his memory's eye. He saw a lifetime.

He saw the patterns of light and shadow all around as he pushed himself out of the earth, but never free of it.

He felt the warm sensuous touch of his "brothers" and his "sisters," present at the birth.

And then he saw himself growing away from them. Watched them wither and die around him with that first winter.

And felt again the need, the awful desperation, that had driven him here. To this city. And, at last, to this building.

And at last, to his death.

Snipe turned to what remained of the group. "Hey, you dipshit," he said hoarsely to Carter Barefoot, who was still bent over with his face in his hands. "Straighten up!"

Carter did not respond.

Snipe nodded to Carlos: "Straighten him up, Carlos!"

Carlos went over and forced Carter into a standing position, pulled his hands away from his face. He slapped him once. "You *listen* when Snipe talks to you."

Carter nodded frantically.

Snipe leaned over and picked up the sheets of notepaper, the pens and the pencils that had fallen to the floor when Klaus grabbed him. He held up the notepaper. "I'll make . . ." he began, and cleared his throat several times. "I'll make a deal with you assholes." He coughed, massaged his throat. "You sign your names," he went on, "and don't give me no trouble and *maybe* I won't let Carlos and Mars-Bar have no more fun." He stopped.

"Yes," said Wanamaker, "I'll sign."

Snipe grinned. They were going to believe his lie. He stepped over to Wanamaker, and offered him a sheet of the notepaper. Wanamaker took it reluctantly.

Carlos, standing close by, said, "Hey, Snipe, I seen somethin' "—he nodded to his left, toward the area where the corridor branched off to the left and right—"over there. You want I should check it out?"

Snipe looked where Carlos had nodded. He saw nothing out of the ordinary—a bare space in the dingy, cream-colored wall between the two corridors, where a fire extinguisher had once been installed; a closed door halfway down the wall on the left, and on the right what looked, in the dim light, like several very large cockroaches moving slowly up the leading edge of the wall. He said angrily, "You just seen a couple roaches, asshole!" and nodded at the edge of the wall.

But he realized in the next moment that what he and Carlos had seen weren't roaches at all; they were fingers—someone's small dark fingers probing the edge of the wall. "Carlos," he whispered, "get that son of a bitch!"

Carlos grinned. "Sure, Snipe!" He moved very quickly. By the time he'd reached the edge of the wall, he'd pulled his knife out and his grin had become a loud, ecstatic, raucous laugh. *Three in one day*, it said, "Shit, damn!"

Snipe listened to the laughter. He couldn't see much because Carlos had turned the corner. But his laughter rang through the building, and it made Snipe feel very good; it even made his throat feel a little better: the phrase, *Laughter is the best medicine*, sprang into his mind, and he wondered briefly where he'd heard it. He turned to the little group, who were all looking in awe toward the spot where Carlos had disappeared. "Laughter is the best medicine," he told them, and then he laughed at himself, but it caused a very sharp pain in his throat, so he forced himself into silence.

It was then that Carlos' laughter began to sound noticeably shrill, almost, Snipe thought—and discarded the idea immediately—as if Carlos were weeping and laughing at the same time. "Carlos?" he called.

And the laughter ended.

The silence that followed was short-lived and tense. It ended when these words, in Snipe's voice, vaulted down the corridor: "You seen a couple roaches, asshole!"

Snipe's reaction was immediate and violent. He reached for Carter Barefoot, grabbed the scruff of his collar, and slammed a fist hard into the bridge of the man's nose. "Son of a bitch!" he shouted at him, spittle flying everywhere, "Son of a bitch! What are you doing to me, what are you doing to me?!" and he slugged him again, in the same place, and felt the cartilage fold up beneath his knuckles.

He let go. Carter Barefoot crumbled to the floor.

And then these words, also in Snipe's voice, came down the corridor. "Son of a bitch! What are you doing to me?! What are you doing to me?!" And Snipe looked up at Mars-Bar, standing only a few feet away. "Mars-Bar?" he asked, because the look on his face was a look of deep confusion and awe, as if he were watching the sun rise in the west or the Atlantic Ocean turn itself inside out. "Chrissake, Mars-Bar . . ." Snipe said.

And he saw Mars-Bar back away from him, his eyes wide, his lower lip trembling, his fists clenched hard at his side. He saw Mars-Bar cross himself quickly, desperately. He turned to look at what Mars-Bar was looking at.

The child was standing, motionless, naked, and blank-faced, well into the light, several feet away. Her mouth, her hands, and her arms were coated with Carlos' blood.

She opened her mouth. She said, "Son of a bitch! Son of a bitch! What are you doing to me?! What are you doing to me?!"

And Aunt Sandy, just to the right of the child, put her hand hard to her stomach.

Bill Meese broke into an awkward run down the corridor, where Carlos had disappeared, stopped, turned, and ran the other way, past the child, past Snipe, past Mars-Bar. He was screaming all the while.

Aunt Sandy vomited.

Wanamaker passed out, falling in a heap over Carter Barefoot.

"This is a private place, you know," the child said, in a voice that Snipe did not recognize.

And then Mars-Bar was gone, after crossing himself again several times and murmuring incantations to his mother. Snipe listened to his panic-stricken curses echo hollowly in the building, and, finally, fade away altogether.

That is when he realized that except for the inert bodies of Wanamaker and Carter Barefoot, he and the child were alone in the corridor. That all the other old people, along with Mars-Bar, had run.

It had been barely twenty seconds since the child had appeared. And a little more than a minute and a half since Carlos announced that he'd seen something down the corridor, that maybe he should check it out.

But Snipe hadn't run.

Snipe couldn't run.

Snipe was riddled with fear, and by the deep certainty that he was experiencing his last few moments of life.

And so, despite his view of himself, he said to the child, he pleaded with her, "I don't want to die." And as he said it, he told himself that what he was really telling her was that he didn't want to die the way Carlos obviously had.

She said to him in his voice, "I don't want to die," and he heard, though she didn't say it, one other word, "either," tacked on to the end of the sentence.

"I don't want to hurt you," he whimpered.

She repeated it.

"So I'll go . . . I'll go . . . I'll go . . ." But he got stuck on the phrase, and could not complete his sentence.

The child had vanished.

Crying with fear, Snipe ran back to his makeshift office, where he locked the door, bolted it, then ran to the windows and bolted them.

From the Rochester *Democrat and Chronicle:*

THEY'RE ARMING THEMSELVES IN MANHATTAN

In the wake of recent numerous unexplained and brutal murders in Manhattan, the Manhattan Islanders appear to be ready to fight back. According to Deputy Police Commissioner, James Hefter, gun sales have skyrocketed an incredible 1000% over the same period one year ago, and request for permits have quadrupled.

"I must emphasize that, above all, caution be exercised," says Deputy Commissioner Hefter. "I understand the need of the average citizen to protect himself, but he should be assured that these killings are not beyond the capabilities of the New York City Police Department to deal with. We are, as a matter of fact, looking into numerous leads at this very moment, and though I cannot promise that a break in the case will emerge today, or even tomorrow, I can assure all of you that these killings are not, as some have claimed, the work of madmen. To the contrary, they display a pattern and a predictability that madmen are not capable of."

The killings began a little over one week ago, when two young women on their way home from work . . .

Chapter 60

The two cops cruising 12th Street near Third Avenue were discussing a TV show that last aired many years ago but was still being shown as reruns. The show was called "Barney Miller," and the cops loved it. One of them, a tall, well-muscled guy in his late twenties, identified very strongly with Wojohowicz, the Polish cop on the show; and his partner, for reasons of intellectual vanity, identified with Dietrich, the curly-headed, wise-cracking character who always seemed to have quick answers to obscure questions. The partners liked the show so much, they adopted the characters' names as nicknames.

"It's fucking timeless, you know what I mean," "Dietrich" said.

And the one who identified with Wojohowicz agreed. "Timeless is *the* word. The little things might change— but not the real nitty-gritty of everyday police work. "Wojo" was the rookie, barely a year out of the Police Academy, and still aching with enthusiasm, while his partner, the one who thought of himself as Dietrich, had been with the force nearly a decade. Although Dietrich's enthusiasm had waned long ago, he got a kick out of Wojo.

"The streets are very quiet tonight," Wojo said, his tone heavily portentous.

Dietrich forced back a smile: "Yeah," he whispered, "the streets are very quiet."

"It's those murders, I'm sure of it. They keep people at home."

211

"And that's really the best place for them," Dietrich observed.

"I suppose," said Wojo, obviously unconvinced. "It's just kind of . . . sad."

"Sad?"

"Uh-huh. A city like this . . . I mean a great city, a truly *great* city like this, and no one is out enjoying it."

"It's bad for business."

"Very bad for business." Wojo paused, then looked back toward a narrow alley they'd just passed. "I saw something."

Dietrich brought the car to an abrupt halt. "Where?"

He inclined his head to the rear, unbuckled his gun. "That alley."

"You want to check it out?"

"Yeah." He pushed his door open, vaulted from the car, and took up a position with his back to the closed and locked grating of a store front. He had his gun drawn; his arm was bent, the gun's barrel pointing upward.

Dietrich watched, half-amused. This wasn't the first time that his partner's enthusiasm had bubbled over. He got reluctantly out of the car, and moved quickly over to where Wojo was standing. "What'd you see?" he whispered.

"Movement," Wojo answered.

"Movement? What kind of movement?"

Wojo glanced quizzically at him as if to say the question had been impossibly stupid. "Su*spici*ous movement, of course."

"Oh." Dietrich nodded toward the alley, about twenty feet away. "You think we need backup?"

"Naw," Wojo answered, and began inching toward the alley. Dietrich followed.

They stopped several feet away from the alley. Wojo yelled, with great authority, "This is the police; whoever is in the alley, show yourself at once."

Silence.

Wojo repeated, "This is the police; whoever is in the alley, show yourself at once."

They heard the unmistakable and chilling sound of a shotgun being cocked.

Dietrich pulled out his gun. "Stay put!" he ordered his partner. "Stay right the fuck where you are!" And he crossed in front of him so the toe of his shoe was beyond the edge of the wall and into the alley. He said crisply, "You got ten seconds from right now to drop that weapon and come out of there! You got eight seconds. You got six seconds." They heard the shotgun clatter to the pavement.

"Okay," said a man's voice, "okay. How was I to know—he appeared, hands behind his head, at the front of the alley. He was a tall blond man, and he looked very scared—"you were cops. How was I to know?"

Dietrich threw him against the far wall. "Spread your feet!" he ordered; the man did it. Dietrich frisked him; there was a small calibre handgun in the man's pants' pocket and a long-bladed knife in a holster tied to his leg. Dietrich sniffed at the barrel of the gun; apparently it hadn't been fired recently; then he cuffed the man, and started leading him back to the car. Wojo fell in behind, the shotgun in hand.

"You're a goddamned one-man army," Dietrich said to his prisoner.

"Yeah?" the man said, "Well I got a permit for the .22, I got a permit."

"And the shotgun? Do you have a permit for that?"

"I don't *need* a permit for it."

"Sure you do."

"Since when?"

"Since about forty years ago. What's the matter, you don't read the papers?"

They got to the car; Dietrich opened the door and pushed him in. He leaned over. "What were you doing in that alley?" he asked.

"Protecting myself," the man answered. "And my family. I got a right to do that."

Dietrich sighed. "Yeah," he said, "sure you do." And he closed the door.

Wojo was disappointed. He said to Dietrich, on the way to the precinct with their prisoner, "Whats'a matter—you think I woulda gotten myself blown away, or something?"

Dietrich shook his head. "No. I'm sorry. It was a touchy situation; I thought I should handle it."

From the back seat they heard, "So what's gonna happen to me?—I'm going to get thrown in jail, or what?"

Dietrich answered, "Just for the night. You'll get an appearance ticket in the morning. The judge will probably ask for bail."

"Jees," the man said, "I can't afford that."

"Then he'll probably waive it," Dietrich said, then to Wojo: "You've never come up against a shotgun before, have you?"

"No," Wojo answered, "but neither had you, your first time." He was noticeably glum.

Dietrich thought a moment. "You're right," he said. "I'm sorry . . ."

"Hey you guys," the man in the back seat said; and there was a note of urgency in his voice. "Hey you guys," he repeated, "there's some—"

"What's the problem?" Wojo broke in; he glanced back, through the metal screen that separated the front and rear compartments. "You know, you're damned lucky you didn't get yourself blown away, my partner here—"

"But there's someone—" The man's voice had grown shrill and incredulous. "There's someone . . ."

"Someone what?—for Christ's sake," Wojo said, as if growing very impatient. He retrieved a flashlight from the glove compartment, shone it through the screen; the light fell on the man's face; "My God!" Wojo breathed. "My God!" because the man's face was a mass of blood.

Dietrich said, "What's the problem?"

And that is when the man in the back seat screamed. And Dietrich, reacting in a very human way to something so loud, so harsh, and so sudden, craned his head around, felt adrenaline coarse through him, and with the kind of strength he would not normally have been able to summon, hit the brake pedal all at the same time.

It was an unfortunate reaction.

The man in the back seat was dead by then; nothing could have been done for him, though, of course, Dietrich could not have known this. Because the patrol car had not been in for service in over a month, when Dietrich slammed the brake pedal, the front brakes locked and the car went into a right hand spin. Dietrich took his foot off the pedal at once—he was an excellent driver—and watched helplessly as the car careened toward the back end of a big U-Haul van illegally parked only yards away.

He wanted desperately to say "Forgive me!" to his partner—frantically shining the flashlight around the back seat—but had time enough only for the word "Forgive–" And then the car slammed head-on into the back of the U-Haul truck, its speed on impact just a hair above thirty miles an hour. The car jackknifed and broke in two at the middle; a fire broke out in the engine compartment. Incredibly, the gas tank remained intact.

The cop who identified most with Dietrich died instantly. The other cop made it halfway to Bellevue Emergency. Before dying he whispered these words to the attendants working furiously over him: "The child–" They radioed this information to the investigating officers, who reported back that no child had been found.

Chapter 61

At The Stone

Snipe had always thought that Channel Three News anchorwoman Gwen McDonald was "a fox," and he'd made a point of watching her show when he got the chance just to utter obscene suggestions at her.

He was watching her now, in his little makeshift apartment (which had once been Lou's apartment). He was not uttering obscene suggestions at her. He was staring vacantly at her, or, more correctly, at the TV screen, which he'd allowed to become a large, bluish blotch in his line of sight. He was listening to her words—"and so, as a result of the greatly increased number of guns on the street, Commissioner Hefter has pledged that police presence will be, as he puts it, 'formidably enhanced,' to protect us, so it would seem, from ourselves"—and he was saying to himself, over and over again, "I'm gonna die in here, I'm gonna fuckin' *die* in here!"

He'd locked himself in the apartment two days ago. He was down to three cans of Campbell's Vegetarian Beans, a dry, Kraft Macaroni-and-Cheese Dinner, and half a loaf of Wonder Bread, which was rapidly turning to mold.

He had stopped being scared. He was merely coasting, letting Fate take him for its grand ride. He found that he was thinking quite a lot about his mother, although he hadn't seen her for almost ten years. He found that he was remembering her voice, which soothed him, and her body, which soothed him too. He found that he was remembering some of his last words to her: "I don't want no one to hurt *me*, Mama, that's why I do those things!'' And he remembered her response, ''Yes,'' in that fine, soothing voice, ''I understand that.''

He was having no regrets. He was not capable of it.

He was merely coasting. And listening. And waiting.

Georgie MacPhail was giving very serious consideration to the possibility of carrying Winifred Haritson out of The Stone and then to a hospital. Bellevue wasn't far away. For sure, she weighed no more than ninety pounds, if that much, and though it would be an effort, he could probably do it. He thought that he cared enough for her to do it; he cared enough, in fact, to have asked her what she thought of the idea.

''Not much, Georgie,'' she'd answered. ''Because you'll have some questions to answer and I don't think you want to answer any questions, do you?''

He made no response.

''And besides, Georgie, you probably could carry me that far, you're a strong boy, but I can guarantee you that it wouldn't be a joyride for either of us. I hurt, Georgie. I hurt bad. I hurt so bad I can't move, so if you try to carry me even a couple blocks to the hospital, I'll be screaming and carrying on every step of the way. And that's something I don't want to do, Georgie.''

He stayed quiet.

''And haven't you heard, Georgie, people are shooting other people left and right out there, so the hospitals are probably all filled up. What would they want with a tired old woman like me? Save the beds for the people who can use 'em, Georgie.''

All of it, Georgie thought, was true enough. But still, he didn't want to see her in pain. He didn't want to see her die here, in this dingy room.

Chapter 62

Evening: At Central Park; Near Bethesda Fountain

Seth could feel her shivering next to him; he could sense the fear in her, and the need; he sensed that she was slipping away from him and he wanted desperately to say to her, *Stay with me, Elena.* And so he did say it, in his way. And found that she had already slipped far enough that she did not hear him.

It was cold in Central Park, as cold as it had ever been during that time of the year, and he could feel that the winter would come early, nipping at the heels of autumn.

He told himself, *I am a creature of the Earth, and my own kind number in the hundreds, in the thousands all around me.*

It gave him comfort. It warmed him a little. Because he could hear them, and their voices were even louder than before. They were voices that were shrill, on the verge of breaking. And he knew it was because of him.

Which made what was happening to the children all right. They had done their work. The city was turning on itself—a snake biting its own tail.

He should have guessed that their deaths would come. That the children could not survive here for very long.

This place, this city, was not theirs. It never had been. Like fish flung onto dry land gasping for breath, they were grasping for the Earth, their mother, and finding a million square miles of asphalt instead.

He could not have expected that they would adapt.

He felt Elena push away from him suddenly. He looked;

he saw her stand. He said to her, surprising himself because he had never used the words before and they sounded strange coming from him, "I'm sorry." She did not acknowledge him. She turned and soon was lost in the darkness.

Chapter 63

Jim Hart thought it was like looking at a whirling carousel that has various scenes painted on it, and that if his eyes panned its movement, the scenes became visible, if only for the very briefest moment.

Marie Aubin was in one of the scenes. She was lying very still, on her back, and someone—perhaps himself, Jim thought—was weeping over her.

And Fred Williams was there, in another scene. He had a scowl on his face; he was mouthing the word "candy-ass."

And Marie was there again, leaning over him, saying, "Jim, I can't carry you by myself, you've got to help." And he was singing, "If that diamond . . . ring turns brass . . ."

And, in another scene, a tall man was watching him from across a short stretch of water.

He saw the same man again. In a place crowded with cars and people. A place where small, dark, and beautiful faces with exquisite, unblinking pale blue eyes watched, and watched, and watched. As if they were faces on grandfather clocks. Which is what he let them become, what he let his mind turn them into, because the faces on grandfather clocks are hungry for no one.

The scenes on the carousel were like scenes from history. They were static and dry, and the noises they made were noises his mind made for them, out of his brain's catalogue of sounds:

And he remembered this, too:

He was a city dweller. He had told them that. "New York may be a hellhole—I know it's a hellhole—but at least you know where to hide, and from what, and with whom!" For Christ's sake, that was true, that was . . . modern American anthropology, it belonged in National Geographic . . .

. . . And he had told them—slowly, steadily, as if teaching them something that required their deep attention—that people (people in general, but not all people) had long ago built cities in order to shield themselves from the wildness all around them. And gradually, over the centuries, they had produced children and grandchildren and great grandchildren who were increasingly dependent upon the cities; until, at last, a whole new life-form had developed; the city dweller . . .

. . . Just like some birds were cliff dwellers, and some fish were bottom dwellers (but not all birds, and not all fish), so some people were city dwellers. But not all people. What was simpler? But they—Fred, and Marie, and their friends—hadn't understood that, or believed. They had told him he was intellectualizing his weakness; they had challenged him and laughed at him, and had, finally, dragged him here, where he had no business being, where the goddamned stinging rain was surely going to kill him unless he got out from under it.

He watched the carousel spin, watched it cast off its scenes from history, and he ached as he watched, as if his entire body had been frostbitten and the blood was returning to it at last.

It was sanity and awareness and knowledge coming back, and it scared the hell out of him.

In another part of Bellevue, Whimsical Fatman—who was mending nicely, much to the surprise of his doctor—was listening to a couple of the other patients as he moved his wheelchair past them down the corridor. They were saying something about "the city falling apart," which, he thought, had been going on for a long time, anyway, and "people getting nervous as cats," which, he thought, they had always been, and that "the only comic relief is these streakers, these fresh-air fiends. Christ, they're seeing 'em everywhere, I guess," he said, and laughed. But beneath the laughter, he sensed an air of confusion and befuddlement.

Whimsy got to the door marked WARD R: PERMISSION TO AUTHORIZED PERSONNEL ONLY. He remembered the face he had seen in the little square window, the man who was the spitting image of W.C. Fields. But the window was empty now.

Lenny Wingate looked up from her desk at the couple who'd just come in: "Yes," she said, "can I help you?"

"I'm here to see my daughter," the man said.

"Her name and ward number, please?"

"Marsha Campbell. Ward R."

Lenny looked the name up; "She's not an outpatient, is she?"

"No," Sam Campbell answered.

"You are her mother?" Lenny asked the woman.

Joyce Dewitte shook her head. "No. A friend."

"I'm sorry, but—" Lenny began, and Sam interrupted, "We've made prior arrangements. I believe there should be a note there–" He leaned over Lenny's desk, saw her flip through the patient roster. "Yes," she said at last, "here we are. Let me confirm this with her doctor, please. You're a little early"—she checked her watch; it was 6:10—"but I don't think there should be a problem. If you could wait over there, please." She nodded at the reception area, packed with people.

Sam nodded reluctantly.

John Marsh came very slowly into Dr. Halloway's office, his gait stiff.

Halloway nodded at the rococo couch; Marsh nodded back and went over to it. He sat on the edge.

"Pardon me," Halloway said, "for disturbing your dinner. I wanted to talk to you, Mr. Marsh."

"You have . . . no right to keep me . . . here," Marsh

said, and realized dimly that his eyes were beginning to tear; he felt as if his brain had been filled with pudding, and his limbs encased in mud.

"That's not precisely correct, Mr. Marsh, but that's not why I called you in here." He paused, turned away, so Marsh could see only his profile. "You are a very disturbing individual, Mr. Marsh. And you have said some very disturbing things." Marsh noted dimly that Halloway's voice was quivering. "We're going to be taking you off the medication you've been receiving. It seems to be having an adverse effect on you."

"Are you letting me out of here?"

Halloway ignored the question. "You're a very long way from home, aren't you, Mr. Marsh?"

Marsh said nothing.

"Penn Yann?—that's in the Finger Lakes Region, isn't it?"

Still, Marsh said nothing.

"And as far as we've been able to ascertain, you really have no way back."

"I've got my truck," Marsh grumbled.

Halloway checked a file on his desk. "Oh yes. Miss Wingate—one of our Admissions people—did mention that. Apparently the police have impounded it."

"They had no right—"

"Probably not, Mr. Marsh. But the fact is, they did impound it . . ."

"And that woman, that 'Miss Wingate' has got my dog, too." Despite his drug-induced lethargy, Marsh felt anger welling up inside him.

"You're very attached to that dog, aren't you?"

Marsh said nothing.

"And even to your truck, I imagine, isn't that so?"

Marsh still said nothing.

"You very much resent me, don't you?"

"Yes," Marsh answered at once, "I do."

"And I would guess that you don't like this hospital very much, either."

"It's a hellhole."

Halloway grinned. "You probably feel the same way about this city, if I'm any judge of people, and I am."

"It's a hellhole, too."

Halloway took a breath, held it, then said on the exhale: "Then it would probably be a real godsend to you to be able to leave it."

"Yes."

"I can make that possible, Mr. Marsh."

Marsh shook his head. "No," he whispered.

"Oh but I can. I am not without—"

"Seth is here. In this city."

"I am going to ask that you not persist with that, Mr. Marsh. I am going to *tell* you not to persist with it." His voice was quivering again; he turned his head and looked Marsh squarely in the eye. "Remember, please, Mr. Marsh, as I said, that I can get you out of here. However, if you wish to stay with us here at Bellevue for, let's say, another few months, or even another few years, we can make that possible, too. *I* can make that possible, Mr. Marsh. And, conversely, if you wish to leave, if you wish to be *able* to leave, with your dog, and your truck, then I can certainly make that possible, too. Do you understand what I'm saying to you?"

Marsh did not answer immediately. But he did understand. He understood only too well. At last, he said, "I understand."

The doctor smiled, and turned his head again so his face was in profile. "Yes, I believe that you do. That will be all for now."

Marsh left and went back to his room.

A Partial Transcript of the 7:00 P.M. Channel Three News Update:

". . . and this just in: The bodies of three children, aged ten to twelve years have been found in three separate areas of Manhattan tonight—on the fringes of the West Village, on East Houston Street in the Bowery, and in a tenement house on 129th Street. Details at this time are sketchy, but it has been learned that each of the bodies—two boys and a girl—was nude, and there were no outward signs of cause of death . . .''

A Partial Transcript of an 8:15 P.M. Channel Three News Bulletin

City police report that several carloads of armed men have been spotted in various locations on the lower east side, and near the West Village . . .

Chapter 64

"It's because we're such an integrated city," Snipe heard the balding, bearded man on the TV say, "and I don't mean racially. I mean, we're such an *interdependent* city. If the subways go out, Wall Street closes down. If the traffic lights fail, or the sewer systems backs up, or a transformer out in God-knows-where blows itself to pieces, then we're in deep trouble. And now, with people left and right arming themselves—often illegally—we are just perpctuating the fear that caused us to arm ourselves in the first place."

Snipe thought he had never enjoyed anything quite so much: The city, his city, was about to fall apart right in front of him.

He wished he could look out one of the windows and see mobs running through the streets, torches in hand, screaming "Death to all!" But he knew it wasn't as bad as that. Not yet, anyway. Of course, if he got lucky. . . .

Then he heard, below the noise of the TV, from behind, from near the door, in his voice, "Hey you, dipshit!" He remembered using the words on Carter Barefoot just before beating the crap out of him. He heard again, again in his voice, "Hey you, dipshit!"

And so he did not bother to turn and look. He knew who it was; he knew what it was. And he knew what it wanted.

226

7:40 P.M.

Georgie had been pounding on lots of doors. Wanamaker's apartment was empty, and Aunt Sandy's apartment, too. Wilson Gruscher had pleaded so poignantly, from behind his locked door, for him to go away that at last he had, and Carter Barefoot, also from behind his locked door, had whimpered something about meeting him "on the street— ten minutes!" which Georgie thought was probably a lie, but he had little time to worry about it.

He was tired. Bone-tired. And Winifred Haritson was a lot heavier than he had supposed she would be.

"I hurt, Georgie," she pleaded. "Oh I hurt." She said the words every half minute or so, as if discovering her pain anew each time. Georgie wished fervently that she'd stay quiet, and so he told her, time and again, "I know it hurts, Mrs. Haritson. I know it hurts."

He was carrying her piggyback style, her skeletal arms crossed in front of his neck. Her head was down, so her cheek rested against his shoulder; she wept constantly, and softly.

Georgie imagined, now and then, that he could feel her pain.

He slowed his gait when he approached The Stone's main entrance doors. The lobby was all but pitch dark— he could see the vague, dark yellow mounds of an old couch and chair and, in one corner, the suggestion of a phone booth, sans phone, which had been ripped out long before. He looked through the double doors at the street. It too was dark. And still.

He heard a scream then, and he stopped walking. He listened. He heard it again, from his left, from down a short hallway. From Lou's apartment, he realized. Where Snipe was. He thought it had not been so much a scream of pain as a scream of frustration—*Goddammit, Goddammit, why does it have to end now?*

He listened. He heard nothing else. He went to the doors, pushed them open, and carried Winifred Haritson out to the street.

He turned right. He stopped. Someone was standing a couple yards away. "Who's there?" he said.

"It's me," he heard. "Carter Barefoot." His voice sounded very nasal, because his nose had been turned into pulp by Snipe. "Where we goin', anyway?"

8:00 P.M.

Jim Hart was cold. He had pulled the sheet and blanket over himself, but he was still cold. He was convinced that the hospital had turned the heat off. Maybe it was part of the therapy. Keep the patients cold and numb.

At any rate, it would explain the creepers of fog swirling into the room.

He said to John Marsh, in the other bed, "Look at that, look at that!" and nodded at the fog.

Marsh looked; he saw nothing.

"They're crazy!" Jim Hart insisted. "The people who run this place are crazy. They want us to freeze. Jesus, aren't you cold?"

John Marsh said nothing.

Jim Hart watched the fog swirl into the room, watched it curl around the bedposts. It was a strange kind of fog, he thought. It seemed to move under a power all its own. And its colors were wrong. Because it shouldn't have had colors at all, he realized.

At Central Park: Near Bethesda Fountain

He said to himself, aloud, "I am a creature of the earth." And for the very briefest of moments he had no idea what it meant.

For the very briefest of moments he saw himself as something he had never been—a man. And for the very briefest of moments he was afraid, because he was cold, and he was hungry, and he did not know what he was doing here, in Central Park, in Manhattan, with the voices of a thousand strange people moving about in his head. ("Oh yes, that was Thursday, wasn't it?" and "Watch for the light; wait till it turns green,'' and ''We have this in a size twelve,'' and ''I know it hurts,'' and ''I ain't gonna do nothing to ya; I just want your wallet, just your wallet!''). And then he knew that they were *his* people, the children of the island, the children of *this* island, and that he was here to call to them. To give their heritage back to them. So they could take their island back.

''I am a creature of the earth,'' he said again. ''And the energy within me is the earth's energy.'' He took one long, deep breath:

He focused that energy.

And on the Upper West Side, in a law office on West 110th Street, the newly installed junior partner of the law firm of Johnson, Bigny and Belles, a young woman named Karen Gears, looked up from her work at a window which faced south and one word escaped her, ''No!'' It was a plea, a word of desperation—keep the dreams away, lock them up in her childhood, where they belong, where, indeed, they had begun, and where she had supposed they had ended.

''It's turned awful damned cold,'' said Carter Barefoot to Georgie MacPhail. ''Awful damned cold!'' He was dressed in old, stretch-polyester brown pants, a faded yellow Dacron shirt—Georgie guessed that it was as old as he was—and a threadbare denim jacket that was obviously doing very little to keep him warm.

The three of them—Georgie, Mrs. Haritson, Carter Barefoot—had seated themselves just inside a storefront. Georgie's plan had been to hail a taxi, which would take them to Bellevue. But the street was unusually quiet, and Georgie guessed, correctly, that people were staying at home in the face of the recent murders in the city.

Georgie could not imagine why Carter Barefoot was complaining so much about being cold. It was cold, sure, but even Mrs. Haritson, before she'd passed out, hadn't been complaining about it. Of course, Georgie considered, she had other things to worry about, didn't she?

''How's Mrs. Haritson?'' asked Carter Barefoot.

"I guess she fainted or something," Georgie answered. He looked at her; she was sitting up; her head was over on her right shoulder, her arms hanging loosely at her sides. "She looks like she's asleep."

"Is she dead?" asked Carter Barefoot.

Georgie put his finger to her neck, felt nothing, put his finger an inch lower; he got a pulse. "No," he whispered, "she's not dead."

Carter Barefoot allowed his head to fall back so it rested against the iron grating in front of the doors. "Where we goin' exactly?"

"Bellevue," Georgie answered. "I'm takin' Mrs. Haritson to Bellevue. They'll fix her up."

Carter Barefoot nodded slightly. "Uh-huh. It's sure awful damned cold."

On the fringes of the West Village, in lower Manhattan, a good-looking, dark-haired, gray-eyed boy was lying on his back on his bed. The lights were out, the shades and curtains drawn. He had always liked darkness.

He was remembering that just two days before, he had somehow gotten Christine Basile, of all people, to agree to go out with him. He was remembering also that barely a month before, he'd celebrated a birthday. His sixteenth, he'd been told. The man who called himself his father had given him an extra set of keys to the car.

The boy was weeping now, and he was whispering to himself, "What a crock of shit, what a damned crock of shit!"

In Manhattan, on West Tenth Street, in a small, bachelor apartment which had been decorated very tastefully in earth tones, and included a wicker loveseat, bamboo shades, and a large, well-maintained fresh-water aquarium, a man named Philip Case—who was apparently in his early thirties—was holding his head and tightly gritting his teeth, trying futilely to shut out the images that came to him in waves, like a tide filled with bad memories.

*   *   *

Sam Campbell was getting very angry. He and Joyce had been waiting—he checked his watch—an hour and a half and he was sure now that the receptionist had forgotten all about him. He patted Joyce's hand. "I'm going to go see what the problem is, Joyce." She nodded, and he made his way to Lenny Wingate's desk. She had her head lowered.

"Hello?" he said.

She made no response.

"Hello?" he repeated. "Do you remember me?"

She looked up slowly at him; he saw that her face was red and slightly puffy, as if she'd been crying.

"I'm sorry," he said, "I just—"

"Yes?" she said.

"I just wanted to know, I was wondering—my name's Campbell . . ."

"Oh, yes, Mr. Campbell." She took a deep breath, as if to give herself energy. "Yes. I called the doctor, everything's okay." She withdrew a pass from her desk, handed it to him; "This is a Ward R pass. You and your wife can both use it."

"She's not—" Sam began, stopped, said, "Thank you; I didn't mean to bother you," then went and got Joyce.

Georgie MacPhail announced, "We gotta keep moving." He thought it was the right thing to say at the right time, but Carter 'Barefoot could not have agreed less. "I'm cold," he moaned. "I'm so cold!" And he hugged himself fiercely for warmth.

Inside the pawnshop, a little aged wisp of a man named Samuelson awoke. He had taken to sleeping in his store only in the past few days, when, as he'd put it, "all hell was about to break loose."

He sat up. He looked around his store. He felt certain he would see that someone had broken in. But the store was quiet.

And then he saw the dark forms at the front door. He moved very slowly, partly from caution, partly from fear, and partly from age. He got out of the cot. He edged sideways toward the back of the counter, where he kept two guns—a Smith and Wesson .38, which hadn't worked right in years, and an Italian-made over-and-under shotgun, almost brand new. It was that gun which he took hold of, broke open, and loaded.

There were a hundred or more Philip Cases in Manhattan that night. A hundred or more Karen Gears. A hundred or more boys lying in their darkened rooms and trying desperately to recall the events of just one or two days before. Because such events were their reality, and reality was slipping from them rapidly.

Because Seth had reached them, at last.

Because he had reached into them.

Into their comfortable and private worlds—the worlds they had created for themselves over the decades and the centuries since the Earth had released them.

And Seth did not like what he saw there. He did not like the fear. And the need. And the desperation.

They had become what they had lived amongst.

They had grown apart from the Earth, because they rarely touched it, and because here there was warmth from the cruel winter, and food in abundance, and sex at every street corner . . .

They had become what they had lived amongst. They had grown apart from the Earth, because they had rarely touched it.

They had grown secure in what they had become, and so had tossed aside what they had been. In stark desperation they had discarded it, and forgotten it. Because it is impossible to be both what they were, and what they had changed themselves into.

Seth had reached into them. Into their comfortable, private worlds. And he had torn those worlds apart.

Sam Campbell and Joyce Dewitte were led to Marsha's room by a psychiatric technician. "You can have fifteen minutes with her," he told them. "Doctor's orders."

"Yes," said Sam, "I understand that."

The technician unlocked the door and pushed it open. Sam and Joyce stepped into the room.

Marsha was sitting up, cross-legged on her bed. She stared mutely at them as they entered.

Sam took hold of Joyce's hand. "Marsha, darling," he said soothingly, "this is Joyce. Do you remember–"

Marsha screamed. It was a chilling shrill noise, as if there were some other person inside her screaming, and she was merely opening her mouth to let it out. No emotion showed around her eyes or in her face. The scream continued, unbroken, for many seconds.

Sam and Joyce stared, transfixed. At last, Sam whispered, "That's not my daughter, that's just not my daughter."

But it was. And deep inside himself, he knew that it was.

And when her screams ended, Marsha broke into fitful weeping punctuated every now and then by, "Oh Daddy, oh Daddy, I'm sorry."

And Sam Campbell, hearing something in her words and in her weeping that he hadn't heard since his wife's death—something very alive and hopeful—ran to her and gathered her into his arms and murmured, "She's come back to me. Oh, Joyce, my daughter has come back to me."

On West Tenth Street, a scream erupted from Philip Case. It was much the same kind of scream that had come from Marsha Campbell and it was a scream done for much the same reasons.

To erase the memories, and the images, and the feelings.
To call back his hard-won humanness.
To blot out the nightmare of what he had been.

On the Upper West Side, the scream did not work for Karen Gears. She threw herself from her south-facing window. Her scream ended abruptly.

On the fringes of the West Village, a boy lay quietly, dreaming again of Christine Basile, his past shut out completely. And forever.

Seth could feel these deaths happening.

And he knew, at last, that he was an imperfect creature who had done an imperfect thing.

He stood. He felt something emerging within himself—something strident, and desperate, and mean.

And for the first time in his life he was frightened.

Because it was late September.

And he was hungry, and cold, and had no idea at all what he was doing here, in Central Park, in Manhattan.

Chapter 65

The first blast from Samuelson's over-and-under shotgun
tore through the glass just six inches above where Carter
Barefoot, Winifred Haritson and Georgie MacPhail had
been sitting. One of the pellets deflected from the metal
grating and lodged in Georgie's right ankle. He grabbed
the ankle, rolled to his left, knocking Winifred Haritson
over, and scurried to the sidewalk. He grabbed Winifred's
foot and pulled her over the edge of the step to him.

He saw then that the back of Carter Barefoot's head was
missing, and he remembered that the man had been prepar-
ing to stand just as the shotgun blast hit. Georgie swore
beneath his breath. Samuelson fired again. The pellets
lashed into a set of windows in a storefront across the
street; the glass shattered; huge, jagged pieces fell inside
the grating.

Georgie swore again.

He heard the distant gurgling hum of a car engine to his
left. Another shotgun blast erupted through the storefront;
it blew away some of Carter Barefoot's shoulder. Georgie
pulled himself to his feet, bent over, put his hands under
Winifred Haritson's arms. The hum of a car grew closer;
Georgie looked to his left; two blocks away an old Cadillac,
its suspension straining under the weight of a half dozen
beefy men, careened his way and stopped in front of the
store. A half dozen firearms of one kind and another
leveled on the storefront; a moment's silence followed,
and then the guns were turned loose. Georgie put his hands

hard to his ears; "What are you doing?" he screamed over and over again as a hundred, two hundred bullets of various sizes, shapes, and velocities tore the storefront to shreds.

And then it was over.

Georgie took his hands away from his ears. One of the men in the Cadillac stuck his head out. "Whatcha got there, boy?—Some dead old woman?"

Georgie shook his head dumbly.

The man laughed. "Well you sure better look again," he said, and the Cadillac sped away.

He turned. He bent over Mrs. Haritson. Her body flowed away from him; her lips parted, her eyes rolled.

Georgie sighed.

He thought that what he wanted most in this world was to be at home. With his mother, and his little brothers, and the ghost—Hiram or Handy.

And so, very slowly—because of the pellet in his ankle, and very determinedly, he started walking north.

At Bellevue—the following morning—10:00 A.M.

John Marsh looked up slowly as the door was pushed open and a big, well-dressed man in his late fifties stepped in. "John Marsh?" the man said.

Marsh answered, "Yes. Who are you?"

"An associate of Dr. Halloway's, Mr. Marsh. He asked me to give you this." The man handed Marsh an envelope. Marsh took it, opened it; he looked questioningly at the man; "There's two hundred dollars in here."

The man nodded and smiled ingratiatingly; "Yes, sir. The doctor feels that's adequate to get you back to Penn Yann. If it isn't—"

"I'm being . . ."

"Released? Yes, sir. Dr. Halloway seems to feel that there is no longer a need to keep you here."

Marsh studied the envelope a moment. "And what about Seth?"

The man's smile faded quickly. "And Dr. Halloway wanted me to remind you, sir, that even in a city this size he would have no trouble at all locating a man who clearly demonstrates that he may be a danger either to himself or to society."

Marsh grinned. "I see."

"Dr. Halloway hopes that you do, sir. Now if you will please come with me, we'll retrieve your street clothes and see to your car."

"Truck."

"I'm sorry?"

"It's not a car. It's a truck. And there's a little matter of my dog . . ."

"The doctor mentioned that as well, sir, and he is sorry to tell you that Miss Wingate, who was holding your dog, is apparently no longer with us."

"No longer with you? What the hell am I supposed to do about that? I want my damned dog back—"

"That is something you will have to take up with Miss Wingate, sir."

"Can you give me her address?"

"I'm sorry, no—it would be no help to you, sir; she has apparently left the city."

Whimsical Fatman was doing very well on crutches. He had only one problem: getting all the way to North Carolina on them was going to be difficult. Even getting out of New York with them was probably going to be next to impossible.

He planted himself on one of several benches just outside Bellevue's main entrance; he thought ruefully that it had been a nice dream.

John Marsh appeared in the entranceway, looked about, and came toward him.

Whimsy raised a hand, waved slightly; "Hi," he said.

Marsh glanced at him, without stopping; "Hi," he said. And then he stopped. "Do I know you?"

Whimsy shook his head; "Not really. We were on the same floor."

"Oh," Marsh said.

"I'm glad they let you out."

"Yeah. So am I." He noted Whimsy's crutches for the first time. "Can I . . ." he began, and thought better of it.

"Can you give me a lift somewhere?" Whimsy coaxed.

A short pause. "That's what I was going to ask."

"You aren't going to North Carolina, are you?"

Marsh smiled. "No. Penn Yann."

Whimsy grinned back. "That's in the Finger Lakes, isn't it?"

Marsh was pleased. "Yes, it is. You're probably the only person in this damned place that knows that."

Whimsy shrugged. "Simple geography," he said. "So what do you say, can I get a lift out of here, anyway?"

"You mean out of the city?"

"Uh-huh. Out of Manhattan."

"Yes," Marsh said.

The orderly, a young woman named Anne, stepped into Room 343. She saw nothing at first. Two empty beds, sheets and blankets in disarray. She flicked the light on. And saw the form huddled in a corner of the room. The form was trembling visibly, and little moaning sounds were coming from it. "My God!" she murmured.

She ran over, touched the side of the man's head. He looked up at her; his face was flushed and swollen from weeping. She lifted his wrist, read the name on the tag there: JIM HART.

He mouthed something incomprehensible.

"I'm sorry, Mr. Hart," she said soothingly. "Can you stand up, please?"

He mouthed words at her again; she understood several of them.

"Can you stand up?" she repeated.

"I'm a city dweller!" he whispered. "I'm a city dweller!"

"Yes, Mr. Hart," she said. "Yes. We all are."

"Don't let them take it away from me, please don't let them take it away from me . . ."

"No one's going to take anything from you, Mr. Hart."

"I'm a city dweller!" He thumped his chest. "I'm a city dweller!"

"Yes," she told him again, "we all are." And she grinned very slightly. "We are all city dwellers, Mr. Hart."

The New York Times: October 5th:

TWO MORE BODIES FOUND

The nude bodies of two children, a boy and a girl, aged ten to twelve years, were found in a tenement house on West 158th Street last night, bringing to eight the number of such bodies found in Manhattan within the last two weeks, fanning speculation that the children may be victims of the West 150th Street killers.

Autopsies are scheduled for today on both bodies; no immediate cause of death was determined, although one of the bodies apparently displayed a number of dark bruises . . .

Chapter 66

The man on the corner of 42nd Street and Broadway
handing out coupons for a free "Relaxo Massage" at "Bette's
Pleasure Palace" in the West Village had several thoughts
going through his head: The first, and most important, had
to do with the weather forecast from earlier in the
morning—a forecast for "rapidly dropping temperatures."
The man was worried about that. Ever since he was a kid,
he remembered now, and had fallen through the ice at his . . .
grandfather's farm, he had been very susceptible to cold.
At that moment, he had no place to sleep for the night, but
if he managed to distribute the rest of his Relaxo Massage
coupons he could stay at Bette's place, which, he had
found, was very warm, and *very* pleasant.

Another of the man's thoughts was that he hadn't really
known what name to give Bette when he'd applied for this
job. He knew his name, of course. Didn't everyone? His
name was . . . David. Everyone called him Dave. They'd
called him Dave since he was in . . . second grade. They
called him Dave because . . . they called him Dave because "David" was so damned *formal* sounding. And it
kind of announced, didn't it, that he was Jewish. Half-
Jewish, really. Because his father . . . Because his *mother*
(he always got that mixed up) had been Jewish. And his
father had been Methodist. Baptist! David Seth . . . Seth
David Goldman . . . *David Seth Williams*. "Dave" Williams.

"Hi," he announced suddenly, and he shoved a leaflet
under the nose of a passerby. "I'm Dave Williams, and

I'd like to invite you to Bette's Pleasure Palace . . ." The passerby took the leaflet. *I'm a good salesman*, the man who called himself Dave Williams thought. *I've got charisma.*

A sudden, chill wind came up, caught the man's leaflets and scattered them around the street. He cursed and scurried after them.

A woman looking on clucked to her friend, "My God, he acts like it's a matter of life and death. If you ask me, he should find a *real* job!"

The man who called himself Dave Williams heard her, though she was a good fifty feet away, and speaking in low, secretive tones—his hearing had always been excellent. He thought, *Don't worry about me, lady. I've got charisma. I'll be okay!*

One Month Later:

DEPUTY COMMISSIONER SAYS KILLINGS ARE BEHIND US

Deputy Police Commissioner James T. Hefter has stuck his neck out and declared that the rash of brutal murders of a month ago are "probably a thing of the past." He goes on to describe the killings as "an anomaly. A hundred years from now civilization may encounter something quite similar. It has happened in the past: Jack the Ripper springs to mind, and Juan Corona"—who, in the early seventies was responsible for the brutal murders of several dozen migrant workers in California—"as well as many others, several unsolved to this day." Pressed as to whether that meant the West 150th Street Killings will go unsolved, Hefter said, "No, we have several strong leads, and they are being investigated." In an unusually philosophical concluding statement, the Commissioner added, "Our civilization, as complex and as vulnerable as it is, probably contributes very heavily to the development of these . . . anomalies. Perhaps it is just a question of . . . adaptation. Perhaps some of us simply find the society *too* complex, and ourselves too vulnerable.'' Asked what he meant, exactly, the Commissioner responded, ''I'm not sure. I'm really not sure'' . . .

Chapter 67

In a Small Cabin in the Adirondacks

Leonora "Lenny" Wingate stroked the big, aged German shepherd as she watched the firelight dance hotly just a few feet in front of her chair. It was a good fire. It would keep her warm. And there was enough firewood piled up that she would have no trouble surviving the winter.

But then, she had never had trouble surviving the winters. She was stronger than the others. She was new. And different.

She was a survivor.

And now, with this dog, and the goodness and gentleness that were part of him, because they were a part of the man, it would be a good winter.

Lenny sensed that the man was out there, beyond the cabin, perhaps not far away. She couldn't be sure. It was possible that he was dead. She had sensed death about him when they'd brought him in—how long ago?—just a month and a half ago? It seemed like centuries.

She glanced out a small window in the west wall of the cabin. The sun was setting. She knew that it would rise and set another hundred times before warmth returned to the land.

Before the Earth produced her own once again.

She sighed.

She continued stroking the big German shepherd.

She thought what a great pleasure it was to be alive.